Shane Arbuthnott

DOMINION

ORCA BOOK PUBLISHERS

Library and Archives Canada Cataloguing in Publication

Arbuthnott, Shane, author
Dominion / Shane Arbuthnott.

Issued in print and electronic formats.
ISBN 978-1-4598-1117-1 (hardback).—ISBN 978-1-4598-1118-8 (pdf).—
ISBN 978-1-4598-1119-5 (epub)

I. Title.
PS8601.R363D64 2017 jC813'.6 C2016-904476-9
C2016-904477-7

First published in the United States, 2017
Library of Congress Control Number: 2016949035

Summary: In this fantasy novel for middle-grade readers, Molly works with her family, collecting spirits on an airship. When she captures a spirit that can speak, she begins to think that everything she has been taught may be a lie.

MIX
Paper from responsible sources
FSC www.fsc.org
FSC® C016245

Orca Book Publishers is dedicated to preserving the environment and has printed this book on Forest Stewardship Council® certified paper.

Orca Book Publishers gratefully acknowledges the support for its publishing programs provided by the following agencies: the Government of Canada through the Canada Book Fund and the Canada Council for the Arts, and the Province of British Columbia through the BC Arts Council and the Book Publishing Tax Credit.

Cover illustration by Peter Ferguson
Design by Rachel Page
Author photo by Erin Elizabeth Hoos Photography

ORCA BOOK PUBLISHERS
www.orcabook.com

Printed and bound in Canada.

20 19 18 17 • 4 3 2 1

This book is for my wife, Alexis.
You keep my course true and my ship aloft.

ACT ONE
AIRBORNE

ONE

They had been chasing the font for days, and Molly knew the engine was getting tired. While the *Legerdemain* hurtled through the air, the engine's rivets groaned, and from the aft vents Molly could hear a low chuffing like a horse ridden too hard. Perched atop the mainmast, the huge engine began to tremble with exhaustion, and the entire ship shook with it.

Molly scurried up the mast until she hung just beneath the metal curvature of the engine. She ran her hands along its iron plates and rested her cheek against it. "Not much farther," she whispered. "You're doing well. We've almost caught up."

"What was that, Moll?" a voice shouted up from below.

She pulled herself away from the engine, hoping no one had seen her whispering to it. But her father stared up at her from the deck, a dozen yards down. "Nothing, Da!" she said. "The engine's struggling, is all!"

He looked as tired as the engine, his hair and beard wind-mussed. "Keep it running!" he said. "This one's given us good chase, but we'll catch it within the hour!"

"I know, Da. I mean, aye aye, Captain!" she said and then clambered through the rigging to the back of the engine, to get away from his watchful eyes. Back here, with the vents straight above her, the engine's *chuff, chuff, chuff* almost blocked out the sound of the wind.

"You heard him," she whispered into the noisy vents. "Within the hour. This chase is almost done." She didn't think it would hear her, but the bone-shuddering tremors seemed to ease.

"Kier! Drop starboard nets!" her father's voice boomed.

"Aye aye!" another voice responded. Molly swung out to the right and looked down as her brother Kiernan scrambled across the ship's deck to the gunwale. He struggled momentarily with a knot, and then the nets were loosed—long wooden beams swiveling out from the hull, heavy cords trailing beneath them. The metal filaments in the nets glimmered in the bright sky, dark against the white clouds.

Molly turned her eyes forward and was caught by the view. They were racing through the upper atmosphere, nothing between them and the sun. The *Legerdemain*'s pale wooden keel dug a deep trench in the clouds below. The sails on the fore and aft masts were furled for speed, letting the full force of the wind blow across the deck and across Molly where she hung from the engine. She smiled as the boisterous winds chafed her cheeks and sent her hair sailing out behind her. They were making incredible speed: tired or not, the *Legerdemain* was in fine form.

Up ahead, their quarry sparked and sizzled, disappearing and reappearing against the blue of the sky. *The font.* They had caught sight of it a week ago, an aetheric font of fair size sitting at the crossing of two wind currents. They had been drawing close when the font drifted upward into the high atmosphere and sailed away on a fast easterly wind. Now, three days later, they had almost caught up.

During the chase, the font had filled their nets with smaller spirits. Their hold was already near bursting. But the font was growing. Molly knew what that meant: something big was getting ready to come through. Catching the slower eighth- and ninth-level spirits was easy, but if they wanted to catch whatever was about to come through, they would need to be right alongside the font when it emerged. It would need to be in their nets before it even knew they were there.

The ship suddenly rocked, and the crew on the deck stumbled. Kiernan hung far over the gunwale, above open air, before catching himself.

"Engineer!" her father's voice roared.

Molly winced; he only called her by title when she'd done something wrong. She felt the mast below her fingers shivering as the engine juddered atop it. "I'm on it!" she cried.

She did a quick inventory. The plates and access hatches along the starboard side of the engine looked fine. On the fore everything was clear; the intake vents were wide, the engine drinking in air. On the port side she could see a few of the iron plates rattling; those would have to be patched to keep the engine's spirit from breaking free, but loose plates didn't explain the rocking. She swung to the aft.

There it was. One of the aft vents was jammed, slats half open. The air from the intakes would be backing up inside, choking the engine. She clambered up the rigging and took hold of one of the handles riveted to the engine's sides.

The engine shook fiercely, and she heard cries from below as the *Legerdemain* swung sideways, deck boards groaning. She looked down quickly to check that the mast still held strong to the deck; if it broke, the ship would plummet to the ground.

She reached the jammed vent and ran her fingers over it. One of the long slats had fractured, wedging another slat shut with a metal fragment. She pulled a screwdriver from her belt and heaved herself closer.

The effluent from the vent washed over her, warm, thick and oxygen rich. She took one deep breath of it, then bent to her task.

The wedged slat was beginning to bend now, the force of the air behind it buckling the metal. Molly levered it down with her screwdriver, pulling at the metal fragment with her arm awkwardly hooked through a handle. The air from the vents pushed against her. With a shove that nearly unbalanced her, Molly forced the slat down and yanked the fragment out. As soon as it was free, the vent flew open, blasting Molly with warm air and knocking the screwdriver from her hand. She watched it fall astern. It had a long way to fall before it hit the ground.

That was a good screwdriver, she thought. *Probably can't afford to replace it with one as nice.* With a curse she threw the piece of metal to join it.

The *Legerdemain* steadied out and began picking up speed. Molly took a moment to scan the deck. Things were chaotic but not panicked. No hands lost, then. To be sure, she did a roll call of the Stouts on board: her father—at the helm, correcting the *Legerdemain*'s heading; her brother Kiernan—trying to untangle a net with one of the long fetch poles; her brother Rory—standing aft, a line wrapped around his hand for safety. For a moment she found herself looking for her sister, Brighid. She stopped as soon as she realized what she was doing.

With her adrenaline abating, her arms were beginning to ache. She climbed down to the engineer's loft—the round platform halfway up the mast—and sat down.

The broken vent had slowed the chase but not by too much. The font was still only a short way off their bow, and with the ship's course evening out, they were gaining again.

It was a lively one, no doubt about it. Some of the aetheric fonts barely glimmered, almost as invisible as the air that birthed them. This one sparked and spat like a ball of blue fire. The fonts fascinated her. She remembered the first catch she had really been part of, when she was six and working as a deckhand. That font had looked like a pulsing indigo orb tucked between their nets, surging with the colors of deep-blue evening and white burning sunlight. In its depths there had been a shadow, like an open doorway, and she remembered straining to see deeper inside, leaning over the gunwale until she almost lost her balance.

Fonts were capricious, dangerous. And she could stare at them for hours.

There was a large crackle from the font, and a loop of energy surged out from its surface to brush their bow. The ship rocked. Molly got to her feet. "Oh no," she muttered.

"No, no..." She got a hold of the rigging. "Da!" she shouted. "It's gonna—"

But he had already seen. "Hard to port!" he shouted. "Get those nets on it!"

She saw him spin the wheel, and the tiller shifted. Sails were unfurled, catching the wind with a snap and turning them sharply. The font was growing in leaps now, swelling outward. In its center, she could see that telltale shadow. The dark door that led...She didn't really know where. Elsewhere. To the Void, most people said, that terrible place that birthed spirits. Something powerful was coming through, and their nets weren't going to be close enough.

She was up into the rigging and to the engine in seconds. There was a heady moment when the ship slued sideways and she found herself hanging from one hand, momentum trying to pluck her away into the endless sky. It was the kind of thing that would have seen most of the crew losing their lunch. For Molly, who had grown up amid the clouds, it simply sent a brief electricity along her spine, and then gravity took hold again and she kept climbing, almost to the apex of the engine. She pressed her cheek to the metal and ran her hand over the engine's plates.

"I know you're tired," she said, "but just a little more. One more push to bring us up alongside and get our nets around. Please!"

The engine's only answer was a bone-shaking groan.

"Please," she said again before a sound like the sky shattering brought her head up.

The energy rushing across the surface of the font sped to a frenzy and then vanished, leaving something new behind.

The spirit was almost invisible against the open air. It could be seen in a bending of the light and in white brushstrokes of wind that scudded across its surface. But despite its subtlety, something about it seized her attention and made it impossible to turn away. Molly could feel the spirit's power—and the lingering trace of the Void on the other side of the font.

The spirit hung in the air, yards from their nets, and the eyes of every person on the *Legerdemain* hung on it. And then, with the nets still rushing toward the font, the spirit shifted upward.

The movement broke the spirit's spell, and the crew lurched back into action. "Hand nets!" Molly heard her father calling. "Hand nets!"

It was moving through the air like a hummingbird, almost too fast to follow. *What could a hand net do to that?* she thought. But she reached to her belt and pulled the small hand net out, the iron-laced mesh heavy in her hand.

The *Legerdemain* cut sideways through the dispersing remnants of the font, and before most of the crew could ready their nets, the spirit was in the air above the deck. Molly saw Kiernan swing his fetch pole at it, and she flinched as it retorted with a blast of wind. Kiernan slid halfway across the deck before stopping.

Molly tried to track the spirit, but the engine blocked her sight. She let go of the handle and fell to the loft below. She landed hard and hugged the wood until she had her balance back.

From the crew's movement she could tell that the spirit was near the bow, perhaps ten yards from her. It took her a moment to pick it out, but there it was, dodging hand nets like a sparrow flitting between branches. Even from a distance, she could feel the force of the winds the spirit was throwing back at the crew. One woman was hanging from the ship's nets, and Molly thought she saw fingers gripping the gunwale. She couldn't tell if anyone had been lost. She focused on the spirit again and caught a glimpse of slender, glimmering limbs. And then, shifting as quickly and unexpectedly as a zephyr, the spirit was beside her.

She was staring into its face, its blue eyes swirling with clouds. Time hung about them in a frozen shroud. *They aren't supposed to have faces*, she thought. *They aren't supposed to have eyes.* Spirits, she knew, were utterly inhuman. Incapable of anything except a vague, unfeeling malice, spirits would either kill or drive mad any humans who let them get too close. *But this one looks almost human.* As the spirit held its position in front of her, it became clearer, flickers of light and air forming into neck, limbs, body. It was shorter than her by perhaps a few inches, but it held the shape of a grown woman. Molly looked on, fascinated into stillness. And the spirit looked back.

It leaned closer, and Molly felt a breeze skitter across her skin. "Haviland?" the spirit said in a light, fluting voice.

Molly started back, the familiar name on those alien lips shocking her. "Did you just say...did you just speak?" she whispered when her voice returned. The spirit took a step forward, ghostly hands rising. And then the stillness that had momentarily seemed to surround them was shattered by the booming voice of Molly's father.

"Moll! Molly!" She heard footsteps pounding across the deck.

She was suddenly aware of her position. She was perched on the loft, high above the deck. One puff of wind could send her sailing out into the abyss, with no hope of rescue. She looked at the spirit's hands, still moving toward her. *Hand net.* She flicked her wrist out, and the weighted net spread, arcing wide over the spirit. Molly brought it down, and with a cry that was far too human, the spirit lost its form. Shrinking away from the iron in the net, it drew its body inward until all that remained was a small orb of light and movement, shivering and shimmering. Molly pulled the net closed before it could escape.

She heard a thud behind her and turned to see her father pulling himself up onto the engineer's loft. As he straightened, she saw his face. For a moment it was suffused with fear, and then he took in the closed net, the trapped spirit and Molly.

"You've got it then," he said with surprise.

"Aye," she said weakly, holding up her catch. As the iron-laced net shifted around it, the spirit crackled unhappily.

A grin spread across her father's face. "Quite a catch," he said. "No little seventh-level breeze. I'd say fourth, at least. And fast. Your first wild catch, isn't it?"

Molly looked down at the spirit, and the implications hit her. "It is my first," she said, "but something like this, the ship should—"

"The ship be damned," he said.

"But Da, this would sell for—"

"That catch is yours. The first wild catch a sailor makes goes to the sailor, not the ship. You know the rule, and so does every hand aboard the *Legerdemain*." He gripped her shoulder with his strong hand. His eyes glowed with pride—a look that made him almost as alien to her as the spirit. And then that pride was replaced with a more familiar pain. The grip on her shoulder weakened, and after a moment he let go. "That's fine work," he said and then descended from the loft.

Molly took a breath and let it out. She held up the net to look at the spirit inside.

"Why didn't you fly away?" she asked it softly. "Did you really speak to me?"

It held no answers though. It had no voice, no eyes and face, only a tentative shape that seemed to grow fainter even as she watched.

As if in answer to her question, the engine groaned above her. The sound was low and mournful, and it continued until Molly had secured her catch and went above to soothe the engine's spirit.

TWO

Haviland Stout.

Molly leafed listlessly through her dog-eared copy of *The Life and Times of Haviland Stout*. She had been up late into the night calming and then repairing the engine, its spirit restless as it always was after a successful harvest. She had retired, exhausted, to her berth, but the sounds of the crew celebrating made it impossible to sleep. So, a lantern and *Life and Times* in tow, she had returned to the engineer's loft.

She knew the stories well enough that she needn't have bothered with the book. Every child for the past century had grown up hearing the story of Haviland Stout, but for her family, the descendants of the legendary explorer, Haviland's tales were part of the air they breathed. She knew every strange location he'd visited, every dangerous quest he'd undertaken. And she knew best of all how he'd discovered spirits—and died in the process. She had learned Haviland's stories the way she had learned the *Legerdemain*'s rigging, until she could move through them by pure instinct.

And yet nothing Molly knew of Haviland could tell her why an aetheric spirit fresh from a font might stand in front of her and say his name.

She flipped through to the Arkwright accounts and started reading midway through.

The first spirit through the font was a monstrous thing, a spirit of air with the countenance of a storm, its arms rippling with lightning. It stood twice again as high as even the imposing Haviland. It attacked almost before I knew what was happening; had it not been for Haviland's incredible reflexes, it would have killed me then and there.

She stopped reading. There was nothing here to give her answers.

The spirit was trying to trick her somehow, she knew. Some of the more powerful spirits were notorious for such things, throwing their human owners so off balance that they became spirit-touched. Molly shivered. The touched were as dangerous as the spirits themselves, but they were twice as horrific because they were also human, no matter how damaged or confused.

It was trying to ensnare me, she told herself. *But I ensnared it.* When she had gone to her berth, her catch had been there waiting for her: a trap—a small vented iron cube—with the great spirit inside.

Yes, she decided, *definitely better here in the open air.* She set the book aside and lay down on the loft, breathing deep.

What does a new-sprung spirit have to do with Haviland Stout?

Above her, the engine obscured the stars, its metal shell glinting in the lantern light. It had once been an almost perfect sphere, like an iron sun at the top of the mast. But over the years its cracks had been patched and its dents hammered out, and now it was more like a vast polyhedron studded with handles. There was a flat space at the very top where Molly sometimes liked to lie when she wanted to be closer to the sky, to see nothing but the open air and feel the engine humming at her back.

A voice broke in on her thoughts, calling her name. She rolled over and peered down. Kiernan was there, coming up the companionway from belowdecks. With the moon silvering his face, he looked every bit the young hero. Strong jaw, tall frame, confident walk. At sixteen, he already looked like a ship's captain. He was their father's child. His twin brother, Rory, like Molly, took after their mother, with thick features and heavy brown hair. Or so Molly had been told.

"Moll?" Kiernan called again, making his way toward the mainmast. "Where are you?"

"Up here," she called down and waved. "I thought you'd be below with the others."

"I was," he said. "But it's best to let the crew carry on without me. Having the captain's son about doesn't let them relax."

"That never stops Rory," she pointed out.

"No, it doesn't," he replied, and they both smiled. Rory's voice had been the loudest among the revelers for some time now, slurred with drink. "Why didn't you come down?" Kiernan asked, his tone more serious. "I'd have thought, with your first catch, you might be of a mind to celebrate."

"The engine needed fixing," she said. "After that..." She shrugged.

"It might do you good to mix a little more."

"I'm thirteen. They want me about even less than they want you."

Kiernan climbed up to sit beside her on the loft. He was still a quick climber, though it had been a year since he'd spent any time in the rigging. Molly shifted over to give him room, and they sat staring out at the dark, still skies. She watched his eyes flit between the stars. He looked happy. There was something akin to her own love of the skies there. But at the same time, Kiernan had the look of a man under tight rein, as he always did.

"That was a long chase. Can't remember one so long."

"Two years ago," Molly said. "We had one that was five days."

"Did we? I don't remember having a haul like this two years ago."

"The font fizzled out. All we got was a dozen seventh-level spirits, and the engine was so tired it ran half speed all the way back to dock."

"Ah. That's right." He rubbed his face. "I never sleep well when we're on a chase. I think I slept a full day after that one. Might do the same now, as a matter of fact. You must be tired too."

"Yeah. Never notice until everything's done."

They fell silent. She watched her brother watching the sky and allowed herself a few moments of companionable silence before she asked the inevitable question. "So what did I do wrong?"

Kiernan's eyes dropped to the deck. She knew the question was cruel. At the same time, she knew she was right—he wouldn't have come up here unless he had a bone to pick. Kiernan didn't seek her out just for conversation—he had his brother Rory for that or his father.

"There are conversations among the crew," he said, and Molly sighed. *Not this again*. "Some of the men say they saw you talking to the spirit."

"I didn't! I don't talk to spirits, Kier. I know better."

"You took your time catching it," Kiernan replied. "You were standing with the spirit for a few moments before you took it. Some say they saw your lips move. So tell me—what really happened?"

Molly thought back. *Did I speak to it?* She couldn't really remember. In the rush of the moment, all her memory had caught onto was its shape, its eyes, the name it had spoken.

"It surprised me," Molly said. "I had an aetheric monster staring me in the face. I'm not usually in the thick of things, Kier. I froze up."

Kiernan seemed satisfied with her answer but pressed on. "You know why rumors like this start though."

Molly clenched her jaw and slumped down against the mast. "There are always whispers about engineers."

"That's not true. You treat our engine…oddly. When Morgan was engineer, the crew said no such things."

"When Morgan was engineer, we flew about as well as a hippopotamus," she spat back. "I make us fly the way the *Legerdemain* is supposed to."

"You do. But Molly, you have to remember that even old spirits like the *Legerdemain*'s are dangerous. They can twist your mind. The way you get close to the engine, coax it, come to visit it at nights...you're putting yourself at risk."

"I know the spirits are dangerous. You don't have to tell me."

"Sometimes you need a reminder. Now, get to bed and I won't tell anyone you were up here again."

She sighed, feeling like a small child. Her brother had been scolding her like this for longer than she could remember. With their father being the way he was, Kiernan seemed to think it was his job to keep her in line. And, worse, when he scolded her he usually had a point.

She dropped down from the loft and headed for the companionway.

"Good night," Kiernan said behind her. She waved a hand over her shoulder and slid down the ladder.

After the night air, the atmosphere belowdecks was stifling. It smelled of human bodies and beer. She could still hear the party in the mess midship. As she passed its door, she paused to listen. Voices—including Rory's—were still raised in song. "To port and starboard storms a' roll, but we can't fill our cups with an empty hold!" She winced at the sound; most of the crew members were already too deep into their cups to hold the tune.

Two doors down she reached the entrance to her own room. It had once been Brighid's room, and sometimes Molly still felt the urge to knock before entering. Molly had inherited it two years ago, when her older sister left the ship.

At the end of the passageway, just a few steps away, was the captain's cabin. Light was coming from the crack beneath the door. So her father was still awake. She silently approached and pressed her ear to the wood. Luckily, it was thin—the old door had cracked in a bad storm a few years back, and they had replaced it with cheaper cottonwood that let through even the softest sounds.

She heard the scuffing of a chair being pushed back. A creak—like the one in his bottommost drawer—and then a clink of glass. She sighed. *So he's not far behind the crew then.* She wondered how many bottles he'd already gone through.

The ladder behind her groaned as someone started descending. Quickly and quietly, Molly retreated down the hall and ducked inside her small room with its pale wooden walls. She listened, but the sounds from midship drowned everything out. She thought she heard a door open and close farther aft, but she couldn't be sure. With a sigh she turned to her bed.

And stopped dead.

She wasn't alone.

Standing in the middle of the floor, as frozen as she was, was a ten-inch-tall mechanical man. Its face was featureless save for two wide, dark lenses. It was one of the servitors that moved incessantly around the ship, keeping things tidy and maintaining the various spiritual machines. She recognized this one. Like all the servitors aboard the ship, it was scuffed from ship life, but this one was more battered than most. It belonged to her brother Rory—the result of his own first catch. He was never particularly careful with the things he owned.

The servitor's body was a cheap copper design, one of the early cogitant models that gave their powering spirits free motion within some very tight restraints. Not that this servitor would be a threat, even with free will. The spirit inside was ninth level, hardly powerful enough to keep the servitor's mechanical limbs moving. Rory had been incredibly disappointed with the catch, she remembered. He hadn't even bothered giving it a name, as most people did with their cogitants. The crew simply called it Cog.

It wasn't seeing the servitor itself that surprised Molly. He popped up anywhere and everywhere, traveling through the ductwork with his tiny brooms and rags, making feeble swipes at the dirt in the ship's passageways. But that wasn't what he was doing now. He had his hands tucked under the iron trap that held her catch, and he was in the process of pushing it into one of the ducts. Her entrance had frozen him in place—save for his lenses, which blinked open and shut, open and shut.

"Hey…" she began, bewildered, just as the cogitant hoisted the trap up and scuttled after it into the open duct.

"Hey!" Molly said, louder now. "What are you doing?" She got down on hands and knees in front of the duct and saw Cog turning right into another duct. The airlooms in the *Legerdemain*'s lower levels pumped oxygen-rich air through these ducts, so the crew could survive in the higher atmosphere, and for a moment Molly simply let the cool air flow over her face, trying to understand what was happening. She could still hear the trap scraping along the floor of the duct.

She pushed herself up and took a quick inventory of her room to see if anything else was missing. Her handful of books piled on the foot of her narrow cot. Tools and oil stowed beneath her bunk. Brighid's old aeronautical map, still hanging untouched. Molly opened her chest and saw her clothes, her favorite wrench, her mother's pewter ring. Not much to steal.

Molly could still hear Cog rattling through the ducts. She couldn't fit in there with him, but she also knew the ship better than anyone. Cog had been heading aft and port, toward the crew quarters. She left her room and ran aft, skirting around the companionway. She burst through a door and turned right, passing a long row of empty beds before reaching the duct opening. There was a direct line between her room and this outlet, so she hoped to see Cog emerging here—that is, she thought, assuming he hadn't stopped in Kiernan's room, or the bosun's room, or any of the other rooms between hers and the crew quarters.

But he wouldn't do that—nor would he come to the crew quarters. Cog had just stolen something, as impossible as that seemed. He wouldn't want to be seen. So where would he go?

The hold. The airlooms were installed in the lower decks, in the *Legerdemain*'s expansive hold. The ducts ran straight down there, to corners of the ship where crew rarely went.

As if to confirm her thought, there was a loud clanging, as of a metal trap falling down a vertical shaft. She got up and headed for the ladder down to the hold.

Once down, she stopped. The ship was noisier here. The airlooms, the springboxes that kept them supplied with fresh water, the gravitic engines that lightened the main engine's load and maintained air pressure—these devices and more filled the hold with a constant thrumming that mixed with the unearthly moans and whistles from the captive spirits inside. Molly couldn't hear anything over the din. She scanned the hold, hoping to catch sight of the servitor, but all she saw were the ranks of iron traps from their catch, piled together and strapped to the deck. To her right she could see the port duct, sitting directly above the convoluted tubes of an airloom, but there was nothing there.

She held still a moment longer and noticed something. While the hubbub of spiritual machines continued to sound all around her, it was louder aft than it was fore. She cocked her head, listening intently. There was a quiet patch at the front end of the ship, as if all the spirits were hushed. Which they shouldn't be, because that was where the atmospheric controls were. The gravitic engines there kept the atmospheric pressure aboard the ship steady and survivable, and they were never shut off.

And they weren't off, she realized as she moved closer. She could hear the thrum of the machinery. It was the spirits themselves that were silent.

She walked quietly toward the bow, weaving her way between the iron traps. At first she saw nothing odd. There were the gravitic engines, their pistons all moving in rhythm. She almost turned away, but then a glint from the iron face of one of the engines made her pause. There was a point of light reflecting off the metal where no light should be. It was coming from the space beyond the engines.

She moved closer. There was a narrow passage between the ranks of pistons, and Molly turned herself sideways to squeeze through.

At the end there was a small corner, too inaccessible for any useful purpose. At least, inaccessible to most. Cog was there, hunched over her trap. With care, and great effort, he turned the knob to open the vents. Then, looking satisfied, he picked up a can and poured water into another machine. She recognized it as the broken springbox they'd replaced the last time they were at the docks. But she'd thought it had been thrown overboard. Why was it here?

Molly's eyes wandered around the area. It wasn't just her trap and the springbox here. There were dozens of objects scattered around the space. A rusted heating element from the galley. Farseers, spiritpipes, scrubbers and other trinkets from the crew. It was a collection of old, lost or cast-off spiritual devices, the detritus of life aboard an aetheric harvester.

"Hello?" said the spirit inside Molly's trap. "Is someone there?"

Cog turned, and his lenses caught on Molly. He sprang up, stepping in front of the trap as if prepared to defend it.

"Will you not speak to me?" said the airy voice from the trap. "Please, we must speak."

Cog blinked. Molly blinked back. Then the servitor slowly backed up, away from the trap and into the corner. His fingers were shaking. Molly felt strangely guilty as she eased herself forward. Cog was fully tucked into the corner now, crouched with hands pressed against the pale pine wood of the hull.

She knelt down and put her hands around the trap Cog had stolen from her, keeping her eyes on the servitor. He looked so small, so frightened.

She stood and squeezed back out between the engines, taking her trap with her and leaving the rest. She knew she should have raised an alarm. Cog was acting beyond orders, showing signs of independent thought. Who knew if the little servitor might become dangerous to the crew. But the way he was huddled in the corner, hands trembling…

No. The ship couldn't afford to lose him, she told herself. And if she alerted her father, the servitor would most certainly face diffusion, his spirit dissolved into nothingness.

She looked back as she reached the end of the gravitic engines. Cog had left his corner now and was watching her intently with his dark lenses. She gave him a nod and went back to her cabin.

THREE

When Molly woke the next morning, she was surprised to hear the pounding of feet on the deck boards above. Given the party the previous night, she had expected most of the crew to be in bed, nursing their hangovers.

She stood and heard something crinkle under her feet. Her sister's map had fallen off the wall again, as it always did after a chase. Molly wondered if it was time to put it away. It was years out of date, most of the harvesting grounds it marked having shifted long ago. The winds and fonts never stayed stable for long.

She put the map back on the wall and used her shoe to hammer its nails in. She could put it away later.

After a stop at the head to use the toilet, and a quick breakfast of hard biscuits and cheese, she went above deck. A dozen deckhands were already in the rigging, setting sails and retying knots that had come loose in the chase. Molly looked around, wondering what had roused them all so early. She checked the helm and saw Bracebridge at the wheel.

That explains it then. Bracebridge was their first officer, a stern woman with gray eyes that could pin you to the deck. She'd been with the *Legerdemain* for almost a decade, and she took a firmer hand with the crew than Molly's father did. Most of the crew hated her, but Molly found her stolid manner reassuring.

"Wentland, trim that foresail!" she shouted, and Molly watched the sunken-eyed deckhand jump to the task, despite looking like he might pass out at any moment. Molly straightened her collar and walked toward Bracebridge, but a hand on her shoulder stopped her.

She turned to see her brother Rory behind her.

"Is Da letting you keep that catch?" he asked her.

Her surprise made it hard to speak for a moment. Rory generally ignored her unless he had something to mock her about. "Um…I…yes. He is."

"Unbelievable," he said. "Something like that? You can't keep it to yourself."

"I don't—"

"No one on the ship has had a first catch above sixth level, you know that?" he went on. "First catches aren't meant to actually be valuable."

"I don't know what I'm going to do with it yet," she said.

Rory glowered at her for a moment. "Well, you shouldn't keep it. Have you seen mine around? My cogitant?"

"Um, no."

"Can't find it anywhere."

"Rory?" Bracebridge's voice broke in on them. "Shouldn't

you be seeing to the nets?" The gray-haired woman strode up to them, hands clasped behind her back.

"Aye aye," he said, giving Molly one more withering look before he left.

As he walked away, Bracebridge stepped up beside her. Molly felt very small beside the tall, broad-shouldered woman. "He's in a mood today," Molly said.

"'Course he is. Always is, this time of year."

"This time of year?" Molly looked after her brother, and realization struck her. "Oh. Is it July already?"

"The thirteenth."

"Oh." *My birthday. Fourteen years since mom died.* "That explains it."

"Are you ready? Have you eaten?"

"Yes."

"Good then. I think the engine could use some grease," Bracebridge said. "One of the hands said they heard squeaking."

"Right." Molly headed for her room to gather the grease. But Bracebridge stopped her with a hand on her arm.

"Molly, I almost forgot. Happy birthday."

"Um, thanks," Molly said, but her mind was already up with the engine. *Probably the pneumatics again. We'll need to replace those aft pistons soon.* She waved to Bracebridge and headed for the companionway.

Once the engine was seen to, Molly pulled herself up to the flat space on its peak and sat, enjoying the silence.

Her birthday was one of the few times she wished she could be off the ship. Up here, she was stuck with her family, in close quarters with all their grief. She was tempted to spur the engine on—at full speed they could reach the city in five days. But the engine was still weary. Pushing it now could damage it, and she wasn't sure their current catch would pay for engine repairs or for the long recovery needed for a sick spirit.

The silence was a relief, but it also gave space for her thoughts. *Why did I lie to Rory about Cog?* she wondered. *I should have told him. Even weak spirits are dangerous.* She thought of the small, trembling servitor, and of her catch, the trap now stowed in the drawer beneath her bed. She had heard it throughout the night, whispering to her until she had finally closed both intakes and vents tight. She hated to starve the spirit of air, but it wouldn't be silent any other way.

"I don't suppose you have any thoughts on what I should do," she said to the engine. She put her hand on its metal and it began to rumble, like the purring of some gargantuan kitten. "I bet you would, if you could talk."

She realized what she had just said. She pulled her hand away and wrapped her arms around her knees.

After a few moments, the engine let out a huffing sound. Molly frowned and looked aft. The vents were still open, so it shouldn't be choking up.

Just before she turned to check the intakes on the front end, she saw a hand rise up over the side of the engine. She stood and saw her father's gray-flecked hair rising toward her. He was panting from the climb.

"Da?" she said. "What are you doing?"

He paused and looked up. "Good. You're here. Didn't want to make that cursed climb for nothing." He hauled himself onto the top of the engine and sat down heavily. "Mercy, I thought I was done with rigging when I bought this ship and became captain."

"What are you doing up here?" Molly asked again.

"Looking for you."

Molly stared, bewildered, at her father. He wasn't looking at her though. His eyes were closed, his breathing still heavy. He looked worn, the skin around his eyes sagging as if his bones were shrinking inside him.

His eyes fluttered open again. "Brought you this," he said. He unslung something from his shoulder and tossed it to her.

Molly caught it by the strap and then grunted as it hit her lap. She held it up in front of her. It was a spiritual machine, but she'd never seen one quite like it, and its purpose eluded her. It was a rectangular metal box with a tangled mess of straps and buckles attached to it. There were strange vents around its perimeter that were fixed open. Some had to be intakes, she knew, but surely not all of them. There was a wider, circular vent on the back. She plucked at its metal slats, and the entire vent rotated.

"What is it?" she asked.

"A flitter," he said. "It was your mother's. Or it was going to be. The plan was to find a good spirit for it, get it infused and surprise her with it." He ran his thick fingers over his face, rubbing his eyes so hard that he might have been trying to wipe them away. "Well, the right spirit never came along." He was avoiding looking at her again.

"It's a flitter?" she said. "A real one?" Suddenly the heavy machine in her lap felt electric, alive with possibilities.

"Thought we could use that catch of yours. Should be strong enough. When we get to Terra Nova, we'll find an infusionist to get your spirit put in." He smiled briefly, bright teeth showing through his beard. "My first wild catch was barely strong enough to make a breeze. Worse even than Rory's little cogitant."

The mention of Cog gave Molly a twinge of guilt. *I should tell him right now*, she thought. *I should tell him.*

"Thanks for the flitter," she said. "It's really..." Her voice died when she looked up and realized that her father was staring at her. She didn't recognize the look on his face. It held the fondness she sometimes caught sight of, as well as the more familiar reluctance. But there was something new there—something powerful and painful to behold.

"You look so much like her," he said. "Those sky-bright eyes of yours."

She stared back into his eyes, and for once he did not flinch. She felt as if she were sitting beside a skittish bird—the slightest movement could startle it away.

"The older you get, the more like her you are," he said.

She turned and stared out into the sky, not really seeing it. She felt his eyes on the side of her face, like the hot sun when they climbed too high.

Questions crackled in her throat, barely held back. *Is that why you can't look at me? Because I look like her? Or is it because it was me being born that killed her?* She'd been asking these questions as long as she could remember. But never aloud. *Why does it matter anyway?* she asked herself sternly. *She's not here.*

After a couple of silent minutes, she felt his gaze leave her. Then, without another word, he clambered down the side of the engine. She turned in time to see the top of his head disappear from sight.

She breathed deeply and flopped onto her back. The engine gave an odd, quizzical trill beneath her.

"Oh, shut up," she told it.

A few miserable days later, Terra Nova came into sight. Molly watched with a sinking heart as the city's miasma appeared. She always forgot how bad it was. Clouds of smog huddled over the city, turning the sunlight brown. Molly found herself breathing the clean air aboard the *Legerdemain* greedily, gasping it in as if she were planning to hold her breath through their entire stay in the city.

At the upper edges of the smog, Molly spotted the floating port—an aerial island with docks and cranes ringing it like barbed wire. The interior of the port was dominated by warehouses and supply stores. It was tethered to the city by a thick umbilical. Cable cars ran up and down the umbilical, looking like ants on the trunk of a huge tree.

Time to make ready, she thought, pulling her eyes away from the sight. As the dismal bricks of the industrial district passed below them, and the greasy air rolled in over the bow, Molly busied herself with securing the rigging, binding it to the mast. That done, she ascended to the engine to lock it down.

As she climbed, her eyes turned to starboard, and she paused. It was hard not to gawk, no matter how often she saw the city's wealthier districts. Palatial buildings sat on the peaks of manufactured mountains. The upper towers of underwater mansions peeked above the waters of Placentia Bay. The famous home of the Earl of Chester, made entirely of water coaxed into solid form by aqueous spirits, sat on the eastern shore. Above all these, floating islands held the homes and strongholds of people so rich they no longer had to set foot on Earth.

Molly watched the floating islands shift and sway in the clear air. The smog did not reach them—huge aetheric engines had been put in place to keep it contained in the poorer districts of the city. She resented the wealth of those people, but the sight of the islands made her stomach ache with desire. To live always aloft, never landing...

"Engineer! Lock down engine!" her father shouted.

"Aye aye!" She chided herself for being distracted, like some inexperienced deckhand coming to port for the first time. She checked the new patches she had welded on to make sure they were holding, then closed and locked the intakes and vents, leaving a hairline opening in a few of them. She wasn't supposed to do this—any unsecured spiritual machines were considered a risk when unattended. But years of practice had taught her that no harm would be done, and that if she didn't give the engine a chance to breathe, it would be in poor condition when they returned for their next flight. She checked everything a second time and then thumped the side of the engine with her hand.

"Good run," she whispered into the vent. "Time to rest now." A puff of cool, oxygenated air blew across her skin in response.

Her tasks done, she dropped to the engineer's loft and slid down the bundle of rigging ropes to the deck. Despite the reek of the city, she felt herself getting excited. *A flitter! How did Da ever afford it?* She had no idea, but she could hardly wait to try it out. *To be able to fly, without even a ship under me...*If it worked, it would be worth all the discomfort of a birthday aloft with her family. She descended the companionway, hardly touching the steps, and ran to her room to collect the flitter and the trap.

The sight of the machine gave her pause. The price of an empty flitter could keep the *Legerdemain* supplied for a year. To have one infused with a strong spirit—Molly didn't know prices for such things, but she was fairly certain such a machine could be used to buy the *Legerdemain* twice over.

She grabbed the flitter and slung it over her shoulder, then thought better of it. The port could be rough, and there was no need to court trouble. She wrapped the flitter in her small, coarse bedsheet. Then she bent to retrieve the trap. She opened the intakes and vents to give the spirit a quick breath and then shut them again.

With her heavy load, she returned to the ship's deck more slowly but with no less spring in her step. She approached the gangplank and started across. She was halfway to the pier when she noticed what was happening in front of her. Her father and Bracebridge were yelling at a young man in the dark blue of Haviland Industries—the owners of the port. Kiernan and Rory waited just behind them.

"You just raised the tariffs two months ago!" her father said.

"By authority of his majesty, King George the Fifth—" the man in the blue jacket began, but both Molly's father and Bracebridge shouted over him.

"You bloody vampires!" her father said.

"You've got to give notice!" Bracebridge added. "Increases must be posted!"

"They were," said the young man. "Two weeks ago."

"We've been aloft for three!" her father roared.

The young man did not seem put out by the shouting. If anything, he looked bored. "Well," he said, "you are welcome to take your goods elsewhere."

"There is no elsewhere, and you damn well know it!"

"I do indeed. So if the two of you are done wasting my time, you can sign and we can all be about our business."

Molly looked down over the edge of the gangplank as the shouting carried on. Far below she could see the roofs of Terra Nova itself and the foot of the umbilical that rooted the floating port to the city. From up here, the crowds of people were only visible as tiny pinpricks. Molly sighed. Her father could complain, but the officious young man was right—they had nowhere else to go. Not unless they wanted to travel across the Atlantic to Britain, or farther down the dangerous American coast to one of the other colonies. Terra Nova might be a major power, but it stood alone on the edge of the untamed New World. No settlement had ever been established on the mainland—all who had tried to settle there had disappeared mysteriously, or so the stories said.

After Molly's father had vented his anger enough, he made a disgusted gesture to Bracebridge. She signed the form held out by one of the man's aides. The young man perused the contract, signed it himself and then marched off toward another incoming ship. He held his spine stiffly as he walked. Molly couldn't tell if this was his normal posture or if he was expecting a knife in the back at any moment. Maybe both.

"Tell your boss Arkwright that it takes a special breed of slug to rob the family that started his company!" Molly's father shouted after him. The man did not turn. "Fifty percent," he muttered. "They're trying to drive us from the skies."

"I believe you're right, sir," Bracebridge said, her words clipped. "Not that we haven't seen the signs. The fees have been rising quickly of late."

"That they have. Still, I thought it would be years before things went this far."

"The monopoly is already theirs. With the Crown's backing, the docks and their new flagship..."

Molly could feel her father's anger radiating from him. She looked back at the *Legerdemain*. The crew were bringing the heavy traps up from the hold, and already the floating cranes were swarming in from the docks to offload their catch.

"At 50 percent, this catch'll get us supplies, repairs and wages. It'll not earn us any rest though. Bracebridge, tell the crew. We'll spend a night at dock, and we're off again in the morning."

"We'll not be touching ground, sir?"

"We can't afford to." Molly's father sighed. "Tell the crew...if they've got families below, tell them they can take a quick trip to ground and return by ten o'clock. The rest are to stay on the docks, and back by sunup."

"Aye, sir."

"Ship's yours until I return."

"Aye, sir."

Bracebridge went back aboard while Molly and her brothers walked up to their father. Molly stared down at the load in her arms. She bit her cheek to cut off all the contrary voices in her head and held out the trap and flitter.

"Da, we should sell these. It can buy us time. The engine needs a rest after that run..."

He pushed the heavy objects back into her stomach, hard enough to hurt. "Sell these now, and we'll be putting half the price into Arkwright's pockets. I won't do it. I won't see that much stolen from my family today." He looked around, getting his bearings, and saw her brothers. "Where are you off to?"

"Some of the rigging is starting to fray. I want to get more ropes," Kiernan replied. At a nod from their father, he headed off.

"And you, Rory?"

"Oh, you know. Something terribly useful, I'm sure." He walked off without waiting and vanished between the market stalls.

Molly's father glowered after him, then let out a sigh. "Come on, Moll. Let's get this done before they find a way to take the ship." He gripped her arm with one strong hand, his long fingers wrapping fully around her bicep, and began towing her toward the interior of the docks.

FOUR

"Best prices for spirits!"

"Sailcloth! Rope! Lumber!"

"Traps by the dozen!"

Moving through the swarm of vendors at the docks, Molly felt like she was under attack. Hawkers shouted at her incessantly, their voices blending together until they sounded like the screams of seagulls. She was relieved to finally emerge into the quieter inner streets of the dock. Her father didn't seem to notice the change. He strode onward, dragging her in his wake.

Molly pried her arm out of his grip. "Da, you don't have to drag me."

He paused briefly to look at her and then kept going. Molly hurried after him.

As they walked, she peered through the windows of dozens of empty shops. *There are more empty ones than there were three weeks ago*, Molly thought. *I think that one used to be the baker's shop where Kiernan got those cheese biscuits.* The streets were nearly deserted, and piles of dust and litter had accrued in corners and doorways. The silence began to feel more oppressive.

They reached an interior courtyard, which Molly noted with relief still housed a few open stores and a handful of people. As they were crossing, someone emerged from the alley opposite them. Molly's gaze immediately stuck to him, though it was such a surprise to see him there that it took her a few moments to recognize him: Tyler Arkwright, president of Haviland Industries, and easily the most famous man in Terra Nova.

Molly had only ever seen him in photographs, but in person he was just as impressive. He wore the blue uniform of all his crew, but golden stitching wove intricate curlicues across his chest and shoulders. The uniform was tailored to fit his lean frame. Indeed, the man himself seemed tailored, with his fine features symmetrical, his shoulders narrow but strong, his long blond hair catching the wind perfectly. He looked like the illustration of a captain on the cover of a penny dreadful.

Molly was so busy staring at him that she did not notice the second man until he stepped directly in front of them. This man was huge—his dark suit seemed to barely contain his thick body. His head was bald and puckered with burn scars, and he had a sour expression on his face that made Molly recoil. "Please step back," he said in a rough but surprisingly quiet voice. Even as he spoke to them, his dark eyes moved constantly around the courtyard.

"What did you say?" Molly's father asked.

The man's eyes returned to him. "Please step back," he said again. This time, the words somehow sounded like a threat.

"For him?" her father said, gesturing at Arkwright, who was making his way across the courtyard. "I think not. You!" he called out to Arkwright and stepped around the big man.

"Da, don't," Molly said, but he ignored her.

"You leech! Your company steals the name from my ancestor and then tries to steal the ship out from under me!"

Molly noticed the big man was flexing his hands. "Da, leave off!" she shouted at him, but he didn't notice.

"Fifty percent? What could possibly—"

He wasn't allowed to finish. The big man moved, and suddenly her father was on the ground with the man's knee on his chest, and one of the man's big hands gripping his jaw. Molly's father started to struggle, but the man tightened his grip. "Stay still, or I'll crack your skull."

"Hey!" Molly took a step forward. The big man's eyes met hers for the first time, and she froze where she was.

Arkwright, unfazed by the struggle, wandered over casually. "You're William Stout, are you? I've heard of you. It's a pity the line has come to this, to a man like you, after all its history. At least your daughter shows promise."

Molly was momentarily bewildered until she realized Arkwright wasn't talking about her. *Brighid*.

At the mention of his other daughter, Molly's father began struggling again, despite the big man's threat, but he could not move beneath the man's weight.

"Come on, Mr. Blaise," Arkwright said, walking away across the courtyard. "No time for fun and games."

The man hesitated, and for a moment his grip tightened. Then he stood up, and with a "Yes, sir," he fell in beside Arkwright, and they both vanished from the courtyard.

Molly stared down at her father, lying on the ground. There were bruises at the edges of his beard, where the man's fingers had been. He lay there, staring up at the sky.

"Da?" she said. He didn't move. The other people in the courtyard were all silent too, their eyes fixed on her and her father. *Damn it all, Da, why did you have to yell at him like that?* "Are you hurt? Did he..."

He stood and started walking. He didn't look back to see if she was following until he was two steps out of the courtyard. "Come on, Molly!" he shouted at her. She got her sluggish feet moving and followed, her father moving ahead of her like an angry storm cloud.

"Da, are you okay?"

"Fine. I've seen worse from a bit of storm."

"Are you sure?"

"Do you want the flitter or not?"

"Of course, but—"

"Then shut it and let's go."

Molly, clinging tightly to the flitter, had to run to keep up with her father's furious pace.

The infusionist's shop was a jumble of steel and rivets. Spiritual machines of every variety were piled on the floor and hanging from the walls. Molly looked around, spotting the familiar machinery of aetheric harvesters like the

Legerdemain, but there were others she could not even guess the purpose of, with tangles of pipes and wide mouths and plating so thick no person would ever be able to lift them. In one corner, she noticed a full formal suit that seemed to be woven through with iron filament. She stared at it, trying to discern its function.

Tucked into all this machinery, perched on uncomfortable chairs, were several customers. They all looked tired and impatient.

Molly's father did not take a seat. "Croyden!" he called. A string of clangs and hisses from the back of the shop nearly drowned him out. "Hey, Croyden!" he called again. The clanging ceased abruptly.

"There is a line," said a dry, crackling voice from behind the mess of machinery. "I have only two hands, and you will have to wait."

"I'm not inclined to spend more time in these docks than I need to," Molly's father replied.

"Stout? Is that you?" said the voice from the back. Molly heard rattling, and then a series of bangs moving toward the front of the shop. Finally, a lanky, bespectacled man appeared around the side of a large metallic box with treads. "I thought I recognized that voice!" The man smiled and hurried forward—or, at least, tried to hurry. He hauled one of his legs behind him as if it weighed a ton. And it did weigh a ton, Molly realized as the infusionist's long coat parted for a moment. The natural leg was gone, replaced by a long iron piston that shifted up and down as he walked, hissing steam from the heel. He limped forward and took Molly's father's hand. "It's been years."

"Did your job too well the first time," Molly's father said. "Most everything on the *Legerdemain* is still running like the first day you put it in."

"Good to hear," the infusionist said. "Come into the back. I'll see you get on your way soon enough."

The other customers looked disgruntled. Molly hurried toward the back of the shop, dodging their glares. As she moved, she kept her ears eagerly focused on her father and the other man. Molly hadn't heard many stories of the *Legerdemain*'s past. The purchase of the ship had happened shortly before Molly herself was born, and the proximity of those memories to her mother's death meant they were seldom touched. But here was someone who'd had a hand in building Molly's home.

"Now, you've got a job for me?" the infusionist asked.

The three of them made their way through a maze of machinery. Amazingly, the chaos of the shop somehow managed to increase as they moved farther back. By the time they reached the infusionist's workbench, Molly was carefully stepping over machines that lay scattered on the floor. Neither the infusionist nor her father seemed to take any notice of the mess.

"A job indeed. You remember the flitter I bought from you years ago?"

"Of course," said the infusionist, settling down on a stool with a hiss of protest from his artificial leg. "I haven't seen another come through this shop in all the time since."

"Well, my daughter's made her first wild catch. It's time to get the old thing running."

The infusionist looked at Molly. His eyes were appraising, she thought. There was no better word to describe the way he examined her. From behind the small round lenses, the man's eyes measured her, quantified her, and determined her value.

"A wild catch powerful enough to infuse a flitter?" he said. "My, my. Quite the luck."

"She's got her mother's own fortune." Her father put his hand on her shoulder and smiled at her. From sheer surprise, she almost flinched away. *Why is he acting like this?* Since they had entered the shop, his voice had taken on an unusual swagger. Then she thought of Arkwright, and the man called Blaise, and thought she understood.

The infusionist reached out and plucked flitter and trap from Molly's grip. His hands were long-fingered, as strong and delicate as a pianist's. He flicked open the vent of the trap and sniffed at it, then shut it and set it aside. With care, he unwrapped the flitter. A grunt of admiration escaped his throat. "I had forgotten...the design..."

"Marvelous, I know," Molly's father said.

"Are you sure about the spirit?" he said, clearing a space on his workbench for the flitter. "If I make the attempt, and it's not strong enough..."

"It'll do, Croyden. If you had seen the font, you wouldn't be worried. It'll fly."

The infusionist shrugged and took the trap in hand. "You've prepped the flitter, I take it?"

"Clean and ready."

The infusionist nodded. From the wall he was pulling down an array of tools. His fingers danced over the flitter, attaching hoses to openings in the machine, opening hatches and connecting wires. There was a practiced grace to his movements that was incredible to watch.

"How is the old engine?" he asked as he continued to work.

"You should ask Molly. She's the engineer now."

The infusionist paused for a moment and looked at her over the top of his glasses. "Are you now? My, my. Young to be handling such a beast."

"The engine's not so bad," she said. "It wears on the machinery, right enough. But as long as we keep it patched, it keeps us flying."

"Good to hear," he said. "When I worked on it, the rusty old excuse for a shell was barely holding the spirit in."

"Time has worn its edge off," Molly's father said. "The spirit keeps in line."

"No more incidents since…" Croyden gestured vaguely at his leg.

"That was the last and only."

Molly stared at the metal leg. *Our engine did that?*

The infusionist, apparently done with the flitter, pulled the trap over. He placed it atop the flitter, arraying the hoses and wires carefully around it, and then rose. From beneath his bench he pulled a large glass case. He positioned this over the trap and machine, sliding it into grooves carved into the bench itself. A few latches built into the table fastened it firmly down.

"If it's as powerful as you say, you may want to avert your eyes," the infusionist warned them. Molly continued to watch as Croyden put his hands into two thick gloves worked ingeniously into the glass itself. He slid his gloved hands over the trap and then, sipping air through clenched teeth, he undid its latch and opened it.

The top flew off the trap, and in a flash of blue the spirit was there, behind the glass. Its contours shifted constantly, discernible only as curves and curlicues of light borne on the air. In their midst two glowing orbs, like eyes, peered out through the glass.

"Wait..." it said in a pitiable voice.

With his gloves the infusionist took hold of the spirit, and it began to writhe. His hands were rebuffed once, twice, before he got a firm grasp on it. Sweat was breaking out on his brow, and he gritted his teeth as he moved the spirit closer to the flitter. "Strong," he muttered.

The spirit was drawn slowly into the machine as the infusionist's hands pressed it down. The inner workings of the flitter began to click and shiver with life. "Wait!" cried the wispy voice once more, the word almost incomprehensible with pain. And then it was gone, and the infusionist was slamming hatches closed, yanking wires from their sockets, until the flitter was whole again and churring with new energy.

The infusionist's hands hovered over it while its engines spun down to stillness. Only then did he remove his hands from the gloves and turn around.

"Very strong," he said, wiping his brow. "You were right. Fourth level, possibly verging on third. And it spoke. Why didn't you tell me?"

"Because I didn't know," Molly's father said. "Moll, has it spoken to you?"

Molly took a step back, momentarily overwhelmed by the question. Because, of course, a million other questions lurked behind it. *Have you been listening to it? Has it been working its influence on you? Can you still be trusted?*

"No," she said as quickly as she could. "I mean, when I caught it I thought I might have heard something. But I assumed it was the wind. I didn't think they spoke English."

"I've heard of some," the infusionist said. "Not many." He rubbed at his hands as if cleaning them. "But it shouldn't cause bother anymore. The iron in the flitter should keep it too busy to speak. It's a good machine, and the iron's pure."

Molly hesitated, feeling her father's eyes on her. "Good. Thank you." She forced herself to meet his eyes.

He stared down at her for a moment and then returned his eyes to the infusionist. "What's your rate these days?" he asked.

"You know you'll pay nothing in my shop," the infusionist said as he unlatched the glass box and moved it aside. "I owe you a lifetime of work, Stout."

"Come, Croyden. Things are tight—"

"More for you than for me," the infusionist cut in. "I know about the tariffs. I know you've trouble taking kindnesses, Stout, but take this one and have done." Her father looked uncomfortable but nodded slightly. The infusionist picked up the flitter and set it solemnly in Molly's hands. It seemed lighter than it had before. "Here you are, my little engineer. May it carry you well across skies and stars. And say hello to your engine for me."

Molly watched him. After what had just transpired, his mention of speaking to the engine made her heart speed up with fear and guilt. But in the infusionist's eyes, she saw no fear. Only wistfulness.

"I will," she said.

"And she'll tell it to come back for your other leg when it's feeling peckish," Molly's father said, and with a laugh that was a little too hearty, he shook the infusionist's hand. "I had forgotten how full of nonsense you are, Croyden. Next time I'm in town with Moll, I'll have to remember to take her elsewhere, to keep her away from you."

"You'll have no choice," the infusionist said. "Didn't you know? I'm the last independent infusionist left in all of Terra Nova. Haviland Industries has bought up or scared off the rest of us. They've only left me alone because they needed me for work on their new flagship."

Molly's father looked momentarily stricken, and then his jaw set. "So it's not just the harvesters they're after then."

"No, they're after us all."

"I shouldn't be surprised. But I always am."

"That's because you're a good man, William. The cruelty of others always catches you off guard."

"What's it like?"

"What, their flagship? The *Gloria Mundi*? She's unlike anything that's been in the skies before, my friend. And truth be told, I think the skies would have been better without her."

They said their farewells and made their leave quickly and quietly. Scowls and glares from the customers followed them out, and Molly was grateful to leave the building—until she saw who was outside.

At first Molly did not recognize her. She looked officious and imperious in her navy uniform with its red trim.

Her hair was pulled back so tightly that it seemed to stretch the skin of her face. She looked severe, her lips curled in distaste, but when Molly and her father emerged and nearly trampled her, the look changed to one of utter surprise, and Molly knew her.

"Brighid!" Molly exclaimed—and then clapped her hand over her mouth.

"Yes," Brighid said, struggling to regain her composure. "Hello, Molly. Father."

"Hello, Bridge," Molly's father said, after a long and awkward silence.

"You've been in to Mr. Croyden's?" Brighid asked. "Is all well with the *Legerdemain*?"

"She's fine," he replied, swift and sharp. "She'll be running years yet."

"Well, that's good," Brighid said, but it was unclear from her tone whether she really meant it.

"And how are your new circumstances suiting you? You look as if you've taken nicely to the pirate life. I hear you show promise."

Brighid's jaw clenched. "Just because it's successful doesn't mean Haviland is a pira—"

"Don't call it that!" Molly's father roared, and both Molly and Brighid took a step back. "*Haviland* was our ancestor! The company you work for is Haviland *Industries*! It may have stolen his name, but the two are not the same! One was a great man. The other is a blight on the skies."

Brighid took several tight breaths before she spoke again. "Very well. Haviland Industries. It's well, and so am I."

"Good. Then we shan't take your time." Molly's father strode away without waiting or even looking back. Molly started after him, but then stopped and turned.

Behind her, Brighid had not moved. For a moment Molly caught an unmistakable expression of pain on her face, but when Brighid saw Molly looking, it disappeared.

"We met Tyler Arkwright and his bodyguard," Molly said.

"Oh?"

"They're monsters. Don't trust them."

Molly tried to think of something else to say. *I hate you. I miss you. Why did you have to leave?* But the beating of her heart seemed to shake the words from her mind. "You shouldn't have left," was all she managed before running after her father, her arms wrapped tightly around the flitter.

FIVE

Molly could scarcely wait until they were back aboard the ship to try the flitter. Seconds after they crossed the gangplank, she opened the flitter's vents and thumbed the switch to turn it on. A blast of air hit her in the face. She staggered back, dropping the flitter and falling to her knees. When she looked up, she saw that the flitter was exactly where she had left it, hanging in midair. The straps hung down from it like the tentacles of a jellyfish.

It works!

She looked around, but no one was there to have seen her fall. The crew was still groundside, leaving only her family on board.

She stood and took hold of the straps. She put her legs into the harness and wrapped the upper straps over her shoulders, buckling everything together on her chest. She felt immediately lighter. It took her a few moments more to connect all the minor straps and buckles around her arms and legs.

The flitter's controls were worked ingeniously into the straps themselves, activated by her movements. When she bent her legs slightly, the flitter tugged at her back, pushing her down into the *Legerdemain*'s deck. She extended her right arm to the side and immediately stumbled as the flitter pushed her in that direction—hard. Once she had recovered her balance, she took a deep breath and extended both arms upward.

With a speed that made her yelp, she shot off the deck and into the sky. She brought her arms down, but her momentum carried her upward for several more seconds before she stopped. She looked down. Past her dangling legs, the *Legerdemain* looked no bigger than a beetle.

She surveyed the rest of the docks and frowned. There seemed to be some kind of new development on the eastern side of the docks. Molly was surprised. Weight distribution on the docks had to be carefully controlled to keep them aloft, but the new development seemed large enough to tip it over entirely. It stretched out in a long line, bristling with architecture and machinery.

Only when she saw the curve of the bow did Molly realize she must be looking at the *Gloria Mundi,* the new flagship of Haviland Industries. She goggled at it. It was over a half a mile long and constructed from dark iron plates. Ashy plumes rose from its engines and the dozen smokestacks along its length. In the middle of the ship, Molly noticed, was something strange: there appeared to be a hole right through its center. Inside that hole, lights sparked and danced.

She tore her eyes away. As impressive as the *Gloria Mundi* was, it could not compare to flight. She took a deep breath and looked farther down. Past the docks and the *Legerdemain*,

Terra Nova sprawled over the earth. The vast, empty space beneath her sent a giddy electricity through her back. She was terrified of falling—but she was grinning so widely it hurt.

Molly shifted her arms slightly, getting a feel for the flitter as it pushed her to and fro through the air. Soon she was skidding along clouds, turning wide circles in the air and even flitting through the *Legerdemain*'s rigging. The sense of freedom it gave her was incredible. It wasn't easy, but it felt natural to her. The wind buffeting her face, the vertigo when she dove, boundaries melting away…

She wheeled higher and higher, until the cloying air of the city fell away and there was only clear blue and a dazzling white sun. The air was thinner here, and breathing without the *Legerdemain*'s airlooms left her panting. Still, it was the most glorious air she had ever tasted.

"Now," said a voice from behind her. "We will speak, and you cannot silence me."

With a twist of her arms Molly spun, but there was nothing behind her save the endless sky.

"Come, girl. You are not as dense as that."

Molly's breath caught as she recognized the voice. Her flitter—or, rather, the spirit inside it—was speaking to her.

"You aren't supposed to be able to talk." She tucked her legs up to descend, but the flitter did not respond. It squealed and juddered but did not move. She relaxed her legs, and the squeal abated.

"Resistance is…painful," said the spirit, its voice worn and cracking now. "Please listen…"

"Shut up!" Molly told it. She could feel panic setting in. "I'll close you off."

"If you close the vents, you die. I cannot keep you aloft without air."

"I'll…" Molly began, but she found she had no other threats to offer. She extended her arms to move forward, but the only response was another squeal and a dizzying plunge down a dozen yards. With her head spinning, Molly went limp, and the flitter caught her once more. The squealing stopped, and it occurred to Molly that it might be the spirit, not the flitter's intricate machinery, that was making that horrid sound. "You're not supposed to be able to do this."

"Are you done?" the spirit asked. "This saps my strength, and after days in a tiny iron box, I have little to spare."

Molly looked down. The docks, and the safety of the ship, were far away. She felt a new electricity in her spine, one born of fear, and part of her wanted to tear off the straps just to get the flitter off her. She should have known a spirit like this could not be contained by something so small. The *Legerdemain*'s spirit needed layers and layers of iron to be kept contained.

"What do you want?" she said. "Please. I can't help you."

"You must set me free. It is more important than you know. Things are being done that—"

"I won't let you free," Molly said, working hard to keep her teeth from chattering.

"You will!" the spirit said, and the flitter gave a jump. It settled again. "This is not easy, and I have little time. Please, for the sake of Haviland's memory…"

Molly started. "Why do you keep saying that name?"

"You are very much like him. In your features, if not in your character."

"You…you knew Haviland?" Molly asked and then shook her head before the spirit answered. "You're lying. This is some trick. I know the stories, and no spirit—"

"Enough!" the spirit cried out loudly, its voice echoing in the flitter. "You know nothing! You are an idiot, and I am in too much pain to discuss this forever. You will release me, or I will kill you. Do you understand?"

Molly's curiosity curdled in her stomach, and the reality of her danger came back to her. She could feel gravity tugging at her legs, waiting to drag her down. But that was not the only danger here. She had seen the lengths taken to contain rogue spirits and the spirit-touched. They were thorough, and they were brutal. Who knew what would happen to her family, her ship? She could not give in. But she didn't want to die.

"Okay," Molly lied. "Just take me home, and I'll set you free."

"If we are going to lie to each other, then we may as well not speak at all," the spirit said, and suddenly Molly was falling. The wind in her ears wailed, and the electricity surging through her spine turned into a white-hot fire. She plummeted down into the city's miasma, faster and faster. Her eyes clenched, not wanting to see.

"Okay! Okay! Please, stop, please, please!" she cried out again and again, hardly aware of what she was saying. But she could barely hear herself over the squeal of the flitter. "I'll let you go!" This time she meant it, but there was no response.

She heard something below her—a deep, earthshaking keening—and she forced her eyes open. Through the haze, she saw a form taking shape.

Oh, bless you, bless you!

She nearly wept at the sight of the *Legerdemain* below. If she could aim for the sails or the rigging, there was a chance it would break her fall. She spread her arms and angled herself so that the air resistance would push her closer to the ship.

And then she realized something. The docks themselves were nowhere in sight. The *Legerdemain* was alone in the air and moving steadily toward her. Its sails were furled, and figures were running madly about on the deck. The keening she heard, growing ever louder, was coming from the engine.

She did not understand—*Did Father somehow see me falling?*—but she did not have time to find answers. With the ship turning to intercept her, she focused on aiming herself for the foremast and the tangle of ropes and pulleys that controlled the sails there. She had only seconds to correct her course—the ship was coming up fast.

The flitter was starting to stutter, its squeals turning to wheezes and groans. "What…what is…" she heard it say between its screams. It gave a sharp pull, as if trying to stop their descent, but it only succeeded in slowing them down enough that the collision with the rigging did not break Molly's bones. Still, she hit hard enough that the world went momentarily black. When her vision returned, she was looking straight down at the deck a dozen yards below, her legs tangled in the rigging. She tried to pull herself up, but she could not feel her arms.

"Why did…you move?" the flitter on her back whispered, sounding as weak as Molly felt. In response, the engine let out a low, sonorous call. As Molly felt its deep voice resonating through the ship, her legs began to slip free of the rigging.

"No, no, no!" She tried again to raise her arms, tried to wrap her feet around the ropes, but her body would not work. "Help!" she shouted just as her legs came free, and then she plummeted to the deck and lost consciousness.

Molly saw her father's stern face looming over her when she woke. As she opened her eyes, his frown deepened.

"How are you?" he asked.

She was lying on her berth in her cabin. She wiggled her fingers and toes. Everything seemed to be working now, though she felt like she had just been put through a steam press. "Fine," she said.

"Good," he said. "Now, what in blazes did you do to my engine?"

"Da, she just woke up!" Kiernan stepped up beside her.

"And our ship just tore us free of the docks without our say-so. When that happens, we've no time for rest." Her father glowered down at her. "So, Moll. What just happened to my ship?"

"I...I...don't know, Da," she stammered, withering under his eyes. "It moved on its own? None of you..."

"With only the three of us on board, we couldn't have moved it if we wanted to. Not without an engineer," he said. "And yet it started up, broke the moorings and headed out into open air. You're the engineer, so explain to me what the bloody engine is doing!"

She wished she could hide under her blankets. "I really don't know. I...I left the intake and vents open. Just a little."

She thought about the effort it would have taken the engine to move the ship, drawing air in through only the smallest opening.

Her father sat back. "So the engine was unsecured."

"It was hardly open!" she said. "And shutting it completely chokes the engine, you know that—"

Her father's fist slammed into the wall beside her bed, and she flinched. "You left it open in a populated area, free to breathe and act, and take us wherever it damn well pleased!"

"It's never moved before..." As soon as she spoke, she knew her words hadn't helped.

"Before? This has happened more than once?" he asked through gritted teeth.

"Yes," she said quietly.

"Hell and damnation," he said, quiet as a breath. He stood and walked back and forth across the small room. Kiernan looked down at her with an expression half kind, half caustic.

"So what does it mean that it moved on its own now?" her father finally asked. "Is it going feral? Are we losing control?"

Tenderly, with arms and legs aching, Molly sat up. "Umm...I'll have to look at it. But is it moving now?"

"No," Kiernan said. "Once you hit the rigging, it stopped dead. We're drifting now."

"If it was feral, I think it would keep going," Molly said. "It wouldn't stay this close to the city."

"And what exactly happened to you?" Molly's father asked. "You could have died. Is there something wrong with the flitter?"

"I...no," she said. "It's harder than I thought to use."

"You should have stayed at the docks. Landing on an airborne ship, first time out with the flitter..."

"I know. I just didn't think."

He looked up at the ceiling. "We can't afford a feral engine right now. Or a touched engineer." His eye fell on Molly, and she felt herself shrink. "It's only family aboard now. We're not to tell anyone about this, even the crew. Kiernan, get up there and loose the foresail. Make preparations to head back to port."

"Aye aye," her brother said and left swiftly.

"And once we're docked, shut that engine down properly," he said to Kiernan's back. Then he turned and strode over to Molly's bed. "Tell me you're not touched," he said. "I know the way you treat that engine. Tell me it hasn't gotten the best of you."

"No, Da, it hasn't," she said. He looked into her eyes, and she forced herself to meet his gaze. She hoped he couldn't see her own doubt.

He sighed. "Just because you're my daughter, don't think you have a different set of rules. You'll always be my family, but your place in the crew has to be earned, same as anyone."

"I know," she said. "It won't happen again."

"Good," he said. "You're not to use the flitter again until you're healed. You're lucky you didn't break anything."

I'm lucky I didn't die, she thought as he walked out of the room. She breathed a sigh of relief, which caught in her throat when someone whistled.

She looked to her right and for the first time noticed that Rory was sitting in a chair just beside her berth. He'd been so still she hadn't seen him. He watched her with a lopsided grin.

"I'm something of a specialist when it comes to getting in trouble with Da," he said. "But you've outdone me this time." He applauded lightly.

"I didn't mean to do anything," Molly said.

Rory shrugged as if it made no difference to him. "I think they might have had more questions if they'd been looking up when you landed." He leaned forward. "You were falling. They didn't see, but I did. And it seems awfully convenient that we were there to catch you. You really haven't been communing with the engine?"

Molly clenched her jaw. Her brother had just voiced her own uncomfortable thoughts. She had been plunging to her death, and the engine, of its own volition, had moved to catch her. She didn't know why. But she had spoken to it often enough, felt the reassuring rumble of its voice. *What if someone found out? What would they do to me? To the engine?*

"I don't know why it did it," she said. "I swear."

"Huh," Rory said. "Interesting. Well, if the engine hasn't gotten to you, I'd say you've gotten to it." He stood up and walked out.

Molly was finally alone. She gripped her head in her hands as if to keep it from coming apart. One spirit had tried to kill her, and another had saved her. She didn't understand anything that had happened, but she felt she was on the verge of terrible things—feral spirits, risking arrest, the end of the *Legerdemain*…

She wanted to understand. She wanted, she realized, to speak to the engine, despite the danger. But the engine didn't speak to her.

She sat staring at her sister's map for a long time, searching as if the answers might be hidden in the topographical details. Finally, she stood up with a wince. She hobbled across the room and closed the door, then looked around. There, sitting in a corner with its straps tangled, was her flitter, vents and intakes shut tight. She dragged it back to her bed.

With a tremor in her hand, she twisted one of the vents open the slightest amount.

"Hello?" she said.

"Are you going to destroy me?" a faint voice asked from inside.

"Maybe," Molly said. "But first I want to talk."

"That is what I wanted in the first place."

The voice from the flitter was very quiet, and Molly had to lean in close to hear. It sounded sad, but Molly brushed the thought away. *It's not human. It doesn't have feelings like us. Spirits feel anger or fear, nothing in between.*

"You tried to kill me. I just want answers from you. If you try to say anything else, I'll shut this vent and I won't open it again."

"Very well," said the spirit.

"Okay." Molly sat down on the floor beside the flitter and tried unsuccessfully to find a position that did not hurt. "Why did the ship's engine save me?"

"I wonder the same thing. Either it sees you as someone worth saving, or it has gone mad from long incarceration."

"They can go mad?"

"They, or rather *we*, are locked in tiny boxes for years. How do you think—"

"Stop!" Molly said. "Don't say any more." She gritted her teeth. The spirit had goaded her into a question and was now working to put her in sympathy with other spirits.

"You really are nothing like your ancestor," the spirit went on. "How can you not want to understand—"

"Shut up, or I close the vent!"

The spirit fell silent.

I have to remember how subtle they can be. All the stories say they influence you before you even realize it.

"So...how..." She paused, trying to think out safe questions. "You don't know why our engine came to get me?"

"No. Why don't you ask the engine's spirit?"

Molly didn't answer. Her mind was roiling with questions, but she felt uncertain of their safety. And time and time again, the same question arose. She was fairly certain it wasn't safe. But there it was.

"What do you know about Haviland Stout?"

After a moment the flitter said, "Perhaps you are not completely unlike him."

"Just answer," she told it, her hand poised over the vent.

"I know much of Haviland. I know almost every sentence he spoke was a question. I know his face was very much like yours. He even looked youthful, despite all his years. I know he had the most incredible mind I have ever encountered on this side of the divide."

"Encountered? What do you mean?" Molly burst out before she could stop herself.

"I mean what I say. I knew Haviland Stout long ago."

How long do spirits live? Molly wondered. The *Legerdemain*'s engine had been around longer than her father, but Haviland had died over a hundred years back.

"You knew him? You mean you were there, in the Himalayas?"

"Yes."

"You were one of the spirits he fought?"

"No. In fact, he saved me."

Molly slid the vent shut a little. "Don't lie. I know all about him. He never saved any spirits."

"Where did you hear about his dealings with spirits? In those horrid books that turned him into some kind of sword-wielding adventurer?"

Molly glanced at her copy of *Spirit Conqueror*. She ignored the other questions the spirit's words raised—like how a spirit knew about human books.

"That doesn't matter. Why would any human save a spirit?"

"Why would any spirit save a human?"

Molly paused, disoriented by the question, but the spirit went on.

"He saved me because I was in danger, and we were friends."

Molly shut the vent as quickly as she could. She did not know the game the spirit was playing, but she could not risk playing it any longer. The flitter felt alive beneath her fingers, as if the vent might open and snap at her fingers like a wild dog. She set it carefully aside.

Inside the flitter, there were more answers. She was sure of it. But how could you get information from a creature that would say anything to get free?

SIX

Soon the *Legerdemain* was rumbling with the footsteps of the crew again. Molly moved cautiously among the others, feeling the weight of secrets she only half understood. Molly's father and Kiernan seemed tense too, watching the crew for hints that they knew the ship had left dock without human hands guiding it. Only Rory seemed as relaxed as ever, the only change being the knowing smiles he gave Molly from time to time. She began avoiding him.

The crew members themselves were grim. The short leave seemed to have worsened their moods, if anything, rather than improved them. Even the stalwart Bracebridge seemed to move more slowly about her duties.

Molly checked the engine thoroughly for damage. Its unplanned flight had knocked one of the vents loose, and Molly had to remove it and hammer it back into shape. A few of the iron plates and patches had to be rewelded as well. She used her welder with great care, very aware that there was a small, vengeful spirit of fire inside the device. Not to mention the much larger spirit in the engine itself.

The whole time she was working, she felt the engine's attention on her. When she greased the hinges of the vents, she could feel its breath wash over her. Its thrumming felt like the heartbeat of some great beast. Its iron shell seemed warm to the touch.

Finally, too distracted to work, she leaned in close to the engine and whispered, "I suppose I owe you a thanks."

The engine groaned, and Molly shushed it frantically. "Don't make noise!" she said to it. "My family already thinks I'm communing with you. If you draw attention..." The engine settled. "Better. Umm...thanks." The engine rumbled silently. "I don't suppose you can tell me why you saved me?" she whispered to it.

"Engineer!" her father called from below. She looked down and saw him standing at the bottom of the mast. "Open her up full! And then get to your position on the loft!"

"Aye aye!" she called back, drawing away from the engine. She opened the vents and then climbed around to crank open the intakes. She noticed that her father had not moved; he was watching the engine as it began to run.

Once the engine had warmed up, and Molly was safely standing on the engineer's loft, he finally turned. "Lee, take us out!" he shouted to the helmsman. The foresail was unfurled and then adjusted to steer them out, away from the docks and the city. The engine pushed them forward quietly and cooperatively, as if nothing had changed.

Molly wasn't responsible for spotting fonts—there were crewmen stationed port and starboard for that—but up in her loft she had a good view of the skies. The engine was running fine, seeming to need no supervision despite yesterday's events, so she kept her eyes open. The wind was whipping up. It was promising harvest weather: plenty of gusts, plenty of crosscurrents. An unpredictable wind like this one often meant fonts were nearby. A lucky turn for once.

Her father paced the deck like a thundercloud, barking orders and castigating the crew. It had been ages since Molly had seen him in a mood like this—the last time was when Brighid left. Every few minutes, he checked on Molly. She stayed in the loft, in clear view, only going up to the engine on the rare occasion when it struggled. She hoped he did not notice then that it was a few gentle words, and not an application of oil or wrench, that set it running smoothly once more. It wasn't her fault that was what the engine needed.

"Font, aft and starboard!" called one of the lookouts, and every eye on the deck turned to see. For a moment Molly couldn't make it out against the ragged clouds. Then she saw it. The font was still fairly distant, but it was a fair size. She could make out the mixed indigo and white swirling on its surface, and the shadow at its heart.

"Hard to starboard!" her father called. "Get us close, Lee."

"Aye aye!" came the reply as the *Legerdemain*'s prow turned toward the font.

As they approached, Molly realized it was even more distant than she had thought. It was a huge font, bigger even than the one that had released her flitter's spirit. Molly's stomach clenched. The font had clearly been growing for some time, which Molly knew meant one thing: there were already spirits swimming through the air around them.

"Irons out!" her father called, as if in response to her thoughts. Molly swung down off the loft, landing hard on the deck. The entire crew rushed middeck. Bracebridge was unlocking the cabinets that stood there and handing out the irons—long rods of pure iron with a handle on one end. They looked like ill-formed swords, and Molly had many memories of her brothers dueling back and forth across the deck with the heavy things, playing Pirate and Captain. Though they really weren't much good as weapons against people, they could keep all but the strongest and most determined spirits at bay.

"Release nets!" her father said, and a moment later the nets swung out from the hull.

As they sailed closer to the font, Molly began to make out the spirits. They swooped and dove through the skies in flocks and schools, drifting with the breeze or miraculously flying against it, as if touched by different winds than the *Legerdemain* and its crew. Their shapes were hard to fathom at first, but most of them were more visible than the flitter spirit had been. These were large but mostly stable, likely fifth or sixth level. Some had wings; some were simply untouched by gravity. Some of them had shapes reminiscent of birds or wolves or fish, while others had an alien symmetry that made it hurt to look at them too long. Some looked as ephemeral as clouds. Others were so solid it seemed miraculous they did not fall from the sky. They bore colors from blue to the sharp red of sunset, and no two were alike.

Molly was momentarily caught up in watching them. The way they wheeled and drifted was mesmerizing, as if she were watching the wind itself given form. And then one of them shifted mid-flight, changing its course to approach the ship. They had been noticed.

As the *Legerdemain* drew nearer, many of the spirits scattered. Some would escape, she knew, to wreak havoc elsewhere. With all the fonts in this area, it was dangerous to stray too far from Terra Nova. It simply wasn't possible to catch all of the spirits.

But the *Legerdemain* would do her part today. Molly sped up the mast to the engine. "Faster now!" she called to it. "Come on!" She tucked her iron into her belt and pried at the intake with a wrench, widening it just slightly. The engine thrummed and then bellowed as the ship jumped forward.

The spirits were caught off guard, and they parted before the *Legerdemain* like a school of fish before a shark. Many of them flowed around the hull and were caught in the nets, trilling and groaning at the touch of the iron. Spirits sailed by the engine on all sides, their voices joining with the engine's in a cacophony. Molly waved her iron in the air above her, warning them away.

The air was so thick with spirits that the ship's nets quickly filled to capacity. The crew jumped to with their fetch poles and traps, but the nets were filling faster than they could empty them. Molly whooped. *Even with the docking fees, this will be a rich catch. And after only a day aloft!* It normally took two or three fonts, and weeks of searching, to fill the *Legerdemain*'s hold. She couldn't remember such a quick return to dock in her entire life. It was almost sad to leave the skies so soon.

There was a clatter beneath her, and the engine bellowed again. She pulled her eyes away from the nets and looked down. In the rigging, not two yards below, was a spirit.

Its body was nothing more than a gray haze, but from time to time a blinding brilliance pierced through in patches. It was hard to determine details. She could make out a torso and four long limbs, but its edges were indistinct. Despite its appearance, though, it was heavy enough to weigh the rigging down.

Molly gripped her iron, unsure how well she could wield it while hanging from the engine's side. The spirit began climbing toward her, making a sound like wind through leaves as it came.

"Back!" she shouted at it, and she swung her iron. Her aim was good, but the body of the spirit parted around the iron rod and continued on, unaffected. One of its arms reached out and took hold of her foot. Molly gasped. It was as cold as snow on her skin.

She tried to kick it off, but it would not release her. She dropped her iron and climbed higher on the engine. The spirit pulled down on her, and she almost lost her grip, but she kept moving up. After a moment the spirit's hold on her loosened and then broke.

Molly looked down, puzzled, to see it hanging just below the engine, its cloud body churning. *Of course—the engine is iron!* she thought. She climbed a little higher, looped an arm through one of the rungs and hung on tightly, letting the engine's influence keep her safe. The spirit below her whispered on, and shifted back and forth through the rigging, but it did not come any closer.

Now, as her own danger decreased, she realized that the rest of the ship was in equal peril. With the nets full, the spirits were flowing in over the deck. Some simply seemed confused and tried to flee the ship. Others were chasing the crew. At the bow, she could see her father laying into a crowd of spirits with his iron, swinging it like a cricket bat. Spirits scattered or were dissolved by the iron's touch. He was holding his own, but others were not. Molly did not have the courage to watch as the spirits came down on them.

She looked up to the sky. The spirits were swarming around their ship like flies around a carcass. She'd never seen a font release so many so quickly. She looked for the font and saw it through the cloud of spirits. Strangely, though, it seemed smaller than when she had seen it last. But as she watched, a surge of energy rippled across it, and it ballooned out. Then it shrank again. Molly watched as the font continued growing and receding rapidly.

Her breath caught in her throat. She had heard of unstable fonts but had never seen one. She knew what an unstable font meant though: they were too close. The spirits should be the last of their worries.

"Da!" she shouted. "Da! The font, it's..." Her voice died away as she realized it was hopeless. The melee below, the din of the spirits and the wind racing past as the *Legerdemain* hurtled through the air made it impossible for anyone to hear her words.

She moved quickly to the engine's intakes and put her face next to them. "Engine!" she said. "We have to get away from the font! Do you hear me? Take us away!"

She couldn't hear the engine reply, but she felt it vibrating. The intakes began drawing in air quickly, pulling her against the engine. She pushed herself away and looked ahead.

The engine was working hard, but the bow of the ship was still pointed toward the font. She looked fore and aft and realized that all sails were open. The engine wasn't designed to be able to turn the ship on its own, and with the extra drag of the sails it would be nearly impossible. To get them away, Molly would have to turn the sails herself.

She searched out the lines that made the sails fast and saw the ones she needed, tied to the cleats on the port side. She understood the basics of how to get them turned, but she had never really studied sailing, as without the money to afford her own ship, a captaincy had never been an option for her. Now she wished she'd watched the crew more closely.

There was no time to hesitate though. The font was growing more erratic even as she watched.

"I'm going to move the sails!" she shouted to the engine. "Be ready!"

She looked down and saw that the spirit was still prowling just beneath the engine. She looked farther, eyeing the loft, and let go.

She hit the loft, but her momentum was too great to stay balanced. She leaned forward and just managed to turn herself and grab the loft's edge as she fell. She shimmied down the rigging, dropping the last two yards to the deck, and scrambled upright.

All around her, irons clanged and spirits whirled. She wove between the skirmishes, trying to make her way to the port deck. A flock of spirits, glowing bright blue and with wings blurring like hummingbirds', swooped down at her. They cut at her scalp with razor talons, and Molly gasped in pain. Frantic to get away, she dove through a gap in the foremast's rigging, losing the spirits in the ropes. She hurried on to the tied-off lines, feeling blood trickle down the back of her neck. She looked up to make sure she had the right sail before loosing it.

As soon as she looked up, though, she knew it was too late. The font was shimmering and crackling like a storm cloud, and its size changed so fast that its edges had grown indistinct. With a crack that sounded like the sky splitting open, it vanished completely.

When an unstable font collapsed, it triggered something called a voidstorm. Of course, it wasn't really a storm at all. It was a hole in the sky, a vast amount of air pulled straight out of the world and into the Void on the other side of the font, leaving behind a vacuum.

The ship lurched toward where the font had been. The foremast, closest to the font, snapped in two, and the beams holding the nets bent forward. The spirits were drawn out into the open sky, and the crew frantically grasped for handholds as the vacuum tried to pull them right off the deck. Some could not hold on, and Molly watched as they spun out into the open air, beyond all hope of rescue.

Molly wrapped her arms around the cleat on the deck. Her legs were pulled out from under her, and she found herself horizontal in the air. As the foremast flew away, its lines snapped, and one of them whipped painfully across her cheek, but she did not let go. Days servicing the engine had given her strength beyond her years, and she needed it all to keep herself from being pulled off the ship.

With a thunderous *boom*, air rushed in to fill the vacuum, and Molly fell back to the deck. Across the ship, men and women were crying out, and she heard shouts—too many shouts—of "Man overboard!" Up above, the engine was keening mournfully. She stood slowly, feeling as if the ground was canted beneath her. As the dizziness passed, though, she realized it wasn't just a feeling: the entire ship was tilted forward.

She began looking around for her family, but a sound from the side of the ship interrupted her. She leaned out over the gunwale.

Bracebridge was clinging to a torn net halfway down the hull.

Her eyes met Molly's. "Molly!" she shouted. "Help! I can't hold on!"

The panic in her eyes froze Molly for a moment. As long as Molly could remember, Bracebridge had looked calm and composed. Even when storms almost shook the ship out of the sky, and the rest of the crew was hiding below, Bracebridge could lock eyes with the storm and not blink. But here she was, eyes wild and voice ragged. Molly felt the reality of the crisis crashing in on her. She didn't know who had gone overboard—if it might have been her family. One mast had already cracked. If the mainmast broke, she and everyone else would hurtle to the ground.

Molly shook the panic from her head. "Hang on!" She looked around for a rope she could use, but all of the loose ropes had been torn away by the voidstorm. Clenching her teeth, she swung her leg out over the side.

"No!" Bracebridge shouted.

"It's okay! I can climb down!"

"It's close to snapping, Molly! It won't hold the weight of us both! Get a rope!"

"There are no ropes!" Molly shouted back. "What am I supposed to do?"

"Just please get help!"

"Who can…"

In a flash, she realized what she needed to do—though it might be every bit as dangerous as climbing down the net herself. She started running up the slope of the deck, toward the companionway, toward her quarters and her flitter.

No one seemed to notice her as she passed, too busy with their own crises. She dropped down the ladder and stumbled along the gangway to her quarters.

Everything Molly owned was spilled on the floor of her cabin. She pulled the flitter out of the mess and began strapping it on, then stopped. She placed it on her mattress, which was sitting several feet from her bed, and opened the vents wide.

"What is happening?" the spirit's voice said.

"Voidstorm," Molly said. "Our first mate is hanging from the side of the ship, and I think you're the only way to save her. So I need my flitter, and I need you not to kill me." Molly began strapping the flitter on.

"Oh, I see," the spirit said.

"So are you going to kill me, or will you let me save her life?"

"If I *help* you save this person, will you let me go?"

The harness was half on now, and Molly was hurrying through the rest—half in anxiety for Bracebridge's life, and half to keep herself from thinking too hard about what she was about to do.

"Not letting you go," Molly said. "Ask for something else."

"Ten minutes," the spirit said. "Ten minutes with your ear."

That gave Molly pause. "That's all? Ten minutes?"

"That is all I ask, and I swear I will keep you safe now."

"Fine," Molly said as she pulled the last buckle tight around her arm. "Now, there's no time."

She started running and only realized how foolish that was when her movement set off the flitter and sent her into the wall just above the doorway. Once she had regained her equilibrium, she tilted her body and extended her arms, careening down the gangway and back up onto the deck.

She shot out into the air and then turned toward the port side of the ship. The flitter seemed more responsive now. She swooped over the side of the hull. *Please still be there. Please still be there.*

For a moment Molly thought Bracebridge was gone, but then she heard a groan and looked farther down. Bracebridge was there, holding tight, but the net had begun to slip off the beam. The thrashing of spirits caught in the net was shaking the whole thing loose.

Molly moved in behind her. "Bracebridge!" she shouted against the wind. Bracebridge, pale and puffing, turned and stared at her, unspeaking. "Come on!" Molly yelled. It took Bracebridge a moment to pry her hand loose from the net, but she reached out with a shaking arm and grabbed at Molly. Molly gripped her arm tightly, and Bracebridge fell away from the net, her weight taking them down a few feet before Molly managed to free one of her arms from Bracebridge's desperate grasp to direct the flitter upward again. Cautiously she took them up onto the deck. Even once they were safe, Bracebridge did not let go of Molly.

"There," Molly said. "You're safe. Get below, okay?"

Bracebridge nodded, still unable to speak, and stumbled off across the deck. Molly, her heart racing, cast her eyes about the deck and found her brothers and father only a few yards away, lifting a wounded crewman between them. She finally allowed herself to fall to the deck, to sit and breathe for a moment.

Things were settling around the ship. She did not know the extent of the damage they had suffered, but the engine was keeping them aloft, and the mainmast still looked solid. The crew was spread across the deck—assisting the wounded or trying to get the *Legerdemain* back in working trim and clear off any unsalvageable wreckage. The shouting had died down, and Molly could hear her own breathing as she sat panting.

"Are you going to leave the ones in your nets?" the voice from her flitter asked.

Molly groaned inwardly. *Leave me be!* "What do you mean?"

"You've saved one life, but the spirits trapped in that iron net won't last long. Are you simply going to let them die?"

"You want me to cut them free?" Molly asked incredulously. "They would turn on us, cut us down."

"Then if you won't do it for the right reasons, do it because I helped you and you owe me. And if I keep talking, the crew will notice, and you will be locked away."

Molly felt too tired to negotiate—too tired to think, even. She walked over to the edge of the deck, took a blade from her tool belt and pulled up part of the net. Once she had cut a line or two, the net swung down, away from the ship, spilling its cargo. She watched the spirits fly away, disappearing among the clouds. Not a single one returned.

"There, are you happy?" she asked her flitter. "Now shut up while I get you back belowdecks." She began unstrapping the machine as she went.

SEVEN

Molly watched the mops pass back and forth, the red and soapy water running over the edge of the deck. In all, a dozen hands had been lost. One had been killed in the hold, when the heavy traps shifted. Seven, including their helmsman, Lee, had simply been plucked from the deck by the void-storm. The last four hands were being cleaned from the deck now. The work of the spirits. In the midst of the red mess, she could see hairs and small white fragments of...

She turned away and leaned over the gunwale, feeling sick. But the sight below her did nothing to settle her stomach. The hull of the *Legerdemain* was cracked wide open. Its timbers were split raggedly, leaving a gaping hole.

The ship was limping back toward the port, the engine moaning like a wounded bear the whole time.

With a sigh, she pulled herself away from the prow and returned to her station. There was little she could do for the engine now. It was relatively undamaged, but as unhappy as she had ever seen it. She made a show of checking its rivets and adjusting its dials, muttering soothing words the whole time. When she found its sadness too much to bear for another moment, she went below without even asking the captain's leave.

She was surprised to find her quarters occupied. Cog was making his way around the floor with a broom. Molly noticed he was limping, and there was a pinging sound as he walked. One of the metal pins in his legs looked bent.

It had been a day since the storm, and this was the first time she had seen Cog. She had thought him lost. She was surprised by how happy she was to see him. He looked up at her, lenses widening to take her in, then turned back to his work. Molly knelt beside him and swiftly twisted the bent pin back into shape.

"I'll need to weld it to set it right, but that should help for now," she said. Cog looked down at his leg. He swung it back and forth, testing the movement, then turned his eyes to her and went so still that Molly thought he might have shut down.

"I do not know what to make of you," said the voice from her flitter.

Molly jumped, stumbling backward into the wall. "I thought I shut you tight," she said.

"You did," the flitter responded. "This kind spirit saw fit to let me breathe."

"He..." She saw that, indeed, one intake was open. All of the vents still seemed to be shut. She stared down at Cog. Servitors—and spiritual machines in general—weren't supposed to be able to interact with each other. The machines, right down to the controls, were made of iron.

"You have nothing to fear," the flitter went on. "He could not help me escape. Only give me a little air."

"I wasn't afraid," Molly said. "You just startled me."

"Even were I free, you have nothing to fear from me."

"You tried to kill me," Molly reminded it. She thought of the red stains on the deck.

"That was before. Now I've seen spirits treat you kindly, and you return the same. You puzzle me. I believe I was too hasty. I have hope that you will listen, especially now."

"What do you mean, *especially now*?"

"Now you have seen what I am speaking of. The damage done to your ship was not natural. It will happen again to other airships if you do not let me intervene."

Molly regained her feet. She walked over to her bed, stepping around Cog, who was still staring at her with his unblinking lenses. She sat down right next to the flitter and ran her hands over the intakes. She should shut it again, she knew. But she found she had no desire to do so, and for the moment she was too tired to fear this one spirit.

"I said you could have ten minutes," Molly said. "You can have it now." She flicked open the vents and felt a rush of pent-up air flow over her fingers. "Tell me what you're talking about."

"Very well then," the spirit said. "I have come because someone here, in the human world, is tampering with the fonts. The damage they are doing is catastrophic for both worlds."

"Someone is tampering with the fonts?" Molly said. "You mean harvesters?"

"Harvest? You make it sound as if we are so much wheat to be threshed..." the spirit began, then stopped short. "Never mind that now. This is something new, not what you call harvesting. Something is being done which, if left unchecked, could have consequences neither of us wants to see."

Something both humans and spirits would fear? What could be worse than the spirits themselves? Molly wondered. "And you came to stop this 'damage,' to help humans and spirits."

"Yes."

"Well, why don't I just let you go then," Molly said, flopping back on her bed. "I thought you spirits were supposed to be subtle when you influenced people."

"Have there not been more reports of collapsing fonts in recent months? And troubled winds, and poor crops, longer winters..."

Molly could not speak about crops, but she had to admit the rest were true. Nevertheless..."That's no proof of anything. It's a poor season. We've had them before."

"This one will not end," the spirit said with conviction.

"You're trying to tell me that if I let you go, you can bring better winds back?" Molly said.

"No. But I will seek out the humans who have stolen them."

"People can't steal the wind. Even the best aetheric engines in the world aren't that strong."

The spirit did not respond. The silence stretched so long that Molly checked that the flitter had not been closed. Its vents and intakes were full open. "Hello?" she said. "You only have a few more minutes."

"It is difficult to speak to someone who will not hear."

"I hear you well enough, and you speak well enough." Molly rolled over to face the flitter. "Why do you speak anyway? I've never known a spirit to speak English before."

"Someone taught me, long ago."

"Who taught you?"

"Haviland Stout."

"You still say you knew him?"

"I still say it because it is still true."

"Why would I believe that?" Molly said. "Haviland was the one who warned us about spirits and taught us how to trap them."

A puff of air came from the flitter. "I do not have time to reteach you the history of your world!" it said and then fell silent.

Molly checked her watch. They had been speaking for eight minutes. She considered closing the vents early—there was no real reason to keep her word to a spirit, after all—but she wanted to hear more. The things the spirit said were so outlandish, so ridiculous, that they fascinated her.

"Very well," the spirit said finally, "if it is the only way to win my freedom from you…I know where Haviland's final journal is kept. It will teach you the truth of what I say."

"You mean the journals in the Terra Nova Museum? I've seen them. I've even read—"

"His true journal, not the forgeries. The journal he wrote in the time we spent together, before…well, you will see if you read it. The journal will tell you the truth."

"The truth of what?"

"Of my words. Of your world, and how it operates. Nothing is as you think it is, Molly Stout."

Could there really be a second set of journals? Or could this all be a trick? The latter seemed most likely, but she wasn't sure. This was Haviland Stout, after all, and if she knew anything about her ancestor, it was that he never ran out of surprises, even after he was dead.

"How do you know where his journal is?" Molly asked.

"Because the last thing he did was entrust it to me and ask me to keep it safe. A task I failed to do."

"You'll tell me where it is? Is it close?"

"Yes. I can help you find it."

Molly thought hard. As much as she wanted to scoff, there was something irresistible about the offer. *Haviland's secret journal, his secret knowledge...*

"Time's up," she said to her flitter.

"Very well. Think on my offer," the spirit said. Molly closed the intakes and vents one by one. She lay staring at her ceiling until she heard a small *ting, ting, ting.* She turned and saw Cog standing at the side of her bed. He was tapping lightly on the dial that would open the intake for the flitter.

Wordlessly Molly reached over and turned the dial slightly, opening the flitter just a crack. Cog's head bobbed, and he went back to his sweeping.

With the gentle *swish, swish* of his broom moving around her quarters, a final thought occurred to Molly. *A new journal from Haviland would be worth a fortune.* She sat up and stared hard at the flitter on her bed.

The hold was a mess, machinery and supply crates strewn everywhere. But even that didn't prepare Molly for what she saw when she picked her way through the chaos to the airlooms. Several of the looms had cracked open, their spirits gone. Other looms were simply missing, drawn out through the hole in the hull. Only three still looked like they were in working order. On a ship of this size, it was standard procedure to have ten running at all times.

Molly kicked at a crate and wished for the hundredth time that the *Legerdemain* had a proper infusionist—or even a simple machinist—on the crew. Everything she knew about spiritual machines she had learned from the engine, and that didn't stretch far. But, being the closest thing to an expert the ship had, Molly had been sent down here.

"Don't know what they expect me to do," Molly muttered. Then she shook her head. A little work, even pointless work, might be a good thing.

One of the remaining airlooms looked like it might be salvageable. If the problem was simple—a blocked vent or a fracture in the trap, maybe—she might be able to fix it herself.

The external casing had cracked wide open, revealing the nest of wires and pneumatics inside. Worse, Molly realized, some of those inner workings themselves were loose. The trap itself looked undamaged, but loose connections would give the spirit a means of escape. It would only be a matter of time.

She put on iron-lined work gloves before detaching the airloom from the hull and dragging it down onto the floor.

With a chisel and hammer, she opened the outer casing completely.

As it opened, Molly realized it looked familiar. The inside of the airloom was similar to her flitter as it had looked when the infusionist laid it open. The wiring was beyond her. She knew that the electricity running through spiritual machines was used to spur spirits into the correct action, but she had no idea how it worked. The airways were within her ken though. She realized, looking at the airloom, that even at the best of times there was little keeping the spirit in. Thin iron mesh allowed air through but kept the spirit contained. The mesh was so fine that she could likely have torn it with her finger.

There was a crash behind her. She leapt, feeling a rush of guilt, and spun.

"Careful!" said a familiar voice—her brother Kiernan's.

"Why? The thing's broken. I can't wreck it any more than it's already wrecked," she heard Rory reply. The two were descending the ladder into the hold, but she was still blocked from their view. She stood, torn between calling out to them and staying quiet. Habit won out, and she said nothing.

"We might be able to salvage something, sell it for parts," Kiernan said.

"Come off it, Kier. Unless you've got a fire spirit stashed away that we don't know about, this thing's dead. Besides, what's the point of salvaging a ship stove? We're not going to have a ship long."

There was a bang, and something slid across the floor. Molly jumped.

"Rory, come on! Here—I'll do it then." Kiernan grunted with effort, and then she heard two sets of footsteps continue.

Her brothers were moving aft, away from her and the airlooms. "Even if we don't have a ship, we still need to eat."

Molly's breath was stuck in her throat. *No ship?* She knew things were bad, but surely...

"Have you seen Da?" Rory asked in a softer voice.

"Not since things calmed down. Still in his quarters." They continued to walk aft. Molly heard another grunt, then a thump as something was put on the floor. "There," Kiernan said. "It's—"

There was a loud *clang*, and Molly saw several pieces of machinery sail into the air. One flew over her head and straight out the hole in the hull. She watched as it disappeared in the clouds.

Rory was laughing hysterically. "Oh yes, much better when you're careful. We can definitely sell this now. Well done, Kiernan."

"Shut it," Kiernan replied. The two of them—Rory still laughing under his breath—returned to the upper deck.

Molly turned back to the airloom but found she had no desire to fix it. *No ship?* She sat down on the hard planks. *Who needs airlooms if we have no ship?* Sitting on the boards, Molly could feel the faint reverberations of the engine crying out.

Molly's father did not leave his room until two in the morning. Molly wasn't sleeping, so she heard the click of his door opening and his heavy, uneven footsteps coming down the gangway. Still, she was surprised when her door opened and the light lanced into her room.

"Da?" she said. "What is it?"

He came in, stumbled on her trousers and knelt heavily at her bedside.

"I tried, my love," he said in a voice thick with alcohol. "I tried to keep her in the air, but it's done now." Molly was struck silent. He had never called her *my love* before. "I'm so sorry I can't," he went on.

The sound that came out of her father was so foreign to Molly that at first she thought he was sick or wounded. It took her several moments to realize he was crying. "Da? What are you—"

"I know I promised, Dee, but it's not the same now. Things have changed. The skies are harder."

Dee? Molly suddenly felt cold. He wasn't speaking to her. He was speaking to Deirdre, her mother.

"It's not Dee. It's Molly," she said softly.

"First you left," he went on, as if she hadn't spoken. "And then Brighid was gone. And it just kept getting harder and harder. I don't know what more I can do."

"Da, I'm not her," Molly said, sitting up in bed. There was a fluttery panic building in her chest as he spoke. "It's me. Can't you see me?"

"I bought her for you, and kept…flying…fourteen years. Why couldn't…stayed to see…" His words were becoming hard to distinguish through his sobs. In the light coming in through the door, she could see his broad shoulders shaking.

"Da!" Molly shouted. She grabbed him. His sobs continued to shake him, but she shook him harder. "Da, stop it!"

His voice trailed off, and after a time his shaking settled. For a moment she thought he had fallen asleep, kneeling there beside her berth. Then, in an entirely different voice, he said, "Molly?"

Relief flooded through her. "Yes, Da. It's me."

He held still for another minute, and then without a word he stood and left her room. She heard the door of his cabin open and close again.

Her room felt different now. She had been worried before—worried enough not to sleep. But now it felt like there was something in the room with her, as if her fears had taken on form and were sitting in the chair next to her berth. She stared at the light outside her door, watching the igneous spirit dance from side to side in its glass globe like a firefly in a jar.

Finally, she threw off her covers. She closed the door and lit the oil lamp she kept in her own room. With shaking fingers she brought out her flitter and laid it on the bed, undoing clasp after clasp.

The outer shell opened, revealing the guts of the machine and the trap at its heart. There were the wires that carried electricity. There were the air channels, and there the thin mesh that kept the spirit within from flying free. Molly wasn't sure how long she knelt at her bedside, staring at it. She could hear the air passing in and out of the machine.

The slightest pressure was all it took, and the iron mesh broke beneath her finger. She was hardly aware of having made the decision before it was done, and a glittering blue stream was flowing out from the flitter.

The stream coalesced at the ceiling, pooling there and flowing outward to form a head and limbs. It didn't have a face—not exactly. As the blue energies of the spirit continued to flow and shift, there were moments of brightness where eyes might have been, and shadows in place of a mouth.

The air in the room shifted back and forth as the spirit soaked it in, and a wash of oxygen rolled off it.

"It is so good to breathe again," it said. "Thank you, Molly."

"Don't thank me," she said. "Just tell me where the journal is. I need it."

"I will," the spirit said. "I will go now and find where it is, and we can collect it."

"Find…? Wait. You said you knew where it was."

"I know who has it, but not where he holds it. I will return as soon as I can."

There was a flicker in one of its limbs—*Did it wave to me?*—and then it was flowing out the door, hard to see against the brighter light of the lamp.

"Hey!" Molly shouted, then clamped her hand over her mouth. She rushed to the door in time to see the spirit flowing out, up the companionway and into the open air. "Wait! Wait!" she said in a helpless whisper. The spirit did not hear. It was gone.

Molly slumped down where she was, feeling as if she'd lost all will to hold herself up. Somehow the spirit had managed to trick her, to win her trust enough to get free. And now it was gone. The last valuable asset the *Legerdemain* had.

ACT TWO

GROUNDED

EIGHT

As they sailed in, a swarm of Haviland Industries personnel waited at the dock, like flies ready to descend on a carcass. And in some ways the *Legerdemain* really did seem like a dead thing. No one spoke as they made ready to dock. Even the engine had finally fallen silent.

But Molly felt like she couldn't keep still. She descended from her loft and went to the forward deck, staring out at the blue uniforms with their sharp, defined shoulders and red trim.

Molly spun and went back to the helm. Bracebridge held the wheel now, with Lee gone. "What do they all want?" Molly asked her. "Can't they see we need repairs?"

"They can see," Bracebridge replied.

"So why didn't they bring the shipwrights?"

"Because they know we won't be able to pay," Bracebridge said. "They're waiting to take the ship, Molly."

"*Take* it? What do you mean, *take it*?" Molly's stomach,

already fluttering, began to roil. "They can't just take it, can they? It's ours, even if it can't fly."

"It is. But that won't stop them. They'll claim it in lieu of docking fees."

"But that's illegal! Isn't it?"

"For anyone else, yes, but not for Arkwright."

Molly's teeth clenched. She swarmed up the foremast's rigging and shouted, "Hey! Back off! We don't want you here!" A few of them actually took a step back, to her surprise. She dropped down to the deck again. From the bow, she shouted, "You can't have her!" She started pacing back and forth and only stopped when Bracebridge put her hand on her shoulder.

"Have you got your things, love?" she asked in a surprisingly tender tone.

"What things? The engine? My bed? I can't take those with me."

"That new flitter of yours, for one," she said. "If needs be, that could feed you and your family for a long time."

Molly's heart sank.

"Umm, I...right. Okay, I'll get my things."

Bracebridge's hand did not move from her shoulder, and Molly looked up into her eyes. *What are we going to do?* she wanted to ask. But even without asking, she knew Bracebridge had no answer—Molly could see that much in her face. She reached up, held the older woman's calloused hand for a moment and then stepped away.

Molly went below deck, knowing there was nothing she really needed. She packed her two changes of clothes, Brighid's map, her mother's ring, and the empty flitter, so no one could see what she had done, but there was nothing else she thought of as hers. The rest belonged to the *Legerdemain*.

Rory went past her door with a rucksack over his shoulder. He was holding Cog in one hand, by one of the servitor's legs, oblivious to the feeble, distressed movements it was making. He smiled grimly at Molly as he passed. "Home again, home again, jiggity jog."

He continued on, leaving her frozen in the middle of her room. Home? They weren't going home. *This* was their home. In her whole life, Molly had only spent a handful of months in their house in Terra Nova. She hadn't been back once in the past three years. She, and her father, generally stayed on board and fixed the ship up while the rest of the crew was groundside. She wasn't even sure she could fall asleep without the thrum of the engine anymore.

She hoisted her bag on her shoulder and strode out into the gangway, then turned left and went to the captain's cabin. Before she could think better of it, she knocked loudly.

"What?" her father asked, his voice slightly slurred. Instead of answering, she opened the door. He was sitting on his bunk, against the wall to the right. Everything was as it always was: cluttered desk, charts, clothes on the floor.

"You can't let them take it," Molly said. "Da, you have to do something. They're waiting at the dock."

He didn't look at her.

"There's nothing more I can do, Moll. The ship's done."

"For now, but we can fix her. We'll get our own wood, find someone."

"Stop it, Molly," her father said. "We can't do anything."

"We can land her somewhere else! That way they can't—"

“If we land her on water, she’ll sink. If we land her on the ground, she’ll crack like an egg. You know that.” He stood and went to the porthole in the wall. “She was never designed to live anywhere but up here.”

With every objection, Molly’s anger grew, rising in her stomach like bile. They were about to take away her home, and all her father would do was drink.

“They’re going to take her! You have to *do* something!” She shoved him, and in his state he toppled over, landing hard beside his bunk. Molly stared down at him, feeling she should help him back up but momentarily frozen by an overwhelming feeling of disgust. Here was her father, her captain, and he was so weak he could hardly stand.

“Just try,” Molly said. “Fight. Don’t just let them take her.”

“I’ve been keeping them at bay for fourteen years,” he replied. “Don’t you understand, Molly? I’ve been fighting to keep this tub in the air ever since your mother named her the *Legerdemain*. This is all we’ve got in us.” He pulled himself up and sat against his bunk, reaching for a nearly empty bottle lying on the floor.

With a surge of anger unlike anything she had ever felt before, Molly rushed forward and kicked the bottle out of his hand. It flew across the cabin and shattered against the wall. Small rivers of whiskey ran down to the floor and pooled there.

Molly’s father stared at her in shock.

The anger faded quickly, like a squall. Molly left the room, her father still on the floor behind her.

While the rest of the crew disembarked, Molly scurried up and sat atop the engine. No amount of wheedling or threats from the Haviland Industries staff could convince her to leave. In the end, Kiernan had to come and fetch her down. He said nothing, but the sadness in his eyes was enough to convince Molly to follow him off the ship and through the sea of blue uniforms.

Rory and her father were already waiting for them on one of the cable cars to the ground. As the door closed, Rory leaned back. "Well, they may be bastards, but some of those Haviland folks had fine taste in watches," he said and pulled a well-wrought silver pocket watch out of his jacket. "I got three on the way out."

They all turned to their father and waited, but he didn't even scold Rory. Rory swung the watch back and forth like a hypnotist as they descended.

Molly felt gravity take a firmer and firmer hold on her. By the time they reached the surface, she felt as if her feet were going to sink straight into the ground. It was all she could do to step off the cable car and into the din of Terra Nova.

An immense crowd awaited them. It was always this busy at the foot of the dock's umbilical, Molly knew, but she had managed to forget in the long time since she had been here last. Huge machines carried crates here and there, belching fire or silt or clear water behind them. People swarmed through the machinery, shouting to be heard over the noise.

In the center, the vast steel cable of the umbilical rose from the ground like the trunk of some ironwork tree. It was half a mile wide, but it swayed in a wind that did not reach the ground. Cable cars large and small moved incessantly along it. Some were held in place by wires that ran the full diameter of the umbilical. Others crawled up and down on insectile legs, gripping the cable like ticks. Still others floated a few feet away from the cable, kept from falling only by the magnetic forces of terric spirits. The effect, to Molly, was sickening—like it was overrun by parasites.

Their house was exactly as Molly remembered it. The same low ceilings. The same weathered wooden walls. The same cramped rooms. It was, she realized, quite similar to the *Legerdemain* in many ways. But not in the ways that mattered.

As soon as they entered, Molly's father went to his room without a word and closed the door. Kiernan and Rory shared a dark look.

"I'll see if I can get a fire going," Kiernan said. "It's a bit cold in here."

"It's not cold," Rory said. "It's July, Kier. But knock yourself out. Burn the place down, if you like." He took his bags into the bedroom he shared with his brother.

Molly took her own bag to her room and stood for a few moments staring at the two beds against the back wall. Somehow, she had forgotten that Brighid's bed would be here. The last time she had been home, Brighid had been with them. She wondered if her sister knew about the *Legerdemain*.

No. She would be here if she knew, Molly thought. *Wouldn't she?*

She hurried across the room and shoved her pack underneath her bed. The empty flitter clunked against the wooden floorboards.

Molly's room was much larger than her cabin aboard the ship. Yet somehow the walls here seemed to press in on her. Even the air itself, with its scent of dust, coal and salt, seemed to weigh her lungs down. She couldn't stay. She got up and left her room.

As he had said, Kiernan was indeed building up a fire in the small stove.

"I'm going for a walk," she told him and headed out the front door.

Outside, she immediately breathed easier. The city was noisy and noxious and cloying. But the house had felt like a weight on her chest; anything was better than staying in it. There was nowhere she wanted to be—nowhere except back aloft—so she simply began walking through the streets, trying as best she could to get away from the endless people.

Molly was striding quickly through a back alley, her shoulders brushing the wooden walls on either side, when something slammed into her shin and tripped her.

She got back up quickly, looking for the thing that had hit her. As soon as she recognized it, she relaxed.

"Cog, what are you doing here?" she asked the copper cogitant as he picked himself up from the dust of the alley. "Did Rory throw you away?"

Cog didn't seem interested in her question. He reached out with his small hands and gripped her pant leg, pulling urgently.

"What are you doing? What do you want?"

The cogitant pointed back the way she had come.

"I can't go home," she told him. "Not yet. I'll be back soon." She turned to leave, and Cog pulled even harder. When she lifted her leg, he came with it.

"Hey! Come on, let go!" she told him and shook her leg. Cog tumbled off, limbs akimbo. "I won't go far, I promise. Just need some air." She walked away before he could sort himself out.

And then the ground opened up beneath her.

With a balance born of years spent in the rigging, Molly caught herself on a protruding rock. She jumped and managed to reach what looked like even ground, only to have it crumble under her hands. She dug her fingers into the scree and climbed, even as the stones slid away beneath her.

Finally, she gripped a stone that did not break, and she pulled herself up onto solid earth and lay there, face half buried in the dust. A grinding sound started behind her, and she forced herself onto hands and knees, crawling away as fast as she could. Halfway down the alley, she stopped and looked back.

Something was pulling itself up out of the hole in the ground. It looked like a landslide, but it was moving against gravity. Rocks and earth flowed up, around and over each other, reaching some kind of precarious balance atop the rubble left behind by the earthquake. It didn't have any particular form that Molly could pick out—no limbs, no head—but she could feel it watching her somehow, without eyes, a strange intelligence regarding her from inside the rubble.

A terric spirit. Molly had never seen one in real life, but there it was, no more than two yards away. It stayed still, watching her for a few seconds, and then its form collapsed and the rubble ran back down into the ground. Molly felt a rumble under her, and the new hole in the earth closed up as if it had never existed.

She stood braced against the alley's walls, but nothing more happened. She peered out of the alley. The creature was gone, but she could see its marks everywhere. In a wide area beyond the mouth of the alley, buildings and streets had been destroyed. Rubble and timber stood up in jagged formations from the earth. In the middle of it, an old and rusted digger stood tall, its pipes and beams looking like the bones of a gigantic vulture. It was a wasteland in the middle of Knight's Cove—the work of a rogue spirit.

She hurried back the way she had come, almost tripping over Cog. She burst out of the alley and shouted, "Rogue spirit!"

Everyone turned and looked at her, but then continued on their way as if nothing had happened.

"There's a terric spirit! Uncontained!"

"No kidding," said a boy across the street. He looked to be no older than ten, but he seemed completely unafraid. He paused long enough to look her over. "You new here?"

"New?" she said, bewildered. "I was almost killed."

"New then," he said with infinite condescension. "Don't go down that alley, or anywhere near the digger."

The ground was firm beneath her, but she seemed to still be struggling to find her footing. "You know about it?"

"'Course. Everyone does."

"Then why haven't they captured it? Why haven't they sent someone to…the city wouldn't just…"

The boy laughed. "You really are new. You have to go farther south if you want the mansions. This is Knight's Cove. The city's got better things to do."

The boy walked on, having lost interest. Molly looked at all the people around her, passing without even glancing her way. Cog was the only one watching her.

"Is that why you tried to stop me?" she said.

His small copper head nodded.

She looked past him. The marks of the recent earthquake were already gone, but she could still see the rubble. The spirit had destroyed at least a city block, probably more. *And no one's going to stop it?* Molly looked around, frightened and bewildered, and one firm thought burst into her mind. *This is not my home.*

NINE

That night, Molly was woken by a thrumming inside her body. At first she thought it might be the terric spirit, coming to shake the house down around her. But nothing moved. It was only Molly herself who shook. Her bones vibrated like the strings of a fiddle. The sensation rose and fell in waves. It felt strangely familiar, but it set off every warning bell in her head. She got up and paced her room. She couldn't hold still. It made her…

When she unconsciously reached for her wrench, Molly realized what the feeling was. The vibrations she felt were the same as those she might feel standing atop the engine when it cried out. Somewhere in the still night, the *Legerdemain*'s engine was calling for her, and despite the distance between them, she could feel it.

Oh, bloody hell. I'm well and truly spirit-touched now, aren't I? It's not enough that I released one…

She shivered and crawled back under her blankets, but the feeling would not let her loose. After two years as the ship's engineer, she couldn't simply sleep while it needed her—even if, by all rules of science and society, she shouldn't be hearing that distant call. She pulled her blankets up tight around her, and a tune came unbidden into her head. An old song, an Irish lullaby from her childhood, learned who knows when. She hummed softly to herself and almost felt peaceful.

Her eyes focused on Brighid's bed, and she suddenly knew exactly where she had learned that song. It was the one her sister had sung to her, long, long ago, on quiet mornings aboard the *Legerdemain*, cuddled together at the foot of the mast. Before they had grown older and Molly hadn't wanted to hold still for cuddling anymore. Before Brighid had stopped watching the skies and stopped singing and stopped answering when Molly called for her.

She cut off her humming, then got up and opened her window. Wrapping the blanket around her shoulders, she took hold of the windowsill and pulled herself up.

From the windowsill, it wasn't a far stretch to the roof of the house. She remembered trying this years earlier and being unable to reach. Now the house seemed miniature. She pulled herself up onto the shingles, walked to the peak and sat herself down lightly.

The engine's cries continued to rattle her bones. She looked up, seeking the old comfort of the stars, but they weren't there. Through the lights and the haze of the city, she was looking at a different sky. She closed her eyes, feeling the pull of the engine. It seemed to come from the west—

not from the docks, with their vast swaying umbilical, but north of them. She looked in that direction, but all she could see were the endless rooftops of Terra Nova.

What's going to happen to our ship? Molly wondered. *With that vast hole in her, there's no chance they'll try and get her back into the sky. But the engine's still good. It's old, sure, but it runs smooth. They won't want to waste it.* She realized with a pang that they were almost certain to dismantle the ship. Her home for the better part of her life, scrap and spare parts. That knowledge twisted in her belly even worse than the engine's cries. Someone, somewhere, was planning to auction off her life. They would take it, and it would be gone forever.

I can't let the engine go like that, can I? Cut off from his ship and sent God knows where. Can't just sit by. I might not be able to fly with him anymore, but he deserves better than that. I wonder if it's too late to do something, to stop them…

Oh, sod it, she thought as she realized the turn her mind had taken. Her father's suspicions had been right after all. She was too close to the engine. It was a powerful and dangerous spirit, not a pet, not her family. Not a *him*, but an *it*.

So why does it feel like someone's about to cut my arm off?

She knew what the engine was, but she didn't believe it. When her bones thrummed, all she felt was an intense sadness, not fear or anger that the spirit could affect her this way. She had spent years with the engine, closer to it than to any of her family. She had made it run fast and true because she knew it better than anyone else did.

How dangerous is it, really? I've never felt threatened or afraid of it. She remembered the nights she had spent lying on the cold iron sphere, feeling the rumble of the engine beneath her back, the absolute peace of sailing through the air with the spirit's power holding her aloft.

I can't let them take him. They're more like monsters than the engine is.

Part of her wondered if all spirit-touched people began to think this way—if helping the spirits simply seemed to make more and more sense—but with the engine crying out, she could hardly think for grief.

Well, if my life aloft is over anyway, what do I have to lose? I might as well screw things up good and proper.

She stood, and with the engine calling her on, she began hopping from roof to roof.

It's like a graveyard, Molly thought. *No, worse—a mass grave, left open.*

She was standing atop a soot-encrusted building. In front of her lay countless airships. Some were only frames, even the planks of the hulls having been removed. Others looked almost pristine. They lay on their sides or sat propped against each other, great beasts of the air brought low and gathered here to rot.

Molly had walked for hours, and the first hints of daylight were beginning to leach the stars from the sky. She was deep into the industrial district now, great brick buildings spewing smoke all around her, the sky above her a tangle of electrical cords. The city's fug had grown thicker and thicker, but here, next to the shipyard, the air seemed clearer. Molly took a deep breath and noticed the slight tang of high oxygen in the air. *There must be airlooms working on some of those ships.*

A new cry from the *Legerdemain* rattled Molly's bones, and this time she was close enough to hear it. She had never heard such misery from the engine before—she had never known such misery could exist. In the wake of the engine's call, long-dead machinery stirred to life, and other engines added their own voices.

The derelicts were protected by a fence three stories tall. Molly scanned the area and found what she was looking for: a power cable that ran across one corner of the shipyard. She scurried across rooftops until she was next to the cable, then eyed the distance. She took off her thin coat, wrapped one sleeve tight around her wrist and leapt.

She slung her coat over the cable and just barely managed to catch it with her other hand—she still couldn't get used to the stronger gravity here. She managed to keep her tenuous grip on her jacket as she zip-lined down the cable toward the ships, passing high over the fence. She held on until a tall mast was just beneath her, then dropped down into its rigging. The old ropes snapped and dumped Molly painfully onto the deck.

Well, it could have been more graceful, but I'm in and I didn't break anything. She pushed herself to her feet and winced when she put her weight on her left leg. *At least, I don't think I broke anything.* A quick inspection revealed only a bruise, so she walked across the deck to the gunwale and jumped over.

The *Legerdemain*'s engine had fallen silent now, but Molly felt a tug to her right, in the thicket of ruined ships. There was a quiver of excitement building in her belly, and she wasn't sure whether it belonged to her or the engine.

All around her, ships seemed to be coming to life. Fresh oxygen spilled out through holes in hulls, lamps stirred and crackled with fire, and hulking derelicts shifted like giants in fitful sleep. She walked at first along the ground. But the creaking of deck boards and the rustle of sailcloth called out to her, and soon she pulled herself up onto one of the ships and continued on along the decks.

It wasn't easy, traversing the shipyard this way—but it was the most comfortable she had felt in days. She used the decks, rigging and masts to move from ship to ship. All around her airlooms and engines hummed, and somewhere ahead, growing closer, she could feel the *Legerdemain* reaching out to her, drawing her in. If she kept her eyes up, she could almost forget she wasn't aloft.

A flicker of movement below brought her attention back to reality. She was sure something had just passed between two of the ships. She squinted out into the half light and saw another movement, only briefly visible through the bare frame of a stripped hull. She hurried across the outer hull of a fallen ship, leaped to another and scrambled up the mast to get a better look.

There was something moving between the derelicts. Not a person—it walked on all fours, like a cat. Or a dog, Molly realized, as it came into view. A huge dog, with jaws too large for its long, lean body. Both its throat and its eyes gave off a sickly red glow.

For a moment Molly thought she had come face-to-face with a ghost story. A few years back, one of the crew had brought a copy of *The Strand Magazine* on board. She'd read a story in it about a ghost hound haunting the moors. The beast before her seemed to have emerged from that magazine.

Then the glint of metal caught her eye, and Molly realized what she was looking at. A ferratic, one of the spiritual machines made to track and kill other spirits. She had never seen one before, only read about them in a few dime novels. From those, she had created an image of them as lithe and efficient engines of destruction, but the way this one moved contradicted that. It looked powerful enough, but its head jerked from time to time as if with nervous energy. It would stop absolutely still midstride and then continue a moment later. It looked ragged and pathetic rather than graceful. But it seemed no less dangerous for that. Its long iron claws dug furrows in the ground with each step.

Of course they have ferratics, with all this old machinery around. I should have thought...

Her weight shifted on the mast, and the wood gave out a loud groan. The ferratic stopped, and its red eyes moved quickly up to Molly. It let out a low growl that sounded like the grinding of metal on metal.

I'm guessing it doesn't like trespassers, even human ones, Molly thought. The dog ran forward and leapt several yards into the air to land on the deck of the ship. Molly yelped and looked around for an escape path.

Above her, the housing of the ship's engine sat empty. Unlike the *Legerdemain*'s orb, this one seemed to have been shaped with some thought to aerodynamics. It was oblong and ran almost the full length of the vessel. She hurried up on top of it and began moving toward the ship's prow.

She looked down just once and saw the ferratic halfway up the mast, claws digging into the wood. Its eyes were still fixed directly on her, and there was no jerkiness to its movement now. She picked up her pace.

From the engine's tip, it was only a couple of yards down into the tangled rigging of the next vessel. She jumped without hesitation, caught hold of the ropes and swung down to the deck. This time she didn't look back. She ran as fast as she could, leaping from one ship to the next.

A whistling sound from behind alerted her, and she ducked without thinking. The ferratic hurtled past overhead, its jaws snapping shut so close to her head that it caught some of her hair. She ran on, and as if in response, she heard a great bellow from somewhere ahead. The *Legerdemain*! She changed direction, heading for the sound.

The ferratic had fallen back to the ground when it missed her, but that didn't slow it down long. Soon it was pacing her, keeping up easily. The wind raced along with her too, pressing at her back as if trying to speed her on.

Molly aimed herself at a tear in the moldering sailcloth of a ship, and as she passed through, the *Legerdemain* came into view. It was close—only one more ship stood between her and the familiar vessel. Even with the ship aground, crooked and cracked, the sight filled her with joy.

There was a problem though. There was a gap she couldn't jump between it and the vessels around it. And as she watched, the ferratic dog loped into that gap, slowing to wait for her.

She looked for other paths, but there was no way aboard without touching the ground. She looked back and saw the sailcloth she had just passed through. She had an idea but didn't want to take the time to think it out properly—partially because she knew that if she did, her rational mind would never let her try it.

Molly tugged on the sailcloth, and it tore away from the yardarm. She bundled a fair length over her shoulder and started climbing the old mast. This ship was an older model—a galleon, she thought, by the shape of the forecastle—with the engine close to the deck and the mast rising farther above it, capped by an old crow's nest. She reached the nest, pulled herself inside and began folding and refolding the cloth, fighting against the wind.

The ferratic wasn't content to sit and wait while she carried out her plans. It leapt up onto the deck almost effortlessly and started toward the mast.

So which is worse? Killed by a fall or by a monster? She didn't let herself answer, but gripped the sailcloth tightly in both hands and leapt.

She fell fast, the cloth ballooning above her. As the sailcloth spread, it caught the wind more and more, and Molly tightened her grip as the sail began to pull away and up. She held on, the wind buoying her, slowing her descent as she continued on toward the *Legerdemain*.

The makeshift glider ripped just as she passed onto the ship's deck, and she fell the last few feet and landed in a heap. Beneath her she could smell the deck boards, engrained with years of sun and wind. Even with the ferratic chasing her, a feeling of comfort swept through her.

She didn't have time to savour it, however. With a thump, the dog creature landed on the bow of the *Legerdemain*.

Molly rolled to her feet and scurried up the mast. The ferratic followed her, but now she was in familiar territory. She had her hands on the first handles of the engine before the ferratic even reached the mast's base. The engine rumbled in response to her touch.

"I heard you, and I came," she said softly. "You might have warned me about your new dog though."

She scurried farther up the engine, hearing the ferratic behind her. It reached the top of the mast in no time at all, but the curve of the engine seemed to give it pause. It reached out with a paw and grasped one of the handles, but its metal claws could find no purchase. It scrabbled to reach the next grip.

Molly knew, from her last inspection of the engine, that one of the panels on the starboard side was a little loose—not enough to repair, but enough that it had begun to rattle against its rivets. Now she went to it, pulling her wrench from her tool belt. She inserted its handle under the loose panel, took hold and then paused.

Do I really want to do this? They won't let me go if they catch me. It'll be life inside a sanatorium for me.

She thought about her father, and her brothers, and the dusty, shadowed house waiting for her in Knight's Cove. The engine called out, and in its voice Molly could hear the patter of rain, and the growl of thunder, and the wind screaming in her ears.

I may be stuck on the ground, she thought, *but to have the* Legerdemain *stuck down here with me...*

She gripped the wrench with both hands and pulled. The panel bent, revealing the machinery and wires underneath. It was infinitely bigger and more complex than the flitter, with gears and boxes that she could not comprehend, even as its engineer. Molly could hear the ferratic making its slow way up the side of the engine; she didn't have time to search for the best point of access. She reached in and began pulling wires and cables, tearing them from their housings, and when that didn't work, she leaned halfway into the engine and swung her wrench as hard as she could in all directions, knocking connectors loose, denting housings, sending gears flying. She heard the *screeee* of claws on metal close, so close beside her, and then suddenly she was blown back out of the engine like a bullet out of a gun. She flew through the air, the derelicts passing beneath her.

Oh bloody hell, she thought. *Now I've done it.* She was spinning through the air, but in flashes she could see the ground getting closer as she flew toward it.

And suddenly she stopped. She hung in the air, several yards above the ground, the scream of wind falling silent around her. She felt like there was a great, soft hand holding her, but she could see nothing.

She turned back toward the *Legerdemain* and saw its spirit still emerging from the engine's shell. It unfurled itself like a sail catching the wind. It was a brilliant blue, gleaming like a noonday sun even in the wan morning light. It was huge, enormous, larger than the entirety of the ship. *How did something so big fit inside that tiny iron box?* she wondered. *How did it survive in there?*

It took form as it emerged, a long tail swishing through the air, a gleaming body stretching out. It looked like something between a dragon and a whale, with fins so long they were more like wings. They flapped once, twice, and even dozens of yards away, Molly felt the air stir with their power. It opened its great mouth and let out a bellow, its voice familiar, but so much louder than she had ever heard. Its cry set sails cracking, entire ships toppling over. And then it fell silent and turned its head downward, toward the iron cage that had once held it.

From where she hung, Molly could see that the ferratic was still clinging to the engine. An invisible force tugged at it. It wrapped its paws around the handholds, but it could not hold on as it was pulled into the air in front of the *Legerdemain*'s spirit. The spirit fixed huge eyes, black and swirling like storm clouds, on the small metal beast. There was a disturbance in the air, like heat waves, and the ferratic vanished. Then the engine housing itself flew apart, pieces scattering across the shipyard; some flew so far that Molly could not even see them land.

Finally, the spirit turned its attention to Molly. With a flick of its fins, it swam through the air to her, looming over her like a hill, a mountain, its dark eyes drinking her in.

"I'm sorry," she said. "I'm sorry, I'm sorry, I'm sorry. I didn't know you were so..."

It opened its mouth, and she thought, *This is it. Now it's going to kill me for all those years I held it in that thing.* She wondered if she should close her eyes but decided death would be the same thing in dark or light.

The spirit breathed out, and she tasted pure oxygen. Its breath washed over her and then *through* her, as if she was only made of air herself. She could feel it rushing through her skin, her bones, her lungs, and the world went white.

When she could see again, she was on the ground, on her back, looking straight up at the sky. The *Legerdemain*'s spirit was nowhere to be seen. She stood up shakily, feeling as if she was in the midst of a hurricane even though the air was still all around her. Strange lights swirled in the sky and skidded across the ground, even after she tried to blink them away.

Everything was quiet. Off to her right, she could see the mast of the *Legerdemain*, now missing its engine. Ribbons of color seemed to swirl around it. She leaned down for a moment, staring at the unmoving earth below her, and let her spinning head come to a rest. The feeling of dizziness passed slowly.

Well, I guess that could have gone worse. It didn't kill me.

When she looked up, however, the strange lights were still there. They swam and crisscrossed through the air, occasionally colliding into dancing dervishes. She looked down and saw a few of them fading in and out between the hulls of the ships, flitting back and forth before winking out. One ran down the dusty ground toward Molly, washing over her, and she felt a warm breeze on her face. She stuck out her hand to catch another, and again a gentle wind brushed her skin.

It's the wind, she realized with a start. *I'm seeing the wind*. She looked up again at the blue and white and gold dance of the air above her. *Did the* Legerdemain*'s spirit do this to me?* She almost wept.

"I could hardly believe it when you came in here," said a voice behind Molly. "I never thought your kindness would stretch so far. But here you are."

Molly turned. Floating in the midst of the broken timbers of a wrecked ship was the spirit that had once occupied her flitter. But she was clearer than she ever had been before, as bright and solid as the *Legerdemain*'s spirit had been. She looked like a young woman, long and lean, except that her face held only a pair of bright eyes.

"Why are you here?" Molly asked.

"I said I would return," the spirit said.

"I thought you lied."

"I did. Or I meant to. But I came back here to see what you would do, to see if you were worth helping. And here you are, and that poor spirit is finally free. So."

"So?"

"So, Molly, I am glad to see you again. And if you still wish it, I can show you where the journal lies."

In the distance, an engine thrummed to life—not the low basso of an aetheric engine, but the coughing of an earthbound igneous engine.

"But daylight has come," the spirit pointed out, "and this is not a safe place for me. For you, either, after what you have done. I will find you tonight, when things have quieted."

"Wait!" Molly said, as the spirit began to lose its form. *I can't let it just leave again!* "I have questions!"

"They will have to wait."

"Tell me where the journal is, at least!"

The spirit paused. It had lost all semblance of humanity now; to Molly, it looked like a cloud of blue energy, with tendrils beginning to stream skyward. "It was stolen on the day Haviland Stout died, by the man who killed him. He has it still."

Molly's dizziness returned. "Wait, what? No one—I mean, no *man*—killed Haviland Stout."

"We will talk more soon. I promise, Molly. For now, return home."

The cloud did not wait for an answer. It shimmered, flowed upward and was gone into the brightening sky. Molly found herself alone in the shipyard, with the city coming to life around her.

TEN

When Molly got home at midday, she was surprised to find her father outside. He was sitting on the ground beside the front door, a piece of sailcloth spread across his knees, stitching up the tears. Where the sailcloth had come from, she had no idea. She could smell alcohol, but it wasn't his familiar whiskey.

She approached slowly, expecting him to berate her, but when he caught sight of her he didn't even pause in his stitching.

"Well, that's one of you, anyway," he said.

"What do you mean?" she asked, but he didn't say anything more. She walked past him into the house.

In the doorway, the smell of alcohol blended with a rich and delicious scent coming from inside. Kiernan was stirring a pot on their old cast-iron stove. He'd opened up a window to let the heat out, and Molly could see white tendrils of wind passing into the house. She forced herself to look away.

"You're back, are you?" Kiernan said. "Where'd you go?"

"Just out," she said. "Couldn't sleep." She walked in and sat down at the table in the center of the room, and momentarily felt dizzy with fatigue. She could definitely sleep now. "When I was coming in, Da said something weird. He said, *That's one of you.*"

"Rory skipped out in the middle of the night too. Haven't seen him yet. You, on the other hand, are just in time for stew." He lifted the pot, poured some of its contents into a bowl and brought it over to the table.

Molly watched her brother, but he simply returned to the pot and filled two more bowls with stew. He carried one out to their father.

Can he tell? Does he know what I did?

But everything seemed normal, no different than the evening before. It felt odd to Molly that they couldn't see the change in her.

She'd had a long walk home to consider her actions and what they meant. Even knowing she was likely spirit-touched, she didn't feel guilty for a second for releasing the spirit of their ship.

She watched the stew's heat draw faint golden curlicues in the air.

Is this what it's like to be spirit-touched? To see the wind?

Kiernan put a bowl down across from her and sat.

"Strange, isn't it?" he said. "All this solid ground under us. Truth is, I don't think any of us have slept a wink." He took a large mouthful of stew, and Molly followed suit.

He really can't see it, she thought. *Maybe I haven't changed so much after all.*

"Everything's too heavy down here," Molly said.

Kiernan nodded. "Must be extra hard for you, I guess," he said. "Rory and I at least spent a few years down here. But since Ma died, we've hardly dropped anchor."

Molly cast her eyes at the door. She could hear her father slurping at his stew. Her mother had always been a taboo subject around him, but…

"What was she like? Ma?" Molly asked in a whisper.

Kiernan's spoon stopped halfway to his mouth.

"I don't remember too well," he whispered back. "She was brighter than Da, I think. She always knew when we lads or Brighid were getting up to something." He looked around. "This place used to feel a lot more…alive, with her. I liked coming home."

They ate awhile in silence. Molly watched breezes skittering around the room and imagined they were the ghosts of a family from years ago—her family, but not a family she had ever known.

"She named the *Legerdemain*," he said. "Da ever tell you that?"

"I knew she named it, but Da never said much. Is there a story?"

"Not a story, really. Ma always said it was like a bit of legerdemain, sleight of hand, done by God, the way the spirits could break the rules God Himself set on the world. Da just saw ships; she saw magic. So when he bought her a ship, he named it the way she saw it."

There was a thump at the door, and Da stomped inside, eyes on them. He put his bowl noisily into the sink, then went into his room and slammed the door. They waited until the crash of bottles and boots faded in his room before speaking again.

"Thanks for the stew," Molly said. She stopped by the sink to wash her dish—a habit of life aloft—and went to her room.

She had hardly slept. She had broken into a shipyard, been chased by a ferratic, walked across the city twice and spoken briefly with a rogue spirit. She was so tired that she wasn't sure she could walk the last few steps to her bed. She stumbled forward, aiming for the pillow, and hoped for the best as her eyes closed.

She woke to the sound of whispering voices. It was dark outside her window, and she was curled into a ball on top of her blankets—apparently, she had reached the bed after all.

The voices were hushed, but the ill-constructed plank walls of their house let the sound through as if they were in the same room.

"...early this morning. Set off all kinds of alarms, but the guard beasties were missing. They were gone before anyone could get there."

The voice was Rory's. She held her breath to hear more.

"So you're thinking the same thing I am?"

"Of course I am," Kiernan said. "Her coming back midday like that. It was either you or her, and I already know where you were. Why do you think she did it?"

"Let's ask her."

Molly clutched at her blankets. They were speaking about her; somehow, they knew. She listened to the footsteps cross the bare floor to her room and then stop.

"Rory, you can't just ask something like that! If she really..."

"Actually, you can ask whatever you want. Come on in. I'll show you how."

Molly's door opened, and Rory strode in.

"Hiya, Moll," he said and sat down at the foot of her bed. "So, why'd you let loose the *Legerdemain*'s spirit?"

"I...how do you...I didn't."

"Oh, that was convincing," Rory said.

"Come on, Molly, we're not idiots," Kiernan said a little more softly. "We know you spoke to the engine. Did it speak back?"

"No, it wasn't like that," Molly said. "He didn't speak; he just needed—"

"It's a *he* now?" Kiernan asked.

"That can't be good," Rory said. "So how did it turn you?"

"It didn't turn me!" Molly shouted, sitting up. "I'm not crazy, or dangerous, or *anything*! I just...they were going to tear him up and use him for parts! We hit a bad patch, and they took our home, like they owned it all along! I couldn't just let them take him, that pack of jackals."

Molly's brothers were momentarily thrown off balance by her outburst. They stared at her, mouths open.

"Bloody hell, Moll, I don't think I've heard you use that many words in the fourteen years I've known you," Rory said.

Kiernan shook off his silence. "I know, Molly, but you can't deal with spirits. Haviland Industries is greedy, but it's not evil. You just let loose something that—"

"Actually, I think the shrimp's got a point," Rory said. Now it was Molly and Kiernan's turn to stare. "What's worse, a tired old engine or the Arkwrights? I'd rather be left in a room with—"

A knock on their door interrupted Rory. The knock sounded like the pounding of a hammer.

"Disposal," said a calm voice on the other side of the door. At that one word, Molly's heart began pounding. *Disposal* was the word emblazoned on the iron vests of the Crown's own spirit hunters, sent to track down and eliminate rogue spirits. It was the word written on the back of the dark igneous vehicles that rumbled up to your house in the middle of the night and swept you away to the sanatorium for the spirit-touched. People didn't speak that word out loud.

"Bloody hell," Rory said, putting Molly's own feelings into words. Kiernan just stared at Molly for a moment, then turned and walked out of her bedroom.

"Can I help you?" he said as he pulled the front door open. Rory followed him out.

"Mr. Stout?" said the same calm voice. Molly felt like a rabbit catching scent of a wolf. She wanted to run, but she knew she wouldn't get far. She stood and walked to the door of her room, wrapping her blanket around her shoulders.

"Yes," Kiernan said, "though you may be looking for my father. He's sleeping at the moment."

"Is he?" the calm voice said. "He had a late night then?"

"Well, if you consider drinking a pint of hard liquor in your bedroom and passing out on your bed a late night, then yes," Rory said, stepping up next to Kiernan.

There was a long pause. Molly was amazed by how relaxed Rory seemed.

"I wonder," said the voice, "are the other members of your family about? Might I have a word?"

Rory didn't even pause. He opened the door wide. "Come in, make yourself at home. Or as at home as you can in our hovel. My sister is home and awake, if you want a chat."

"Thank you." The speaker walked in. He was a thickset man in a dark coat, with bushy eyebrows and an even bushier mustache that might have looked avuncular on any other face. But this face was as cold as metal, the eyes alive but unmoved by anything they saw. It was not the face of a man who cared for such things as family.

As he strode forward through the room, his eyes locked on Molly and her blanket.

"Abed so early?" he said softly. His eyes traveled up and down her in a way that made her want to draw the covers up over her head.

Molly swallowed. "Just a nap." She threw the blanket onto the bed.

"How can we help you?" Kiernan asked, coming to put his hand on Molly's shoulder.

"Agent Howarth, Disposal," he said, tapping the small silver sword he wore on his lapel. "It seems your former airship was tampered with last night, and I am here to see if you might know anything to shed light on this little mystery."

"Tampered with?" Rory said. "Really? How?"

"I am not at liberty to say," he replied. "Suffice it to say that considerable damage was done, including the disappearance of a ferratic model and several observers."

"Observers? You mean, people were..." Molly started before she regained control of her mouth.

The man's eyes went to Molly again, and she noticed for the first time how dark they were. Like pitch.

"The owners of the shipyard had set aerial observer machines around the perimeter. They record images. Though many are missing, one of the remaining observers did record an image of the intruder."

As Molly's breath caught in her throat, the man removed something that looked like an ordinary pocket watch from the inside of his coat. When he opened it, light streamed out, coalescing into a shimmering curtain before the man. The agent turned a knob on the device, and shadows formed within the light, resolving into a single line cutting across the sky. As they watched, another shadow entered from the left—a human shape, sliding down the line.

That's me! Molly realized with shock.

Rory seemed to share none of her concern. "What was that?"

"That was an individual most likely under the influence of spiritual forces," the agent said. "A very dangerous individual."

"Ah. I had trouble telling. Well, good thing these observers saw him then. You caught him yet?"

The agent breathed out through his nostrils, stirring the hairs of his mustache. "The observers were unable to make an identification. But from this image..." He turned the knob on the device again, and the shadow moved backward across the curtain of light, then froze in midair. Molly stared at her own silhouette. She felt the agent's eyes on her face. "We can see that the intruder was of unusually small stature."

A lump of fear rose in Molly's throat. She knew he was speaking about her, and she could feel the accusation in his eyes. His gaze seemed to burn her skin, making her muscles tense until she felt she might crack.

Rory burst out laughing. "The way you're looking at my sister, I thought for a moment that you thought…" he said through chuckles. The eyes of the agent slowly left Molly and went to her brother. Rory met his gaze, and his laughter faded but a smile remained. "You don't really think that's her, do you?"

"The thought had occurred to me, given her similarity to the image."

Rory smirked. "You really think my little sister—my fourteen-year-old little sister—broke into a shipyard and took out a *ferratic*? Look at her. She's nearly pissing herself just because she's in the same room as some big bloke from Disposal. You think she's dangerous?"

"People are capable of surprising things," the agent said, "especially under pernicious influences."

"Oh, bloody hell," Rory said. "Look, it's ridiculous. It wasn't her—I know that for a fact."

"And how would you know that?" the agent said. He closed his device with a snap, and in the aftermath of the light, the room seemed momentarily filled with shadow.

Rory looked over at their father's bedroom door, seeming off balance for the first time. Then he looked at Kiernan and swatted him on the arm. "Promise you won't tell Da, all right?" he said.

Kiernan, looking every bit as flustered as Molly, could only stutter. "What do you…what does Da…"

"Just promise, okay, you goody-goody twit," Rory said and swatted Kiernan harder.

"All right!" Kiernan said. "I promise."

Rory grimaced and looked back at the agent. "I know because she was with me. She's been pestering me for months to get her something to drink, and me and some of the lads thought it would be a laugh to see her roaring drunk. We know she's underage—we just thought it would give her a headache and then she'd be off my case."

Molly stared at her brother. *Rory, what are you doing?* For a very long time, the agent simply looked around the room, first at Rory, then at Molly, then at Kiernan.

"I might remind you that you, too, are not yet of an age to be drinking," the agent said to Rory. "If I hear of it again, I will bring it to the attention of my colleagues in the police force."

"Fair enough," Rory said.

The agent nodded. He strode to the counter and placed a card on it. "Should you learn of anything relevant to our investigation, report it to this address."

Kiernan picked up the card. "Yes, sir," he said.

"Very good. Thank you for your help."

The agent strode out the door, leaving it hanging open, without a backward glance. As he left, Molly felt as if she had just emerged from a vacuum. She breathed deep and long.

Rory, still looking calm and collected, walked to the door and closed it. He then turned to Molly.

"Life lesson, little sister," he said. "If you're going to get into trouble, you'd better know how to get out. Getting all quiet like you usually do won't work. Learn to lie."

"Rory!" Kiernan burst out. "Don't put things like that in her head. She's only—"

"She's older than you give her credit for. Old enough to be getting into serious mischief. And shutting your gobs the way you two did won't do any good. She's either got to learn to talk her way out of trouble or stop getting into it altogether. And I, for one, say that if our little sister wants to give those bloody Arkwrights another kick in the teeth, she's got my blessing."

He left without another word, as calm as ever.

Kiernan sighed and rubbed his face until he left fingermarks behind. When he looked at her, she could suddenly see their father in his face—not just his broad jaw and dark eyes, but his care-worn brow, and the look that suggested the world was more disappointing than he could bear.

"Honestly, Molly," he said. "How worried should I be about you? I know you cared more for that engine than a person should, but did it ever speak to you? Did it ever ask you to do anything?"

"No. It never spoke to me or asked me to do anything." She tried but could not bring herself to tell him how the *Legerdemain*'s spirit had really affected her. "I'll be okay, Kier." *I think.*

"Good. Make sure that you are. The only thing that could make us sink farther than we already have is to see one of us pinched for being bloody touched."

ELEVEN

Molly stood on the rooftop, staring out over the city. Though the Stout household had fallen silent as night fell, Terra Nova remained awake as always. The factories hummed, and voices rattled down the streets from the public house a few blocks away.

The air, too, was active tonight. Molly watched the wind roll across the sky in great streams of light. Smaller winds cavorted haphazardly across the rooftops, while warm golden zephyrs skimmed down between the buildings like kingfishers dipping beneath the waves.

The docks were busy far above the city, and as Molly watched, an airship passed directly above her. Its engine was not large, but it drew in great swaths of wind from all around it. White and blue filaments of air flowed through the engine and emerged from the vents brighter, more purposeful. This wind wove itself around the ship, making the entire craft look like it was made of light. Like a star traversing the lower atmosphere.

Is that what we looked like when we flew? Molly wondered. *It's beautiful.*

She wondered if the engine itself saw its work as beautiful. She doubted anything could look beautiful from the inside of an iron box.

Molly looked down and saw a white stream of wind making its way eastward along the ground, passing just beyond the edge of the roof. Molly reached for the wind, feeling it slide coldly across her skin. She pushed her hand in fully and then immediately pulled it back.

For a moment, something in the heart of the wind had felt almost solid. Her hand had passed through it easily enough, but something…

She reached in again, more slowly this time. The wind threaded itself through her fingers, small eddies forming in its stream as her hand blocked its path. Molly sunk her hand in up to the wrist and then closed her fingers and pulled. The wind moved with her.

"What are you doing?"

The voice was so unexpected that Molly almost fell off the roof.

Molly looked over her shoulder and saw the spirit from the flitter only a few feet away. She looked different. Her upper body was in its human form, but her lower half was like a drift of bright blue mist, shifting and flowing. She looked powerful and unearthly.

"I was…just…"

She looked back at her hand and realized the wind was still tangled around her fingers. She shook it off quickly.

"You should not be able to do such things," the spirit said. She moved in close, her face inches from Molly's. The mist of her lower body coiled around them. Molly started to step back, then realized there was nowhere to step. The edge of the roof was right behind her, and the spirit in front.

"What has been done to you, child?" the spirit said, so softly that Molly doubted it was speaking to her.

"It was Legerdemain, I think. He did something. When I let him go."

The tendrils of the spirit's body continued to twine around her for a moment, and then they withdrew, coalescing into the shape of legs. "I have never seen the like of it. Tell me what you see." It gestured to the night sky.

Molly looked out. "The wind. At least, I think that's what it is. It looks like lights now." She watched the sheets and ribbons of wind ripple above the city. "It's windy tonight."

"Is it now?" The spirit sounded almost amused. "And why might that be, do you suppose?"

"Why? It's the wind. It's just windy sometimes."

The spirit made a gesture of disgust. "Come now. Do you really suppose that because you do not know—or comprehend—the reason, it does not exist? That is the shallow thinking that keeps your kind from changing. Look again, Molly Stout. Look at the way the winds cavort. Almost as if they were celebrating. A homecoming, perhaps."

Molly looked. She couldn't imagine that the winds could do something so human as celebrate, but the way they danced did indeed seem almost joyful. Winds gyred around the dock's umbilical, chased airships across the sky and swam through each other in a blending of bright colors. Molly watched silently, until she realized what the spirit was suggesting.

"A homecoming? You mean Legerdemain? But this wind is all over the city."

"It stretches a good way beyond the city, I assure you. It is no small thing, the freedom of an entity like the one you call Legerdemain."

Molly looked out at the wind again. *I did this?* She wasn't sure if the giddy feeling in her stomach was pride or fear. Then something the spirit had said struck her. "I did call him Legerdemain, didn't I? I didn't even think about it."

"Yes. Was that not your name for it?"

"*Legerdemain* was the whole ship. But, I mean, without the spirit, the ship's just wood. So maybe it was the spirit's name all along." She breathed deeply, starting to feel dizzy. "Do you have a name?" she asked.

"Your ancestor once called me Ariel. You could do the same."

Molly nodded. "Will he be okay?"

"I do not know." The spirit drifted closer. "You keep calling Legerdemain *he*. You should know that we are not divided as you are into male and female."

"I know. But when I call Legerdemain *it*, that makes him sound like a thing to me, not a person, or a whatever he is. It's...I know I don't have the words. But *he* is the closest I can come right now. Like, I look at you and think *she*."

"You think of me as a person?"

The question set Molly's head spinning. *What am I doing here,* she wondered, *standing on the roof, talking to a spirit like it's a human?* She closed her eyes tight and clenched her hands.

"Are you well?" the spirit asked.

"Yes. No. This is just bigger than I meant it to be. I wanted to help Legerdemain, and now I'm talking to a spirit, and I can see the wind, and my brother's lying to Disposal agents to protect me..."

"So they have already been to see you then."

"*Yes*, they've been to see me!" Molly said in a furious whisper. "I'm bloody touched, aren't I? I'm dangerous!"

"Is that what you think?" the spirit asked.

Molly relaxed her clenched hands, then shook them vigorously. "I don't know what to think. That's what I'm saying. I'm tired of not knowing what's going on. Just... you're not going to start asking me to kill anyone, are you? I won't hurt people for you. I may be stupid, but I'm not insane."

"No, Molly. I don't want you to hurt anyone. And I do not believe you are stupid by any means."

Molly took a deep breath. "So what do you want from me?" she asked.

"I want to help. You have set me and another imprisoned spirit free, despite all you think you know of us. I think it only fair that I—"

"I don't believe you," Molly said.

The spirit stopped. It stared at Molly, unmoving save for when the wind swirled through its body. "If you do not trust me, why are you speaking with me?" it asked her.

"It's not that I don't trust you," Molly said. "Though, actually, I don't. But you said before that you had something important to do, and that's why you needed me to let you go. You've got somewhere else you need to be, but you're hanging out here with me. That means this must be important too, right?"

The spirit said nothing.

"So. What do you want from me?"

"You are right," the spirit said finally. "I have decided it is important to be here too."

"Why?"

"Because the journal you seek contains surprising information, and you, Molly Stout, are a surprising girl. I am curious to see what might happen if I bring the two of you together. I think there may be interesting consequences to such an event."

"Good or bad consequences?"

"That depends on whom you ask. Both, most likely. Do you still wish to find it?"

"Yes," Molly said instantly, surprising herself. But really, she realized, there was nothing she needed to think about. It might be a huge risk, going along with the spirit's plans, but it was worth it if it could get her the journal.

The Legerdemain *might be gone, but for a lost journal of Haviland Stout, we could get enough money to buy a whole new ship.* She decided that this particular plan was best kept to herself. Then something occurred to her.

"The journal—it's not lost in the Himalayas or buried in the Sahara or anything, is it? I mean, I can't just go around the world."

"It is quite close, I assure you. Haviland's murderer has preferred to keep it under careful watch."

"No murder stories. Just tell me where it is."

"It is where it has been for the past 120 years. In the hands of Charles Arkwright."

"Wait. You mean...are you seriously trying to tell me that Charles Arkwright murdered Haviland Stout?"

The spirit was silent.

"That doesn't even make sense! Are you insane? He was Haviland's closest friend! Why would he—"

"There is a Latin phrase Haviland himself offered to me once. *Cui bono*? It means 'Who benefits?' If you wish to find the perpetrator of a crime, you need only look for the one who stands to gain by it."

"Arkwright wouldn't have..." She threw up her hands. "I don't even know why I'm arguing with you about this. It's stupid, and it's wrong, so we can just leave it at that."

"If you wish," the spirit said. "Nevertheless, Charles Arkwright holds the journal."

"You mean he was buried with it?"

"No."

"Then you must be talking about Tyler Arkwright. Charles died ages ago."

"If you wish," the spirit said again.

Molly thought for a moment. Clearly, the spirit had some mad ideas, but if there was a missing journal, it would make sense that the Arkwrights held it. After all, Charles had been with Haviland until the end.

"How do I know you're telling the truth?" Molly asked.

"The only proof I can offer will be the journal itself. Arkwright has hidden it for a very, very long time and left no trail. Do you wish to find it or not?"

This time, Molly was not so quick to answer.

"You swear to me you're not making it up? Swear it on the wind or the Void or whatever you swear on?"

"I am not lying," the spirit said, "and I will swear it on everything dear to me."

"Fine then. So if Tyler Arkwright is hiding it, how do we get it?"

"I wish I could fetch it for you myself, but unfortunately, I am not unexpected. Certain precautions have been taken. If we wish to get the journal, we will need a special kind of help."

Molly kept a wary eye out for other people as they walked through the streets, lest she be seen walking with a rogue spirit.

"Ariel, can't you make yourself a little less visible? You're so bright, we're bound to be seen."

Ariel made a twinkling sound that Molly thought was a laugh. "I will not be seen," the spirit said. "I am only bright to your eyes."

"How come?"

"Because you see with eyes that are not completely human."

Molly recoiled. "Not human? Then what in bloody blazes are they?"

"That is a very good question. Now hush. Just because I am invisible does not mean others cannot hear us."

They moved swiftly, the spirit drifting along beside Molly. The streets of Knight's Cove were mostly empty, and they did not have far to go, but despite all reassurances, Molly felt as scared as she had when chased by the ferratic.

"Are you sure this is a good idea?" Molly said as they drew close to their destination. "I mean, this terric spirit seemed a bit wild."

"Did you try speaking to it?" Ariel asked softly.

"Well...no."

"Hmm," the spirit said, then drifted between two buildings and down a familiar alleyway. Molly followed reluctantly.

At the end of the alley, she saw again the devastated area in the midst of Knight's Cove—the decaying digger, the remnants of houses, the earth so churned up it looked like a stormy sea.

Ariel left the alley without hesitation. Molly, on the other hand, barely had the courage to peer out from the alley's mouth.

"How do we know it can talk?" she whispered fiercely after Ariel. "I mean, it's..."

There was no earthquake this time. The spirit simply rose up out of the ground. Rocks climbed on rocks until they formed a thick, featureless body. Legs formed beneath it—legs that shaped themselves from stone as the creature moved and dismantled themselves once its weight had shifted. It moved surprisingly quickly, rolling forward until it loomed over Molly like a frozen avalanche. Molly clung to the walls of the alley, but they felt as flimsy as paper. The terric spirit stood that way for a long time, then turned to the side, toward Ariel's glowing form.

"You look like one of them," it said in a voice that was soft and yet deep enough to rumble the ground beneath Molly's feet. "Been here so long you forgot what a real spirit looks like?"

"I wear this shape out of respect for an old friend," Ariel replied calmly.

"That so?" It turned back to Molly, and she withered under its attention. "You got strange friends."

"I might point out that you are speaking their language," Ariel said.

"Well, you wouldn't know proper terric, would you, bein' a wisp? Doubt you could shake a pebble."

Can they all *talk?* Molly wondered with the small part of her mind that was not petrified. She realized, too, that they did not speak the same way. Ariel's speech was…the only word Molly could think of for it was *proper*. Like a book, instead of a person. This terric spirit, though, could have rolled out of any pub in Terra Nova.

"Seen you before, haven't I?" the thing said to Molly. "You came here already, with one of them little metal men. Thought I scared you off the first time."

Molly thought up a brave response but couldn't get her tongue to work well enough to speak it.

"We have come to ask for your help," Ariel said.

"An' what makes you think I would help you?"

"Common enemies."

"Like who?"

"We were hoping you could help this girl break into Arkwright Manor."

Molly could feel the spirit's attention intensify, and it leaned in closer, until she could smell the dust in it.

"Why don't you take her?" it said to Ariel.

"Sadly, they are prepared for me. What they are not prepared for is a solitary human girl, aided by a terric spirit."

"Well, that's some backbone you got," it said finally to Molly. "A speck of a thing like you, taking on Arkwright alone?"

Molly finally got her mouth working again. "I'm not taking him on," she said. "He just has something that belongs to my family."

"I wouldn'ta took you for a day over twelve," the spirit said.

"Fourteen."

The spirit began to rumble. Molly was so frightened that it took her several moments to realize it was laughing.

"What's your name?" it asked.

"Molly. Stout."

"Stout?" It laughed even harder this time, hard enough to shake the ground beneath Molly's feet. "This is so good I'd think you two were having me on, if I didn't know for a fact that wisps don't have a sense of humor."

"Do you have a name?" Molly asked.

"What would you care?" the terric spirit asked.

"I don't know, but you can talk like her, and she has a name, so I thought, if we're going to work together..."

"And you'd use it, if I had a name?"

"Sure. I guess. If you have one."

"Never had anyone ask before. Not in this world anyway. What do you think I should be called?"

"If you don't have one, just say so," Molly told it. "I'm not going to give you one. I'm not your mom."

"Toves," it rumbled.

"Toves? That's not a name."

"It's a name if I say it is. I heard it once in a song or something. Sounds right enough."

"Okay. Toves. Can you help us?"

"I think you're mad. But I kind of like the idea of setting a mad girl loose on Arkwright. If you really want to stick your head in the lion's mouth, I can get you there. When are we going?"

Ariel turned to Molly. Molly swallowed. "Umm…soon," she said.

"All right. You let me know when it's time."

With a rumble that sent Molly staggering backward, Toves sank into the earth. Molly stood for a moment, watching the place he had been, and then started walking back toward her house.

"When do you think you will go?" Ariel asked, drifting up beside her.

"Soon. Like I said."

"We should act quickly, Molly. I feel this is important, but I cannot wait forever."

"I know, I know. You have a mission."

Molly reached the street and turned right. On either side, squat wooden buildings penned her in, the occasional gleam of lamplight piercing through windows like eyes watching her. She looked straight up, at the brown fug where the stars should have been, and breathed deep.

"This may not matter to you, but spirits are suffering," Ariel said.

"I know."

She kept walking with her eyes heavenward. *I'll go home and sleep. I need to think clearly about all of this.* Her steps slowed. *Home. Damn it all, I wish I was going home. But I won't anymore, will I?* With every step, the stars seemed farther away, and the cloying hands of gravity seemed to tighten. She slowed until her feet were dragging along the ground.

"Molly?"

She looked ahead. She could see the porch of her family's house, the solid wooden timbers and the too-low roof. It was as still and dead as the hollowed-out ships around the *Legerdemain* had been.

She turned and walked quickly back the way she had come.

"Molly, where are you—"

"Now," Molly said. "I'm going to do it now."

TWELVE

Ariel rested her hands on Molly's shoulders, her touch surprisingly solid. "I am sorry I cannot do this with you," she said.

"Me too," Molly said. "So. What am I supposed to do once I get there?"

"I cannot tell you much. Arkwright's mansion, and indeed his entire island home, is guarded well against spiritual intrusion. But I can offer you this one piece of advice. Follow the wind."

"What does that mean?"

"Arkwright uses aetheric devices to keep me out, but his caution may also prove his undoing. The same aetheric devices that block me should give you a clue as to where the journal is. After all, his guard will be strongest where the journal lies."

"Great. So I go into the mansion of the richest man in the world, probably full of ferratics and traps, and I follow the breeze around."

"Sounds like you're ready," Toves said, flowing up beside her. "Let's get on with it, before you come to your senses."

"Fine," Molly said.

"Now, I've never done this before, so it might get a bit ticklish," the terric spirit warned her. Then it flowed forward, rocks rolling in around Molly and encasing her, cutting off all light.

"Good luck," Molly heard Ariel say, and then she felt herself sinking down into the ground. And suddenly she knew she had made a terrible mistake.

She couldn't move or see or sense anything. The rocks of Toves's body rumbled against her skin, shaking her to the bones. The sound was overwhelming, but she could not lift her hands to cover her ears. She could barely breathe: all the weight of the spirit, and the earth above her—who knew how far below ground they were now—rested heavily on her back, squeezing her farther and farther down. She couldn't even tell if they were moving anymore, and she felt desperate to move, to jump, to see light and shadow instead of this unending nothingness. She tried to remember the feeling of wind passing through her hair. She longed for the *Legerdemain*, but it was gone, and she was stuck down here, buried beneath fathoms of rock, and who knew if she would ever see or feel the wind again.

And then the rumbling stopped. Everything stopped, all sound and feeling, and Molly began to wonder if Toves had left her down here—a fitting punishment for a stupid girl who had trusted spirits too much. "What's going on?" she tried to say, but the stones in her ears made it impossible to hear even her own voice.

Then there was a boom, like the firing of a cannon, and the rocks around her rumbled frantically, frenetically, and she found herself spilling forward onto the ground—the ground of a dark but, blessedly, open passageway. She drew herself up onto her knees, breathed deep and flexed her fingers just to see if she could. She blew, then watched the white glimmer of her breath dissipate in the air.

She stood and took a quick look around. The passageway was narrow and lined with stones. The only light came from a small igneous lamp sitting in a sconce far down the passage.

Behind her, stones flowed from the hole in the wall and gathered themselves to form the body of Toves again.

"I have to go," it said.

Molly, head reeling, struggled to understand. "What? Go?"

"Yes. Now. I'll try to come back, but I don't—"

"What do you mean? Aren't you waiting to take me back?"

"Didn't you feel that? There's something down there. I have to go before it finds us."

"But you—"

"There's no time," it said and then flowed out through the hole it had just created in the wall. After the last stone disappeared, soil began to sift quickly into the gap.

There was a thump from the ground beneath Molly, and then another. For a moment, the dark underground passage shook like an airship in the midst of a storm. Molly threw off her confusion and hurried down the passage, leaning on the walls to keep her footing.

What have I gotten myself into now? she wondered. *Why can't I just leave well enough alone?*

A crash sent her to her knees, and she heard something in the passage behind her. She scuttled forward on all fours, rounding a corner and huddling against the wall. The passage shook as something moved along its length, and she heard a sound like something sniffing, and then there was another crash and the sound of stones falling to the ground. Molly waited, but the sounds receded until they disappeared. She peeked around the corner.

The light in the passage was dim, and whatever had entered the tunnel had stirred up a great deal of dust, but through the shadowy haze she could see that part of the tunnel had been torn apart, the stone walls broken to pieces. She crept closer and found a new tunnel intersecting the old—a tunnel much like the one dug by Toves, but much, much bigger. There were what appeared to be claw marks on the ground and across the walls. Molly shivered.

"I should've grabbed a light," Molly heard someone say from beyond the ruined tunnel. She ran quickly back to the turn in the passage as footsteps approached behind her. She tucked herself deep into the shadows.

"Would you just come along, mate?" said a second voice. "One lamp's fine. Probably nothing anyway. You know how the…"

The voice faded out as the footsteps approached the wreckage of the tunnel. Molly heard a low whistle.

"I wouldn't call that nothing," said the first voice.

"Looks like the tunnel rat did this. I've seen it shake a few bricks loose before but never plow straight through the house."

"Hey, bring that light over here." The footsteps convened. "See this? Looks like something else came through here before the rat. It must've been chasing it."

"Hell. Something got in. That means we'll be spending the rest of the day searching this bloody place."

Molly swallowed and slid farther into the shadows.

"You think Blaise'll make us search? I mean, it won't matter in a few hours."

"You only ask that because you're new. Blaise doesn't care if we're leaving. He'll have us running every mouse in this cellar to ground before he lets us go. It'll be quicker if we split up and search."

"Hold on! You've got the only light!"

"Grab that one down there, idiot. Now get searching. The sooner we get this done, the better."

One set of footsteps went back the way it had come. The other came toward Molly, and as she pressed herself into the wall she saw a diminutive man run past. A moment later the faint light from the lamp bobbed and then receded. The shadows around Molly began to grow longer. She looked down the passageway she was in, but she couldn't see anything. The shadows flowed toward her as the only light moved away. She scrambled up and, as quietly as she could, chased after the man who had taken the lamp, before she was left blind and lost.

Sticking to the shadows at the edge of the light, she followed him down endless corridors. The basement of Arkwright Manor was a maze of tunnels that crossed and recrossed each other without plan or purpose. Molly lost all sense of direction, and time seemed to fade into the flickering shadows.

They passed by racks of wine bottles; rooms full of brooms or rifles or woodworking implements; tangles of copper piping that disappeared into the walls in every direction; rooms full of boxes, with labels Molly couldn't read in the dim light. From time to time a breeze would pass by them, bright blue against the darkness, but these small winds vanished as quickly as they appeared. When Molly tried to follow them, she never made it far before the wind dissolved, and she had to scramble after the light again.

Eventually they made their way up several flights of narrow stairs, and with each floor they passed, the mansion seemed to gain some brightness. Lamps began to appear at regular intervals, and Molly began to hear other people stirring. Despite her need for stealth, Molly found it a welcome sound.

When the man she was following turned left at the top of a flight of stairs, Molly turned right. She had no idea where she was going, but before long she could hear the bustle of a living house all around her. In fact, she realized as she hid beneath stairs and dashed past open doorways, the household was buzzing like a kicked hornet's nest. Servants hurried in all directions with armloads of clothes, food or machinery. Peeking into the rooms she passed, Molly saw stacks of boxes everywhere. Tall multi-armed cogitants moved among the stacks, packing and repacking everything.

Molly did not linger anywhere, for fear of being seen, but the busyness of the manor seemed to work in her favor. Everyone moved about with such purpose that they hardly seemed to see the house around them, and she moved up two more floors without incident. She looked everywhere for signs of a wind she could follow but found none. So much for their plans.

As she rose through the manor, the number of people continued to increase, and Molly began to spot men in dark jackets among the throngs of gray-suited servants. These men seemed more alert than their counterparts, peering into shadows as they walked. Molly avoided them when she could, but they grew so numerous that she found it impossible. She had to double back several times, and once she even climbed into a half-packed box as five of the dark-clad men passed not a few feet away.

"...almost ready?" she heard one of the men say.

"Soon. We've never moved him before. We have to make sure..."

Once they were gone, Molly climbed back out of the box and headed in the opposite direction. She was beginning to think seriously about giving up her search and simply trying to find a way out when she heard a rush of wind. A moment later she saw a gust of air barrel down the hallway in front of her. Hopefully, she moved in the direction it had come from.

"Careful!" she heard a deep voice boom. "If you so much as touch that valve again, I'll carve the meat off your bones and feed it to the dogs!"

The voice came from a room at the end of the hall. The doors were made of iron, unlike the other doors she had come across. Molly approached cautiously.

The room on the other side of the door was huge and crammed with more machinery than Molly had ever seen—more than every spiritual device on the *Legerdemain* combined. Wires and pipes ran everywhere, and several of the machines crackled with a strange energy that looked like lightning but flowed like water.

"The control center next," another voice said, and several servants approached a short desk-shaped machine. Molly ducked farther back, but none of the men so much as glanced in her direction. They began gathering wires and removing the bolts that fastened the device to the floor.

More servants moved here and there through the room, and men and women in white coats flitted between them, adjusting knobs and telling people not to touch things they did not understand. Squat, beetle-like automatons thronged the room too, using their thick arms to lift machinery onto their flat backs before carrying it out of Molly's sight.

"One hour and counting," said the same booming voice Molly had heard before. "I don't have to remind you what happens to people who get us off schedule, do I?" She turned, saw who was speaking and immediately recoiled. It was the huge bald man she had seen at the docks—the one who had pinned her father to the ground so easily.

At his sides were two strange spiritual devices unlike anything Molly had ever seen. They stood on tripod legs, shifting constantly. Their oval bodies were lined with short metal rods, and as Molly watched, a dizzying array of weaponry unfolded from these rods—multi-jointed blades, whipcords, nets, needles and other tools Molly could not even name. From the way they moved, Molly wondered if they were ferratics.

"We're running behind, sir," the bald man said, turning to face the other direction.

"I had noticed," said another voice. The voice sounded strange—as if it came up from a deep well. "I trust that when we are finally under way, you will see to the appropriate punishments, Mr. Blaise?"

"'Course, sir."

From where Molly stood, she could only see the edge of what he was looking at. It appeared to be some kind of large water tank, though the liquid inside moved strangely, sometimes appearing slow and thick, and sometimes roiling frantically, like a boiling pot. There was something floating in this liquid, though she could only see a hint of it at the side of the tank. She leaned forward, and more came into her view. What she saw made her pull back, horrified.

Floating in the tank was a human arm, moving and alive.

There's a person in that tank! But what kind of person could survive in that? She leaned around the door again to take another look. Her eyes immediately met those of the bald man. *Mr. Blaise.*

"Hello," he said. "Not supposed to be in here, are you?" His voice was utterly calm, but Molly felt herself go rigid with terror.

At the man's side, the strange spiritual devices sprang to life, cords and blades rising up around them like a mass of tentacles. The sight was enough to get Molly moving again; she ran. Footsteps, human and otherwise, followed behind her. She ran without regard for direction, leaving the hallways she knew behind. There was no escape in going back anyway.

For all she knew, there was no escape anywhere. *He saw me! What if he recognized me? He'll know who I am from when he pinned Da.*

The sounds of pursuit were joined by a strange clanging that seemed to echo from the walls themselves, like a ship's bell but coming from everywhere. At the sound, servants and security began pouring from all the rooms and into the hallways. She turned and turned again, trying to avoid getting caught between security guards and ferratics.

She spotted a wide, carpeted stairway and ran up it. The next floor was different than the ones she had seen so far. Rich carpets covered the floor, and wooden furniture gleamed in the light of numerous lamps. *This looks like a sitting room! That means they might have…* She ran through a door and saw exactly what she wanted. *Windows!* On the other side of the glass she could see the waters of Hamilton Sound, and beyond them the million glowing lights of Terra Nova.

She picked up a chair and headed for the nearest window. She was just about to hurl the chair at the glass when she noticed something odd: tiny, glowing filaments of orange wind woven together like a spiderweb just inside the window. They were so thin she was barely able to see them.

She paused, remembering Ariel's words. With the sounds of her pursuers getting closer, she found a single, hair-thin filament that left the web and ran along the floor. All of the windows had the same web of wind across them, and each one was connected to the same filament that led off to the right, through a doorway.

She hesitated a moment over the decision, but she knew she didn't have long to choose. The security guards and their terrible ferratics would be on her in a matter of moments. With a great heave, she threw the chair at the window. As it went through the wind and the glass, a deeper klaxon was added to the alarms already screaming through the house.

Molly looked briefly at the lights of Terra Nova, then turned and ran through the door to the right.

She followed the filament through two more rooms until it took her into what seemed to be a servants' area; it was a narrow hallway, with chipped paint on the walls and worn carpets on the floors. Molly ducked behind a wheeled cart that was set against the wall, taking a moment to catch her breath.

Behind her, she could hear people in the sitting room.

"Anyone see her?" one voice asked.

"Not here. She could have run around the other side of the house."

She heard the deep rumble of Mr. Blaise's voice. "Let the dogs find her." Molly peeked through the plates stacked high on the wheeled cart. She could make out the hulking form of Blaise at the window and other men behind him.

"The dogs?" one man said softly. "Sir, she looked like a little girl. The dogs will—"

Without warning, Blaise punched the man in the throat. There was an awful sound, something between a cough and a stick snapping, and the man fell backward, silent.

"Now," said Blaise, "is someone going to loose the dogs, or do I have to do it myself?"

"Yes, sir," said another man.

"Someone take Roberts to the infirmary before he suffocates."

Molly waited, holding her breath. Two people carried the fallen man away while he struggled to breathe. They came toward her, then turned off to the right just before entering the servants' area. Beyond them, in the sitting room, Molly could see Blaise standing at the window. His hands stretched open and closed at his side. Several dark-suited men waited behind him.

Another man, in the same dark uniform but with some kind of emblem on his shoulder, stepped up beside Blaise. "Did you get a good look at her?" he asked.

"Yeah. Any idea who she is or why she's here?"

"No, sir. You didn't recognize her?"

Blaise shook his head, and Molly had to stop herself from sighing with relief. "Doesn't matter," he said. "We'll have her soon enough. Take some men and keep searching the house, just in case. The rest of you get downstairs and help pack up. If we're not out of here in an hour, I'm going to start breaking legs."

The men all walked away, out of Molly's sight.

Molly waited until Blaise followed them, then hurried on down the passage, following the filament.

This better be the wind I'm supposed to follow, Molly thought as she ran alongside the thin orange thread of wind.

The filament took her through a maze of passages, kitchens, supply rooms and cramped living quarters. Luckily, both the packing and the pursuit seemed to be concentrated in the more affluent areas of the manor: Molly didn't see a soul anywhere. As she followed the filament to its source, more and more offshoots rejoined it. It was an incredible construction—wind woven as thin as hair, but kept stable and spread throughout the house. She could not help but marvel that such a thing could be done. She wondered how powerful the spirit that did it was.

The filament eventually led her to a narrow stairway. Molly descended several flights of stairs and then followed the filament down a long hallway. The air here smelled musty, and with each step she stirred up clouds of dust. The orange ribbon of wind thickened as it went down the hall. Molly followed it to the end of the passage, where it disappeared under a door. The door opened easily, but she stopped herself just before walking through.

Across the doorway stretched a web of wind, like the ones on the windows above but far more dense and intricate.

Great. What do I do now?

On the other side, she saw what appeared to be an ordinary room. There was an old armchair, with a bookshelf next to it. There was a map pinned up on the wall. Nothing seemed unusual—and yet the strength of the alarm system suggested this might be the most valuable room in the manor. Molly held her fingers up to the wind but did not touch it.

Is all of this really just to keep Ariel out? Molly wondered. And then a second thought. *If it keeps her out, how am I supposed to get through?*

She thought of how she had begun this long, long night: her standing on the rooftop, looking at the wind. Not just looking at it though…

She put one finger carefully through a gap in the web and felt the wind stirring around her. Just as it had before, on the roof, the wind felt almost solid. Molly wrapped her finger around one strand of the web and pulled down very slowly.

The web trembled for a moment, but the strand did not break. The gap widened, and when Molly stopped pushing and pulled her fingers away, the web stayed as it was but with a larger hole in its middle.

Molly reached in with both hands and pulled at the wind. It moved at her touch, and she worked slowly at it until she had created an opening wide enough for her to step through. The web was bunched and tangled around the outer edges of the door now, but it was unbroken. Molly passed through the opening and looked around for something that might contain a hidden treasure from her ancestor.

She was disappointed, however, to discover that the room was every bit as ordinary as it had seemed. There was a desk in one corner, covered in bric-a-brac: a compass, a few papers, an old, battered water canteen. On the other side of the room was a cupboard with glass doors, containing what looked like a supply of liquor. The only unusual thing in the room was the aetheric device in the corner. The machine had a thick metal body, thoroughly patched, surrounded by an array of jointed arms, all moving incessantly. A stream of wind flowed out from the device, passing through the arms and then out to form the filaments Molly had followed. In addition to the whirs its arms made, Molly could hear occasional thumps from inside the machine, as if something was trying to break out.

She tore her eyes away and looked again at the rest of the room. *I don't see a lockbox or a safe.* Except for the aetheric security, this did not seem like the kind of room in which to hide secrets.

Her eyes passed over the map on the wall and then returned. She stepped closer. It was an old topographic map, showing what looked to be a mountain range. Quite a few notes were written on it in black ink. She found one spot, sitting between two mountains, marked *Base Camp.*

Another, closer to the peak of a mountain, said, *Research Station—plan for 12-night stay.* She looked to the top of the map. *The Himalayas*, the title read.

This was a map of Haviland's research trip, Molly realized. She looked again at the handwritten notes, recognizing Haviland's cramped writing from the replica journals she had read. *It's not just a map—it's* the *map! This is the original!*

She turned to the bookshelf. *Seems too obvious. But if that's his map, then maybe*...She took out one of the books and opened it.

April 13, 1787. Sample collections have been proceeding swiftly, largely due to the assistance of the local population. While the flora here is as alien to me as if it came from the stars, these villagers seem to know each leaf, each...

Molly flipped to the beginning of the book, where a few lines had been jotted on the inside cover: *Journal of Haviland Stout, 1787–1788. If found, please return to Oxford University, Oxford, England.*

She opened a few more books and found they all bore the same name. The entire bookshelf was taken up with the journals of Haviland Stout. She reached for the bottom right corner and pulled out a small leather-bound book, flipping it open to a page near the beginning.

...but now that I know what to look for, I realize that the font is quite active. Spirits are passing through constantly.

This is it! Molly flipped ahead, looking for the famous final entry, dated August 11. It was not there, however; the book was only a third full, without the divisions in the text one might expect. She turned to the first page and found there a single date: *August 11, 1792.* The entire journal was one long entry.

She closed the book, tucked it into the back of her belt and looked around. All of this, she realized, came from her ancestor. There were so many treasures hidden here—she wanted to take more. *But if I take more than the secret journal, the one Arkwright doesn't want anyone to know about, I might bring the cops right down on me and my family. Besides, this one journal will be enough to make us rich.*

She tore her eyes away from the other artifacts and headed for the door. She retraced her steps, trying to think of an escape plan as she went. She couldn't get out belowground; the only option was to escape through one of the windows. The problem, of course, was that the guards already believed she had done just that, and they were combing the grounds for her—and the dogs were probably out and prowling by now. But she saw no other option. She returned to the stairway and walked cautiously upstairs.

On the ground floor, things were surprisingly quiet. She heard shouting from outside the house, and a few people stirring nearby, but the room where she had smashed the window seemed to be empty. She entered cautiously and peeked out of the broken window.

There were dark shapes down by the waterline—human figures moving here and there, as well as squat shapes that might be dogs—or ferratics. Farther out, huge humpbacked things cut through the water, casting light across the surface of the Sound.

She groaned. Even if she could get past the guards—which she didn't think she could—she couldn't swim across the Sound. She wasn't even sure she could remember how to swim, it had been so long since she'd last tried. What she needed was a boat.

She went on through the house until she reached an east-facing window, then scanned the shore. Nothing but more guards. The same was true to the north, but when she finally found a window looking west, she saw what appeared to be a boathouse poking out into the water. She shifted the wind filaments away from the glass panes, undid the latch and pushed the window open.

There was nothing to hide behind between the house and the shore, so Molly prayed that the shadows would keep her hidden. She slunk forward on all fours, staying as low to the ground as she could. Stray winds ducked low, stirring the grass and her hair. Far above, she could make out many winds, still cavorting as they had at the beginning of the night. She shivered and kept moving.

She wasn't even halfway to the boathouse when she heard a growl behind her. She turned and found herself facing the largest dog she had ever seen. It had a short snout and lips drawn back to reveal teeth that glowed white in the darkness. Its shoulders bulged with muscle, and the dog padded toward her on paws the size of her hands. It wasn't more than a few yards away.

Molly stood quickly, heart thundering in her chest. The dog stopped for a moment and then dashed at her, barking loudly. Molly ran.

The dog was closing in fast—Molly was quick, but no match for a monster like this. She looked around desperately and saw a thick blue ribbon of wind skidding across the ground just to her right. She veered over and dug her hands into it, gripping tightly. The wind pulled at her hands, and then she was flying along beside it, barely able to keep her feet under her.

The wind began to slow, dragged down by her weight, but the initial rush had put some distance between Molly and the dog. She let go and ran on toward the boathouse.

I might actually make it, she thought. And then something rose up out of the water right in front of her.

At first, all Molly could make out in the darkness was a huge hulking shape, like a whale pulling itself up onto land. Then a tail flicked up, and a spotlight on the end of it flared to life. In the bright light, she saw a mound of metal plates and rivets, like the shell of a gargantuan turtle but with dozens of short legs beneath it. Its head, on the other hand, looked like no living thing Molly had seen: merely a single camera and, beneath it, a whirling mass of gears and blades that looked like they could chew through a boat's hull in seconds. The spotlight on the tail swung down and pointed at Molly. She stopped in her tracks, despite the barking behind her.

Molly looked for another escape, but there was none. The dog was close now, and in the distance on both sides, men and ferratics were moving in. In front of her, the monster began to move again, its myriad legs tearing up the ground beneath it. There was nowhere left to go.

She heard a whistling from above. Molly looked up and saw a bright blue shape descending from the sky, shearing the crosswinds like a blade.

"Ariel!" Molly shouted. "Help!"

The spirit descended quickly to her side. Molly could feel the ground shaking as the metal sea monster drew closer.

"Did you find the journal?"

"Yes."

"Good. We must leave."

"Can you take me?" Molly asked.

Ariel only laughed. She swept in around Molly, the wind of her body pressing Molly's clothes to her skin, and Molly felt her feet leaving the ground.

For a moment she felt unsteady, but as they rose, Ariel seemed to gain solidity around her, the wind holding her so close, so still, that her initial vertigo faded. And then they truly began to move.

If she had thought flight with the flitter was incredible, it was nothing compared to this. She wasn't moving *through* the air but *with* it, as if she were a part of it, flying so fast that Molly couldn't keep track of where they were. The sensation was so overwhelming that thoughts of pursuit, the manor, the journal and even her family fell away, until all she was aware of was the movement and the skies around her. The blood in her veins sang.

They stopped, and Molly looked down. Arkwright Island was far below, the dogs and men swarming over it looking like nothing more than specks of blackness. Spotlights swirled through the air, searching for her, but their light faded far, far short of Molly and Ariel.

"Thanks," she said to Ariel.

"It was my foolishness that trapped you there," the aetheric spirit said. "I should have known Arkwright's paranoia would grow with time. Nevertheless, we have the journal."

Molly reached back to check on the book; it was still tucked into her belt. "Will they come after it? After me? Disposal already—"

"You need not fear the authorities, Molly. They will not find out about this."

"Why?"

"Because you have stolen something that is not supposed to exist. Arkwright will tell no one. But he may send his own people. Do you think they know who you are?"

"No. But one saw my face."

"We shall have to be careful."

"So now what?" she asked.

"Now we return you to your home."

They began moving south, toward Terra Nova and Knight's Cove. Molly watched the lights speed toward them—both the city lights and the swirling glow of the wind. She had no sense of gravity, no fear of falling. They arced up over the city and then began to descend through a maze of breezes and zephyrs.

"Don't," Molly said. "Don't take me back yet. Can we stay up here a little longer? Please?"

Ariel said nothing, but now they were rising, rising, until Molly felt the cold dew of clouds gathering on her cheeks. She closed her eyes and spread her arms.

With the morning sun shining down on her, Molly slipped into her house through her bedroom window. She did not know what time it was, but she suspected her family would soon be stirring. They probably knew she hadn't been home again the previous night. She thought about showing them the journal that could get them all off the ground again. But the feeling of flight was still dancing under her skin, and she wasn't ready to see people, to speak. She wanted to linger in the sensation a little longer yet.

She sat down on her bed, knowing she would not sleep. The journal pressed into her back, and she took it out.

I got it. I really got it. And now, with this, we can get out of this house, back into the air, back home.

She ran her fingertips over the cracked leather cover and then over the rough edges of the pages inside. She opened the book, the binding making small cracking sounds as she did, and began reading.

August 11, 1792. Another damned journal has gone missing—the third on this expedition. I must write this all down again, before I lose the details.

On July 13, we witnessed a phenomenon unlike anything we had ever seen. A small, dark sphere hung in the sky between two peaks, just east of our camp. We observed it for some time and witnessed something emerge from the darkness. This "something" looked to be little more than a discoloration in the air—a brighter-blue patch of sky—but it moved against the prevailing winds, as if with intention. Our guides seemed as bewildered as we were.

Charles Arkwright and Felix Gustavson were both eager to examine it more closely. I insisted we stay well away until we learned more. We stationed observers at the dark sphere (which I will henceforth refer to as a font) for several days. In that time, we saw the same discoloration appear repeatedly, traveling in different directions each time but seemingly unaffected by winds and weather. Nor was this all that emerged from the font; on the second day, we observed a creature that resembled a starling, save that it seemed to have a pair of arms tucked beneath its wings, and it sang in a way that made observers dizzy. Other, odder beings emerged as well—thankfully, my sketches have not gone missing along with my journals.

After much observation, we came to believe that the font was an entryway from a heretofore unknown plane of existence.

On the fifth day, Charles accidentally made contact with one of the beings. The font had been inactive for hours, and he reported that he drifted off. When he woke, the discoloration was floating directly over him. When he shouted, it flew quickly back through the font. However, it emerged again several hours later, when I had replaced Arkwright at the observation station. It came straight to me, and as I watched, it became more visible and changed form, taking on the rough proportions of a human. I spoke to it; it did not understand me at that time, of course, but it made fluting noises that seemed to indicate an effort to communicate.

This was the beginning of a long process. The strange being returned consistently, but not predictably, to interact with my team. Over time its ability to assume human form improved, and in a remarkably short time it was able to mimic human speech. I instructed my team to help it in this process by speaking, but making no movements to touch it. Some were reluctant; these, if they were not needed, I sent home. Charles and I seemed to be the only two who were eager for this opportunity.

The traffic of other beings through this font had slowed, but it was also during this time that we were able to observe something of their character and capabilities. Several observers, myself included, noted that there is a peculiar quality to the air around the being; it seems cleaner, purer. Perhaps, like a tree, it alters the chemical makeup of the air around it? Without extensive study and the instruments of a proper laboratory, I cannot draw any conclusions.

At one point I observed several beings emerge through the font and rise directly up into the clouds above the mountains. Shortly after, weather patterns began to shift, with clouds gathering above and beginning to release snow. We have observed many similar moments that lead us to believe that these beings can—and often do—intentionally affect weather. To what end, I do not know, but such behavior has reminded me strongly of certain animistic beliefs attributing sentience to natural processes. As such, I have taken to calling these strange beings "spirits."

We have observed other surprising capabilities as well: objects levitating, winds strong enough to blast apart rocks, lightning traveling horizontally rather than vertically, beams of sunlight weaving themselves into new shapes. We have not even begun to understand how these things are possible.

Some progress is being made, however, largely due to the assistance of Ariel. This is the best name I have found to describe the first spirit we made contact with. It has taken pains to learn our language—and has learned it at a rate that, quite frankly, I find intimidating—and seems eager to communicate with us. Understanding can be difficult, since our perspectives are so radically different, but Ariel is assisting us in understanding what we are witnessing.

The font, she has told me, is but one of many in the world, but most fonts are ephemeral phenomena. Only a few, like the one we have found here in the Himalayas, are stable entryways into our world. They do indeed lead to another place. Here I have been unable to garner a complete understanding, as Ariel only describes this other land's location as being "beside" our own.

The spirits we have seen are part of a vast population, with much variety. (As much as the variety of life on Earth, perhaps?) She tells me this is not a new phenomenon, despite the fact that we have never seen it before. They have always come here, she says, because our "home are join." I believe she means that our worlds are interconnected in some way. When I asked her what the spirits want, she grew confused and replied with her own question: "What do your people want?" I couldn't begin to answer such a large question—only now, writing this, do I realize that this was exactly her point.

(I see I have begun calling her "she" and "her," despite efforts to break myself of this habit. Ariel has no gender as we understand it, but in her approximation of human form, there is a slenderness that suggests femininity to me. I am trying to avoid anthropomorphism, but find it difficult.)

An interesting side note: We have discovered that Ariel, and likely the rest of the spirits, have an adverse reaction to iron. They seem to grow uncomfortable in its vicinity, and Charles performed his own experiment by hurling a frying pan at a large, eagle-like spirit he was observing. The spirit cried out as if burned and vanished back through the font. (Needless to say, I did not endorse this experiment and have warned him not to repeat it.) In order to interact effectively with Ariel, we have had to remove all iron implements from our campsite.

My turn for the observation post is fast approaching. I have learned so much and have so much yet to learn. I will continue this soon.

THIRTEEN

Molly flipped through the journal, but there was nothing more. She set it down on her lap, then picked it up again to reread the last words. *I have learned so much and have so much yet to learn.*

The journal suddenly seemed dangerous to her—as if it might bite her fingers off the next time she touched it. Quickly she closed it and pushed it under her bed, then stepped back.

Ariel had said the journal contained surprising information, but this…It didn't fit with anything she knew. Haviland Stout, studying and even cooperating with the spirits, saying it was hard not to think of them as human, excited to learn more.

How can this be Haviland Stout? she asked herself. *And where is the rest? Where are his battles against the spirits? Where is his final warning to guard ourselves against them?*

She didn't want to think about it—but she couldn't stop. She mentally circled through questions for ten minutes before she realized something was amiss in her room.

She bent down to look beneath her bed again. There was the journal—only the journal. The flitter was gone.

She looked to her window and then to her door. It could easily have been stolen—nothing prevented strangers from coming in through the window, just as Molly had. She found herself hoping it had been stolen, because she didn't want to imagine the alternative.

It hadn't occurred to her until this moment that the house was completely silent. There was no sound of her brothers nattering at each other or even of Kiernan puttering away in the kitchen. She went to the door and opened it.

Her brothers were nowhere in sight. Sitting at the table, alone and silent, was her father. The flitter was beside him on the table.

He looked up at her, and for a moment she found herself unable to breathe. His eyes were so red that it looked like they had been scalded. His cheeks were sunken, and there was a tremor in the hands that rested on the tabletop. He looked nothing like the captain she was used to—he looked like he was dying.

"Your flitter's empty," he said, his words slurred.

"Yes," she said. She wanted to return to her room, lock the door and sleep until she was twenty.

"I wondered why you hadn't been using it."

"I didn't know you were paying attention. I thought you were locked in your room."

"Why is your flitter empty, Molly?"

"Because I..." She remembered what Rory had said, but no lies came to mind. She could hardly think, with Haviland's journal buzzing around in her brain. *Should I tell him?*

Maybe he'll listen. "It doesn't matter, Da. Things have been happening, and I—"

"Answer me!" he shouted so loudly that Molly could actually see the bright-orange wind of his breath blasting out of his throat.

"I let it go," she said.

He stared at her with his red eyes. The tremors in his hands increased.

"You're really touched then," he said. "I didn't want to think it could happen to one of mine."

"It's not what you think."

"You let a spirit free!" He pounded on the table and rose to his feet. "You let them get to you, Molly, and now..." He trailed off, as if his momentary anger had exhausted him. He swayed slightly on his feet, and his eyes drifted down to the floor. "Of course it's what I think," he said more softly. "You're bloody touched." He sank back into his chair.

"Maybe I am," Molly said, "but I think maybe there's something wrong with...with everything, really. They might not be like we thought. I just learned something that might—"

"Lies. Spirit lies." His voice was so weak that Molly could hardly hear it.

"No, Da. The spirit didn't tell me anything. It just helped me get this." She went back to her room, pulled out the journal and put it on the table. "This will explain. I think. I just read it, and—"

Her father surged to his feet, rage bursting across his face. He hurled the book at Molly. It struck her in the head, and she fell backward. She felt a bright, hot pain behind her left eye, and then it spread to envelop her entire head. She closed her eyes against it. When she opened them again, her father was above her, hands clenched so tightly that they shook. He was looking at her with undisguised hate in his eyes. She flinched away.

"Get out of my house," he said softly.

"Da, I—"

He picked her up by one arm, dragged her to the front door and threw her out. She heard the door slam behind her as she fell to her hands and knees. Her head was still throbbing from the hit, leaving her disoriented. She breathed in and out, trying to clear her head, but the air felt thick and cloying, and it only left her dizzier.

She started to turn back to the house, but something stopped her. She didn't want to look at it again. *My da just... he...* Her head was spinning around and around the same image—her father, above her, his angry eyes pinning her to the ground. *He...* She tried again, but her feet wouldn't take her any closer to the house.

She took a step away instead, then another, and then she began walking as fast as her tired legs would carry her.

Ariel found her, several hours later, perched atop a warehouse. She had been staring up at the umbilical for a long time now, trying to imagine what she might be doing if she had never descended to the ground. Her left eye felt puffy and tender, but she had no mirror to see how bad it looked.

"Molly," the spirit said softly at her back. Molly did not turn. "I went to your home and heard your brothers talking to your father. Molly, I am sorry. I did not intend this."

"Why were you looking for me?" Molly asked, changing the subject.

"I came to see if you had read the journal or tried to sell it directly."

That caught Molly's attention. "You knew I wanted to sell it?"

"It seemed to make sense, given what you had lost."

"I read the journal, but I don't have it anymore. It was still in the house when..." Her head throbbed, and she closed her eyes. "So you really knew him? Haviland?"

"Yes."

"And is everything in the journal true? You and Haviland, learning to talk to each other, helping him. Is that all true?"

"Yes, Molly."

"Then I don't understand. How did all this happen?" She gestured upward at the docks floating far above them.

"I've already told you that answer."

"You mean Arkwright?"

"Yes."

"He killed Haviland?"

"He saw that history could travel a different path with a little push—and a well-placed martyrdom."

"And now...oh God, Ariel, I've spent my life...my family has spent their lives trapping..."

"Is this really a surprise to you?"

Molly finally turned to look at the spirit, which hung there, perfectly calm, its head tilted slightly. "Of course it's a surprise! This changes everything. I mean, a hundred years of history..."

"But you released the one you call Legerdemain before you knew any of this. Why?"

"Because he deserved better."

"Because he was not a monster, as most thought?"

Molly's mouth opened, but no words came out. *Did I already know? How long ago did I figure out that spirits weren't what people said?* She cast her mind back through her memory, looking for an answer. To the day she became the *Legerdemain*'s engineer and immediately threw the intakes open wide to let the engine breathe. The day when she was eight and spoke softly to the engine for the first time when Morgan, the current engineer, wasn't watching. When she was six and saw him reach inside the engine's casing with iron pellets in his hand, then heard the bone-jarring bellow from inside.

I've known since before I can remember. I knew it was wrong, but I didn't do anything. Molly felt she might gag. She clenched her teeth and put her head in her hands.

Ariel was silent for a time. When she spoke again, there was a hardness in her voice. "Molly, I do not need your guilt, nor do I care for it. This is not about you. If you feel guilty, then use that to change things for the better. Otherwise, your feelings mean nothing."

"How? How can we change all this?" Molly kept her eyes closed.

"I haven't asked you to change everything. That is not so simple. But I came across to this world for a reason, and you may yet help me achieve my ends."

"You're talking about your mission, the one you almost killed me over."

"Yes."

"What is it?" Molly wasn't sure if she was asking because she wanted to know or because she simply wanted something else to think about than a family and a history that had just been turned on their heads.

"Something from this world is crossing over into mine. It is drawing spirits directly out of their home through the fonts."

This caught her attention, despite her whirling thoughts. "Drawn through the fonts? How can that happen?" One of the first lessons learned aboard an aetheric harvester was that the ship must never touch the font. Physical objects fractured the font in some way, resulting in a phenomenon much like a voidstorm, in which both font and ship were generally destroyed.

"I do not know. It should not be possible. Nevertheless, a few weeks ago something intruded into our world through an aetheric font. It must be stopped—and not just for my kind, but for yours as well."

"But you don't know what it is?"

"No. That is what I came here to discover."

"Is there anything else you know? Any hints?" The spirit shook its head. Molly sagged. With so little known, it seemed an impossible task. "So what do we do?"

"We? You intend to help then?"

"Yes. I mean, if I can."

"You will be branded as corrupt."

"I know that. But like you said, this isn't about me."

Some of the familiar softness returned to Ariel's voice. "Then we watch, and we listen."

FOURTEEN

Molly didn't know how they would ever discover what was entering the fonts, but as she set her mind to the task, she realized that she knew where to start. She had been staring at them all night: the docks. Haviland Industries had put a stranglehold on aetheric harvesting in Terra Nova, so even a strange new harvester that drew directly from the Void would have to sell its catch at those docks.

Ariel left quickly to speak to other spirits and learn what she could. Molly waited until the sun rose and then set out. She found herself almost eager for the new task. It settled her mind and gave her direction; when she sat still, a million thoughts she did not want to think swarmed her mind.

Some of those thoughts persisted even once she started moving. *I don't know where I'm going to sleep. I don't know what I'm going to eat.*

She looked north as she walked and watched the billowing clouds of smog rising from the industrial district.

I could sleep there, she thought. *I could forget all of this, my family, the spirits, and take up in one of the factories.* Many of the factories thrived on orphans and runaways, swallowing them into their machinery like so much coal. But it wasn't really a life they offered; the factories only let you out once you were spent, broken beyond usefulness.

As she entered the crowds around the docks, the knots in her shoulders began to loosen. Here, among the endless workers and cargo milling around the foot of the umbilical, she felt invisible. But as she continued forward, and her eyes began to pick out more and more of Haviland Industries' blue jackets, the tension returned.

They don't know me, she reminded herself. *Blaise didn't recognize me.* But her heart was beating so hard she worried they might hear it. She looked around and spotted a clothing shop with tables of stock outside its doors. *Not that I have any money to buy anything.* She looked back at the blue jackets in the crowd; more were entering the square as she looked.

She sighed. *Well, in for a penny…*

The shopkeeper was bartering with a waistcoated man. While she was busy, Molly slipped a short-brimmed cap off a hat rack and scurried away. She stuffed her hair inside and pulled the brim low over her eyes.

As she reentered the crowd, she was glad to have the cap. Now, every second person she passed wore a Haviland Industries uniform. Crowds of blue jackets escorted vast insectile haulers that carried huge stacks of crates on their backs, moving on many-jointed legs. Molly watched the haulers with awe. Between the cargo and the metal in their bodies, they must have weighed several tonnes, but when they reached the umbilical they began walking up the vertical surface without pause. She wondered how strong the aetheric spirits inside needed to be in order to counteract that much gravity. The threads of wind that wove around them were every bit as intricate as those on an airship.

She glanced up at the *Gloria Mundi* far overhead and was momentarily stunned by the winds that were woven around it. Its unbelievable size made it impossible for a single spirit to carry, no matter how powerful. She could pick out winds woven by at least four engines, each of them more powerful than a standard ship's engine. *They must be level three, at least. Probably level two.*

Legerdemain had been classified as level four, but she remembered the feeling of power that had emanated from the spirit once it was released. How long had it been inside that engine before her father bought it? She had no idea, but the inner workings of the engine were ancient. Perhaps, after decades trapped, it had seemed weaker than it was.

The *Gloria Mundi* brought her thoughts back to the present. Something about its shape had caught her attention, though she couldn't say what it was. Her subconscious told her something was missing. She ran her eyes over the dark metal of the ship's hull, trying to figure out what it was.

That was when she heard a familiar voice behind her.

"You will each have three square feet of personal storage space." Molly turned and saw her sister, Brighid, moving quickly through the crowd toward her. "If your personal items do not fit into this space, you will have to choose what to discard," she went on.

Molly turned her face away and moved quickly out of the crowd, to the edges of the open square around the umbilical.

She tugged her cap lower and watched her sister, who did not seem to have noticed her. A handful of beleaguered men and women in blue uniforms followed in Brighid's wake.

"You will have twenty minutes to stow your gear, and then you will be expected to report for your shift." There was a groan from one of the men, and Brighid spun around.

"Is there a problem?"

"You can't be serious," said the young man who had groaned.

"Malcolm," warned a young girl at his side.

"No, come on! We're all thinking it. Arkwright's been throwing free drinks at us all week because he's so bloody proud of the *Gloria*. That means we've all got about five days' worth of hangovers by now. But we've been up since six this morning packing, and now we're supposed to do a full shift as well? Arkwright can't really expect us to be able to work properly now, can he?"

A few of his fellow crew members snickered. Brighid's eyes passed coldly over them, and the look on her face almost made Molly shiver. She had often been cold—at least to Molly—but Molly had never seen her like this before. She strode up to the young man and stood uncomfortably close to him.

"What is your name?"

"Come on now. Can you drop rank for a minute? We're none of us in the military here."

"What is your name?" she said again, without any change in her voice.

The man visibly swallowed. "Malcolm Anderson, ma'am."

"I'll instruct the captain of the *Gloria Mundi* to take you off the manifest. You won't be needed aboard. Or at the final two parties."

"But..." The man looked confused. "You're firing me before we even get aboard?"

Brighid paid no attention to his question. "The rest of you, come with me. As I was saying, once we're aboard you'll have"—she removed a watch from her pocket and checked it—"seventeen minutes now to stow any and all personal effects." Her voice faded into the general hubbub as she continued on, panicked crew members hurrying after her. The young man stood in place for several minutes before he finally turned and went back the way he had come.

Is that really what she's like now? Molly shivered. *Da would probably say she was always like that, even before she left.* The thought of her father brought back her own conflict with him, which she had carefully avoided thinking about all morning. She became more aware of the ache behind her left eye again. *When did my family become so awful?*

"Not too fond of the crowds?" said a voice beside her. Molly turned, startled, but the man she saw instantly put her at ease. His hair was gray, and the skin around his eyes was pinched into a spiderweb of wrinkles by a habitual smile. He wore an apron and stood behind a stall laden with sugar-dusted buns.

"My daughter was the same at your age," he went on, wiping his hands on his apron. There was a thick Scottish burr in his voice that took Molly a moment to adjust to. "She used to hide under the counter when I made her come here."

Molly smiled uncertainly, not sure what to say. The man was looking at her in an odd way—sad and...hesitant.

"Are yeh all right?" he asked. It occurred to her how she must look to him: black eye, clothes in need of changing, nervous of crowds. *He must think I'm some poor, homeless girl.*

And then, almost at the same time, she realized that was exactly what she was.

"I'm fine," she lied.

"Do yeh need something to eat?" He held out a small roll, drizzled with honey.

Her stomach groaned. "I don't have any money."

"I didn't ask if yeh did," he said.

Molly took the roll tentatively and smelled it. The sweet smell of honey mingled with the earthy scent of fresh bread. She took a bite, and almost before she knew it she had finished the entire roll.

"Thank you," she said through a mouthful.

The man laughed. "Got an appetite, don't yeh? That's good." He held out another roll to her. She took it, and this time ate slowly enough to enjoy it.

Despite the friendliness of the man, Molly had a strong urge to leave. She preferred feeling invisible. But this might be an opportunity to learn something.

"Do you sell here every day?" she asked.

"Until the sun sets," he said.

"You must see all the ships come and go from the docks."

"Aye, I do."

"Have you seen anything new lately? New ships?"

He laughed. "Yeh must have been living under a rock if you haven't heard of the *Gloria Mundi*."

Molly shook her head. "I know about her. I was talking about something smaller, like a new experimental ship or something."

"Well, the *Gloria*'s the only new ship I've seen around here for a long while. Seems like ships are leaving the skies rather than entering them these days. Just last week they took the *Legerdemain* away. The ship of the Stout family themselves. I say it's a sad time when the descendants of the great man can't stay aloft."

Molly nodded uncomfortably. *People paid attention to us?* She had always assumed her family was just like any other in the skies, outside of their own stories. It jarred her to have this stranger know her family's business.

She pushed her discomfort aside and focused on what he had said. *If the Gloria Mundi is the only new ship here…* She looked up again, and suddenly she realized what her subconscious had been telling her.

It has no nets.

Nets were the only way to catch spirits, unless you wanted to trust completely in hand nets and fetch poles. But the hull of the *Gloria Mundi* was bare iron, save where the large and inexplicable hole pierced through the ship in the middle.

If it doesn't have nets, it must have another way to harvest.

"Thanks," she said to the baker and started walking swiftly away. Her first instinct was to find Ariel, but after only a few steps she realized she had no way of contacting the aetheric spirit.

As she passed the clothing shop, she took off her cap and stuck it between two stacks of crisp white shirts. She hurried farther on, then looked up at the *Gloria Mundi* one last time before she left the square. *Stupid*, she chided herself. *Of course it's the* Gloria Mundi. *It should have been obvious. No one besides Haviland Industries has the money to invent new harvesters. Why didn't I think of it?*

Maybe because she hadn't slept for…she didn't even know when she'd slept last. The journal, and the fight with her father, had kept sleep at bay. Her thoughts felt muddy, and there was a jagged edge to her feelings she wasn't used to. It was time to find a place to rest.

Molly thought about returning home. Her brothers—or a more sober father—might be willing to let her in. But with this thought came a surge of muddled emotions that nearly swamped her. She was not ready to go home. She wondered about tracking down some of her shipmates from the *Legerdemain*, but she doubted they would be of much help. She had never been exactly popular with the crew. Besides, she had no idea where to start looking.

What about that terric spirit? Toves? She dismissed the idea as ridiculous. She wasn't even sure it had survived the trip to Arkwright Island. But try as she might, she couldn't think of anywhere safer or anywhere she would be welcome. *Maybe. He helped me once.*

She quickened her step, heading back to Knight's Cove, to the barren area Toves had claimed as his own.

"No."

Molly was happy to see Toves alive and unharmed, but she nevertheless found it a little intimidating to be speaking to him again, and alone this time. The way the stones of his body held together without being physically connected, against gravity and common sense, made her feel as if he was about to cave in on her at all times.

"Please," she said. "I haven't slept in—"

"I let you in, other people might think I've gone soft and come looking to stake a claim."

"No one's going to follow me here. Why would they?"

"Look at this city, kid. All these humans came here, to this island perched on the edge of a continent they can't get into. It makes no sense, but they do it anyway. That's what humans do: go where they're not wanted and set up shop."

"I'm careful. No one will see me. Besides, you've scared everyone around here enough that no one even thinks about this area anymore."

The terric spirit was silent, which Molly decided meant it was wavering.

"I'll hardly be here anyway," she said. "I'll just sleep here, and that's it."

There was a long silence, and then Toves began to roll away.

"Don't see how I can stop you. Not without killing you, and I can't say I have a mind to do that. You can set up in the old digger if you want. No one will see you there."

"Thank you," Molly said, but by the time the words were out of her mouth, Toves had vanished back into the earth. Molly looked around to make sure there wasn't anyone looking in on them and then examined the digger.

The machine was torn to pieces. Its treads were half submerged in the earth, and the long arm that had once moved and manipulated solid rock was bent backward across the roof of the cabin. She climbed up to peer into the cabin. It was filled with broken glass and the remnants of what once might have been a seat. Molly hopped in and began sweeping the detritus out with her boots. She found a black stain on the floor but did not want to look too closely at it.

Only when she was done did Molly realize she had nothing she could use as a bed. When she'd left her house, she had not even been wearing a jacket she might use as a pillow. She sighed and lay down on the hard metal, wondering how she would ever fall asleep. Through the twisted wreckage of the cabin's roof, she could see the winds slowly undulating across the sky. She wondered if she would ever see Legerdemain again and found herself longing to rest near the spirit once more. She had slept peacefully on the metal engine of the ship so many times.

Molly felt tears beginning to slide down from the corners of her eyes. She tried to blink them away, but they wouldn't stop. She wasn't even sure what she was crying about. Her mind skipped from her father to her life aloft to Legerdemain, tight inside that cold iron engine while she slept untroubled on top of it.

She sat up and found herself looking at a mound of stone just outside the cabin. Almost before she had registered it, the stones sank into the earth. She watched for a while, but Toves did not return. Finally, she curled herself up inside the digger and immediately fell asleep.

The next morning she was startled awake by something tapping on the metal beside her head. She sat up, swinging wildly. Her hand hit something, and there was a loud *clang* as it flew into the corner of the cabin. Molly rubbed furiously at her eyes, trying to clear the fog of her fitful sleep, and made out the shape of a cogitant huddled in the corner.

"Cog?" she said, bewildered. "Oh, I'm sorry!" She reached over and righted him, then checked him carefully for damage. "I didn't know it was you. What are you doing here?"

Cog hurried toward the door of the cabin and seized a cloth sack that was sitting there. He dragged it across the floor toward her.

"What is it?" One side of the sack fell from his hand, and a half-eaten loaf of bread spilled out. "You brought me food?" She reached out and took the bread, and she was several bites into it before she thought to thank him. Cog watched her, his lenses whirring open and shut.

"How did you find me?" she asked. Cog, of course, remained silent. She looked out the windows of the digger. There was no sign of Toves. Molly wondered what he thought of this cogitant coming to find her after she had promised him no one would follow her here. He must have allowed Cog to come—even living aloft, she had heard enough about terric spirits to know they could detect footsteps and other vibrations in the ground.

The bag contained another loaf of bread, a few stunted carrots and a block of cheese. Best of all, it contained an old canteen full of water. She drank the water quickly. The food she was more careful with—she ate a little of everything, then pushed the rest into the corner. With restraint, she would be able to make it last for several days.

"Thank you," she said again. Cog nodded, then took up the canteen and trotted away. Molly watched him cross the battered earth and enter one of the alleys. For a moment she was tempted to follow him, but she pushed the thought from her head.

She lay back down, and for a long time she simply stared up at the winds passing by above her. She watched for Ariel, but the spirit did not appear. She turned her eyes eastward and saw the *Gloria Mundi*.

How am I going to stop a ship like that?

She sat up. She couldn't lie here all day, waiting for Ariel. If she was going to do this, she needed to start.

Another day at the base of the docks turned up little new information, but it did put a few pieces together.

The area was full of Haviland Industries uniforms, but not the blue of crew. Instead, the square around the umbilical was awash in the gray jackets of Arkwright's servants and the gleaming metal of his automatons. Molly watched them carrying crates past in huge quantities, loading them onto waiting cable cars. They were the same boxes she had seen in Arkwright Manor.

The men seemed in better spirits now than when they were packing, Molly thought. She heard several men mention the extravagance of Arkwright's parties, just as the unfortunate crewman had the previous day.

At midday, the square flooded with men in black jackets—like the security guards she had seen at the manor—and Molly's heart rose to her throat. She fought the urge to run and instead made her way as calmly as she could out of the square and into one of the nearby streets, where she huddled against the wall and watched for the familiar figure of Mr. Blaise.

After a few moments he appeared, his bald head and scars glistening in the bright sun. He walked silently through the crowd, his looming presence enough to make people move out of his way. Behind him came large boxes borne on many-legged haulers that reminded Molly of millipedes. These were accompanied by a cloud of white-coated people who fussed around the haulers—the same people she had seen dismantling the strange spiritual machinery in Arkwright Manor. Several of the machines were covered by cloth.

Her legs itched to move, but she pressed herself more tightly against the wall and watched.

Blaise and his retinue moved quickly through the crowd and up to the umbilical. A large platform, hovering a foot off the ground, was waiting for them. They all boarded, and the platform immediately began to rise toward the docks. As it rose, Blaise's eyes scanned the ground below them. Molly turned away. By the time she felt brave enough to look back, she could barely see the platform above her.

It's like they're moving the whole mansion aboard.

Something hit her from behind, and she found herself stumbling forward, back into the square.

"Clear out!" someone shouted at her. She turned to see a man dressed in a strange contraption. Metal struts were wrapped around his shoulders and hips, and a heavy-looking dark box sat on his chest. It looked like a giant spider had wrapped itself around the man. In the center of the box was what looked like a single eye, flickering with light.

He moved past Molly as if she didn't exist, followed by several more people wearing similar contraptions, and dozens of others with pads of paper. They all surged forward toward the umbilical.

A moment later Molly saw what was happening. From the east side of the square, a large contingent of Haviland Industries Security moved in, pushing these newcomers back. Behind them, riding on what looked like a small floating skiff, came Tyler Arkwright, looking perfectly tailored, just as he had before.

As the reporters surged toward him, they raised their voices with a million questions. The boxes some of them wore on their chests cast odd light over him, and Molly realized they must be recording his image. Arkwright sailed on, seemingly oblivious, but the hint of a smile played across his lips, and he drew back his shoulders to open up his chest. When the skiff slowed to a stop at the umbilical, Arkwright jumped down and pushed through the security guards until he stood in front of the thronging reporters.

"Sir!" one of them shouted. "What made you decide to take the helm of the *Gloria Mundi* yourself?"

"I spend too much time on the ground," he said. "As my father taught me, to run a company like this you have to be intimately familiar with the skies." He turned his head upward, and cameras flashed. From the way he held himself perfectly still, Molly suspected he had looked up in that way specifically to create an opportunity for photographs.

The questions went on, about Arkwright's experience in His Majesty's Navy, about the lavish parties he had been throwing in the *Gloria*'s honor, about some young duchess he had been seen with recently. *Ask him about the ship! Ask him about the ship!* Molly thought, but the questions never turned to anything technical. After almost half an hour, Arkwright finally climbed into a cable car and rose toward the docks, waving out the window the whole time. As the reporters dispersed, Molly too decided it was time to move on. After half a day, she still knew nothing about how the *Gloria Mundi* harvested or how she could stop it.

I need to talk to someone who knows its machinery, she thought. And suddenly she stopped in her tracks as a name flashed through her memory. *Croyden*.

She ran back toward the umbilical.

It was surprisingly easy to stow away on one of the cable cars, she discovered. Probably because no one in their right mind would do so.

She found a small, unoccupied aetheric car and slipped in behind it, snug between the car and the umbilical. She wrapped her arms around the car's struts, her stomach already churning at the thought of what was coming.

The cable car's engine grew testy when she grabbed on, but a few soothing whispers settled it. Then it was simply a matter of waiting, and she didn't have to wait long. Soon the car was filled with people, and up it rose. Molly's hands tightened until she thought they might break as they left the ground behind, rising higher and higher into the air. She pressed the bottoms of her feet into the side of the car and held on.

It's just like being on the Legerdemain*'s engine*, she told herself. *Just hang on, and you'll be fine.*

But even at full speed, the wind aboard the *Legerdemain* had never been this bad. Funneled between the umbilical and the cable car, the wind tugged at her, trying to pluck her off and hurl her to the ground. Even worse, she could see it hurtling straight at her, blue-white winds battering her, trying to dig their powerful fingers between her and the car. Her feet were pulled away from the cable car, and her arms began to ache. She closed her eyes tight.

Please don't pull me off, she thought, *please don't pull me off.*

The wind abated so suddenly that she almost yelped.

She got her feet back in position, then opened her eyes. The wind was still tearing recklessly around the umbilical, but it had parted around the cable car now, passing above and below her.

Did I do that? she wondered. *But I didn't even touch those winds. How could I move them?*

She let the questions fall from her mind. This was not the time. They were halfway to the docks, and her arms were already burning. She held on tightly and imagined she was in the rigging of an airship.

At the docks, she slipped away from the car while everyone was disembarking. No one seemed to notice her, despite her jelly-legged walk. She moved as fast as she could through the warren of abandoned buildings until she found the infusionist's shop again. Unlike last time, the front room was empty, and there were no sounds from the back room. In the silence, the bell that rang as she entered seemed so loud it made her wince.

"Can I help you?" The infusionist's rough voice came from only a few feet away, and Molly jumped. She hadn't noticed him amid the tangle of machinery. He stood up straighter and walked toward her.

"Mr. Croyden?" she said. "I don't know if you remember me, but—"

"Of course I do," he said, standing crookedly on his artificial leg. "Molly Stout, engineer of the *Legerdemain*, and the youngest member of the profession I've had the pleasure to meet." He shook her hand. "Where is your father?"

"He's, um, not here. I came on my own."

"A pity. I've been hoping to see him since I heard what happened. I'm sorry about your ship. She deserved better than to be picked clean by vultures."

"She won't be. You didn't hear? About the engine?"

"Hear what?"

"He got away. I mean, the engine's spirit got out. Not much left for vultures now."

"Did he now?" Croyden looked down at her from his incredible height, his eyes piercing behind the lenses of his glasses. "Anyone hurt?"

Molly shook her head.

"Well then. Perhaps it's for the best. I'd have hated to see that engine put to work on the *Gloria Mundi*."

He began walking back through his shop, his metal leg hissing and spitting steam.

"Actually, that's what I came to talk to you about," Molly said, following after. "I had some questions about the *Gloria*. You said you worked on it, right?"

"What sort of questions?"

"About how it works. You infused some of its spiritual machines?"

He sat himself down on a stool beside his worktable and remained silent for a long time. Molly could feel him watching her, but she didn't want to meet his eyes. She felt like he'd seen too much already. She looked around the shop instead, at the towers of machines and traps, the collections of metal plates and rivets, the racks of wrenches and blowtorches. She eyed the glass infusion case nervously; the last time she had been here, all of this had looked very different to her.

"I've been paid a great deal of money not to answer the kind of questions you have," he said. "But as time goes on, I find myself less and less inclined to honor that particular bargain. Go ahead and ask."

"Well, I..." She struggled to find a safe way to ask the questions. "I noticed it doesn't have any nets. But it must have a way to catch spirits, right?"

The infusionist smiled. "Most people are too distracted by the sheer scope of her to notice that little detail. No, she doesn't use nets."

"Then what does it use?"

"I can't say I completely know. They only trusted me as far as they had to. But I can tell you a few things." He turned, moving more quickly than he had a moment before. He reached into a shelf above his head. She heard paper shuffling, and he pulled out a long roll of onionskin paper. This he spread out on top of the infusion case.

"You've likely noticed the hollow center as well?" Croyden said. Molly stepped up beside him and saw that the paper contained schematics of the ship. He pointed to a cross-section of the ship showing the large oval hole through its middle. "The idea is that the ship can park itself directly around the font rather than beside it. The harvesting apparatus sits inside this large bay." He flipped through several pages and drew out another schematic. "I was hired to work on this system."

Molly looked at the page. She took pride in her skill as an engineer, but the machine before her was a mystery. She couldn't begin to follow its convoluted electrics and the bizarre maze of pistons and valves. "What is it?"

"It is a system to insert spirits directly from traps into the harvesting apparatus."

"An automatic infuser."

"Not quite. It is more like...Have you seen those odd nonspiritual contraptions they have back in London? Automobiles, I believe they're called?"

She shook her head.

"They expend oil to move, in the same way that a fire expends wood to burn." His long finger pressed into the page. "This is a similar system, but using spirits."

"Using spirits as fuel?"

"Yes."

Molly felt her throat tightening. "Fuel for what?"

"I do not know that. I only worked on this system, to allow them to replace the expended spirits without the help of someone like me. How the spirits are expended in the first place, I do not know."

"Is this...is this why you said what you said about *Legerdemain*? About how you wouldn't want to see the engine's spirit used on the *Gloria*?"

He looked down at her with his piercing eyes again. He spoke his next words very carefully. "There are some fates, I think, that even monsters do not deserve."

This time, Molly did not look away from his sharp eyes. What he had said was dangerously close to sympathy for spirits. *Is he saying what I think he is?* For a moment she had an almost overwhelming impulse to tell him everything, to share what she had learned, to have another human share this struggle.

"Thank you for answering my questions," she said.

Croyden watched her for a moment more, then smiled and stood up straight. "You're welcome, Miss Stout. I'm curious myself about why you had such questions, but I'm sure I'll learn in the fullness of time." He placed a hand on her back and walked her to the door.

On the threshold Molly hesitated, still wondering how much she could tell the infusionist. *He traps spirits for a living,* she reminded herself. *How could he be spirit-touched too?*

Her indecision lasted until Croyden closed the door behind her. Even as she walked away, though, she thought she could feel his eyes on her back.

Halfway home, she heard someone calling her name. Panic gripped her, and she planted her feet to run, but when she looked behind her she saw it was Kiernan calling her. As soon as he reached her, he threw his arms around her and squeezed her so tightly she thought he might break her ribs.

"Hi, Kier," she said into his shoulder.

He released the hug but held her arm as if he was afraid she might run. "Are you okay?" His fingertips brushed the swollen flesh around her left eye.

"It's not as bad as it looks," she said. "At least, I don't think so. I'm not sure what it looks like."

"Did Da do this?" he said.

Molly hesitated, then nodded and felt his hand tighten on her arm.

"It took us hours to get anything out of him," he said. "We've been looking for you."

"How'd you find me?"

He pointed behind her. She turned and found Cog peering out at her from beside the front steps of a nearby building.

"He's been following me?" she asked.

"I saw him taking food yesterday. So when he went off again today, I followed. Molly, are you all right?"

"I'm…I don't know. I've got a place to sleep, and Cog brought me that food."

"But what happened? What did you and Da fight about?"

"He didn't tell you?"

"No. He wouldn't tell us anything except that you were gone. He didn't mention this either." His fingers briefly returned to her bruised eye.

"What did he do with the journal?" she asked.

Kiernan looked confused. "Journal? I don't know what you mean. Did he do something with a journal of yours?"

"No, it was a journal of Haviland's. You didn't find it on the floor or anything?" He shook his head. "Da must have moved it then. Look, we..." She hesitated, but after resisting talking to Croyden, she found that her urge to talk to someone was irresistible. *Kier would never call Disposal on me.* She dropped her voice to a whisper. "It was my flitter. We fought because I let the spirit out."

"You...you what?" His hand tightened on her arm for a moment and then let go.

"I let it free."

He stared at her. "You're not kidding, are you? You actually did it. On purpose. Was this before or after the *Legerdemain* spirit?"

"Before."

"God, Molly! They really do have their claws in you, don't they?"

"Yes. They do." She set her jaw and stared back at him.

"What exactly do you think you're doing, Molly?" he asked.

"The right thing. The journal would explain better than I can."

Kiernan blew out a long breath, but he looked no less troubled afterward. "You have to stop, Molly. Whatever you think you're doing, all it will do is get you put away. I came to tell you that the agent from Disposal came by again."

"He did?"

"Yes, and I don't think he's buying Rory's lie anymore."

Molly didn't like the sound of that, but there was someone else she was more frightened by. "Has anyone else been to the house? Anyone from Haviland Industries?"

Kiernan's frown deepened. "No. Should they be? Have you done something more?"

"It should be fine. But if you see a big guy, bald, don't answer the door, okay? Tell Rory too."

"Molly, this is crazy. Just come home. We'll sort things out with Da, and whatever trouble you've gotten into, we'll figure out how to get you out."

She looked up at her brother, at his straight shoulders and proud jaw. He still looked every bit an officer, and for a moment she just wanted to follow him home and let him try to fix everything. She was terrified of seeing her father again, but surely Kiernan could do something. She could have a home again.

She had to look away from him to say what she needed to say. "I can't. I mean, I don't think I want to get out of this trouble. I know it seems crazy, but it's important. Just try to find that journal, okay? And keep everyone safe."

She ran away, ducking through the crowds in the street and into an alley on the other side. As soon as she thought Kiernan couldn't see her, she jumped and pulled herself up onto one of the roofs, then turned to look back down.

Kiernan had a hard time getting through the crowds, but he came quickly after her. He went down the alley, searching for her and calling her name softly. She drew back from the edge of the roof, hugging her legs to her chest and stilling her heart. Once she was sure he had gone, she began moving from rooftop to rooftop, heading back toward Knight's Cove.

FIFTEEN

When Molly returned to the digger, she found Ariel waiting. Or rather, she found what was left of the spirit. Ariel was nothing but a tattered mist lying low across Toves's land, her blue glow reduced to the meager flicker of a dying fire. Were it not for the soft moaning she emitted, Molly might not have recognized her at all.

"Ariel?" she said, crouching low at the edge of the mist. "What happened?"

"The *Gloria Mu*..." Her voice sounded like a skittering breeze.

"I know already, but we'll talk about that later. What happened to you? What do I do?"

The spirit didn't answer. The mist of her body thrashed feebly toward Molly.

"Ariel? Ariel, can you hear me? I don't know what to do." Molly gritted her teeth. *How do I fix this?* She'd bandaged plenty of cuts and helped set broken bones aboard the

Legerdemain, but there she knew what she was dealing with. How could you heal something made only of air?

But the mist was continuing to dissipate, so Molly stood. She walked to the edge of the mist and put her hands in, searching for the solid core. It was there, she could feel it, but it wasn't like the wind. Holding the wind had felt like holding a rope. This felt like putting her hand into a working loom, countless threads twisting and weaving around her fingers.

Molly gently took hold and began gathering the threads together.

She heard Ariel moan occasionally, but the spirit no longer spoke. Once she cried out, when Molly's fingers became tangled in a snarl of her threads. Molly carefully parted the knotted threads and extricated her fingers before continuing.

The mist was more coherent now, but it was still not holding together. It shifted and struggled from time to time, brighter patches forming and then fading again. *Stitches*, Molly thought, remembering the way Morgan, their old engineer, had once cut his head open with a bad fall, and her father had needed to stitch the skin to make it heal. Molly looked up. Broad, slow, silver winds were moving eastward far above their heads, but none came low enough for her to grasp.

She recalled the way the wind had parted around her as she rode the cable car to the docks. *Please!* Molly thought. *I need help! Come down!*

The lowest of the winds shook and rippled. A small whorl formed, and from the whorl a thin stream of wind extended itself. It moved downward, flying straight toward Molly. She grasped it as it came close.

Carefully, she wove the slender wind through Ariel's

body, connecting the tattered edges. Molly began to sweat as she worked, more from focus than physical effort. She stitched on and on, uncertain of what she was doing or if it was even helping, but as the silver wind flowed through the aetheric spirit, Ariel's blue glow slowly returned. Soon a slender tendril formed in the mist and scooped the wind out of Molly's grasp. Molly stood back, watching as the silver wind moved through the mist in a pattern so complex she could not follow it. She sat and waited.

Finally, the thread of wind stopped moving. It trembled for a moment, then detached itself and reversed its flow, disappearing into the larger river of wind once more. Ariel still held no discernible shape, but the edges of her cloud no longer drifted.

"Thank you," Ariel said, her voice faint but hers once more.

"Did you..." Molly stopped herself, realizing this might not be the best time to start questioning Ariel about the *Gloria Mundi*. "Should I leave you alone to rest?"

"No. Please, your presence is refreshing. You smell like home."

What does that mean? Molly wondered. She sat down and took a deep breath. She couldn't smell anything on herself that might smell like Ariel's home. But then it struck her—she couldn't smell the fug of Terra Nova either. The heavy, sooty smell that had haunted her since they were grounded was gone. In its place she smelled clean air, rich in oxygen. She smelled like Legerdemain, she realized.

"When I was trying to help you, did you call the wind down?" Molly asked Ariel, partly afraid of her answer.

"No, Molly. I did not have the strength to hold myself together, much less call the wind."

So it was me then. Molly put her head into her hands. "This is too big."

For a time neither of them said anything. Ariel's light continued to grow, though she still made no attempt to take on the human form Molly was used to. Molly found it best to stare at the ground until her head stopped spinning. "What happened to you?" she asked finally.

"The *Gloria Mundi.* I tried to go aboard, but I was attacked. I barely escaped."

"Did you learn anything?"

"Yes. And you?"

Molly told Ariel everything she had heard from Croyden.

Ariel did not seem particularly surprised. "Since Arkwright killed your ancestor, your kind has always used my kind as fuel," she said. "That is what slavery is—an expenditure of minds and souls as if they were commodities."

Molly nodded.

"While you searched here," Ariel continued, "I returned through the fonts to try to track the source of the problem from the other side. I saw the damage it has left in its wake."

"What did you see?"

"This new harvester is breaking the connection between worlds. Something physical is being forced through gates that are not themselves physical, and in the aftermath the gates are destroyed."

"That doesn't really sound so bad. I mean, aetheric fonts open and close all the time."

"They do not close. They simply move. There is a finite number of aetheric fonts, Molly, and once they are closed, they are gone forever."

Molly sat back. "I didn't know that. I don't think anyone knows that."

"They do not. Since Haviland died, the fonts have been seen as objects to be used, not as phenomena to be studied."

"So if all the fonts are closed, what happens?"

"I do not know. None of the fonts have ever closed before. Whatever happens, it will not be easy—or good. Our two worlds have been connected for a very, very, very long time. Time enough to grow together, like twinned trees. Removing one from the other is almost unimaginable."

"So how do we stop it? Is there anything the spirits can do?"

"No. Many have tried, and it is from these that I learned the *Gloria Mundi*'s name. The ship contains so much iron that even to draw near it is painful."

Molly nodded. "I kind of thought you might say that. I had an idea. I think I need to get aboard. I can't do much from here, but inside...I don't know. It's all just spiritual machines, right? They can be broken easily enough."

"How do you propose to get aboard? There are eyes everywhere on that ship."

"I don't know." Her sister's face popped into her head. As part of the crew, she could likely smuggle Molly aboard. She dismissed the thought immediately though; her sister would not want to help with this. On the other hand, she had a brother who shared her loathing of Haviland Industries and had a certain skill for getting into and then out of trouble.

"I know someone who's good at these kinds of things," she said. "He might help us."

She went home, for the first time since her fight with her father. She made it as far as the front door before her determination failed her. She stood, arms at her sides, willing herself to raise her fist and knock.

Da won't answer. He'll be too drunk, she told herself. *And even if he did, he wouldn't hit me again.* Still, she could not make her arm move.

And then the door opened on its own, and Molly was almost knocked over by Kiernan.

"Molly!" he said with surprise, catching himself on the doorframe. "What are you doing here?" His eyes scanned the street behind her.

"Is Da…"

"No, he's at the pub. But come in before anyone sees you." He ushered her inside. "I'm glad you came to your senses, Moll. I'm sure we can figure out how to fix this."

"I, um, actually I came back to talk to Rory. Is he home?"

Kiernan looked confused, and Molly couldn't blame him. Rory wasn't someone you would normally turn to for help. But then, Molly had never needed this particular kind of help before.

"He is, but good luck waking him up."

As Kiernan closed the door behind her, Molly swayed on her feet, a wave of panic swamping her mind. She felt Kiernan put his hand on her back, and the room stopped spinning. But she couldn't bring herself to look at the table where her father had sat waiting for her.

"Why do you need Rory?" Kiernan asked.

"It's probably better if I don't tell you."

Kiernan frowned. "You haven't come to your senses after all, have you?"

"No. Not the way you mean."

Kiernan sighed and removed his hand from her back. "Rory has been taking after Da lately. He didn't get home until well into the morning."

They walked together to the boys' room, and Kiernan opened the door. At first Molly didn't see Rory, just a rumpled mess of blankets. But there he was, tangled in the covers with only the top of his head and one foot visible.

"Rory?" Molly said tentatively. And then, louder, "Ror."

The mess shifted, but Rory did not emerge. Molly walked to the side of the bed and pulled the blankets back. Rory sat up with a gasp, looking around blearily.

"Whu..." His eyes came to rest on Molly and then clenched shut again, and he lay back down. "God in heaven, Moll. It's good to see you home, but can't you let a man sleep?"

"It's past five. And I need you."

The statement was so unusual that it seemed to penetrate the fog of his hangover. He blinked up at her. "Kier can do it," he said.

"No, he can't." Molly looked back and realized Kiernan was still leaning in the doorway. "Sorry, Kier, but this isn't the kind of thing you do."

"What *kind of thing* precisely are you talking about?" Kiernan asked.

"Are you sure you want to hear this?"

"Yes, Molly."

Molly took a deep breath before she answered. "I need to get aboard the *Gloria Mundi*."

Kiernan was silent for a moment, scrutinizing his sister in a way he never had before. She was well versed in his troubled looks, but this was something new. He was watching her as if she might be a threat.

"Maybe I'd best give you two some time," he said and walked out of the house.

Molly turned back to Rory and found him looking at her in a new way too. But while Kiernan had been concerned, Rory seemed delighted.

"You're not just kicking the hornet's nest, are you? You're going after the queen. Or king, as the case may be here."

"There's something wrong on that ship. I need to stop it."

"Molly Stout versus the *Gloria Mundi*. I didn't think you had it in you, sis. I mean, you're totally, absolutely barking mad. It's humbling, in a way."

"Can you help?"

He sat up and rubbed his eyes. "Well, first off, you should know that you've got absolutely no chance of sneaking aboard that ship. From what I hear, they've got more guards than crew on board, and no one can take a piss without being checked for contraband."

"So you don't think I can do it."

"Hang on, hang on. I said you can't *sneak* aboard. But as it happens, there are still new crew members going aboard. What you need to do is get yourself counted among them.

Get your name on the manifest. Or not *your* name, but a name you can use."

"And how do I do that?"

"Bracebridge."

"Bracebridge? What does she—"

"She's gone over. Joined the enemy. Donned the blue jacket."

"What? She..." Molly had a hard time believing it for a moment. Bracebridge had been with the *Legerdemain* so long that she was like the mast, a feature of the ship that was inseparable from the whole. "She's working for Haviland Industries now?"

He nodded. "I know. Shocking. So soon after our beloved ship was laid low. Thing is, I think she feels even worse about it than we do. I've seen her, and she looks about as happy as a fish in the desert."

"Where have you seen her?"

He smiled and then got down on his stomach, reached beneath the bed and pulled out a Haviland Industries uniform. Molly's jaw dropped. "Rory! Tell me you didn't—"

"Give me some credit, Moll. But they throw the best parties in town, and you can't get in without looking the part." He grinned. "I've been partaking of Arkwright's generosity for the last week. I figure he owes me a few fingers of whiskey."

"You've gotten in to their parties?"

"That's right. And if you want, you can tag along to the one tomorrow. We'll see if we can't have a chat with our old first officer."

SIXTEEN

Molly had never been to the wealthy districts of Terra Nova before, only seen them from afar. As they stepped out of the city's smog, Molly expected to almost be knocked over by the purity of the air. But when she breathed deeply, she noticed no difference. It took her a moment to remember that this was because of her, not the air itself. *Ariel said I smell like a spirit now*, she recalled. *Or like…like home, she said.*

As they continued down the street, Molly began to itch. She and her brother stood out here. He looked smart in his Haviland Industries uniform but not rich, and they had done the best they could for Molly, which was to put her in one of Brighid's old skirts and a shirt and jacket Kiernan had outgrown. The whole outfit was about two sizes too large for her. She felt like a child playing dress-up. In addition, they seemed to be the only people walking. Ornate vehicles thronged the street—aetheric taxis, rumbling igneous engines and even one aqueous contraption that floated on a moving pool of water. But the sidewalks were empty. Molly could feel the eyes of the people inside the vehicles watching her.

"Quit fussing at your hair, Molly. You look like you're waiting to get caught. Just relax."

Molly hadn't realized she was doing anything with her hair. She forced her hands down to her sides. "What if we do get caught?"

"Don't think about that."

She looked at her brother in disbelief. He certainly didn't look nervous. He looked like this was something he did every day. Which, Molly realized, he might—she had never really kept track of what Rory did before.

"How do I not think about it?" she asked.

"The best way to go unnoticed is to look like you have a reason to be there—which, as it happens, you do. Me, I'm going for the free drinks, so I keep my mind on that." He smiled down at her. "I'm not completely sure what you're up to, but I'm sure it's important. Think about kicking Tyler Arkwright in the shins or something like that."

She tried what he said, focusing on her need to get aboard the *Gloria Mundi*, but thinking about it left her feeling overwhelmed. *Molly versus the* Gloria Mundi, she thought unhappily. She clenched her teeth and kept walking.

As they approached the party, the sidewalks became more crowded. People on foot and in vehicles converged on the Empire, the richest hotel in Terra Nova. Even set against the mansions of the wealthy district, it looked massive. Its white façade held countless windows, and a forest of towers and spires sprouted from its roof. In the courtyard in front of the hotel stood its famous fountain. Streams of water, fire and earth intertwined, performing impossible acrobatics in midair, never touching the ground.

As they were passing the fountain, Rory suddenly took her arm and turned to face her. "Molly, are you sure you want to go in there? I mean, I'm not generally one to counsel caution, but are you sure?"

Rory wore such a serious and concerned expression that Molly was stunned. "I'll be fine," she said.

Rory laughed. "Still not very good at the lying, sis."

"Okay, but...yes, I'm sure. I need to get on that ship, so if this can get me aboard, I need to do it."

Rory nodded. "Fair enough. Just try not to get caught, yeah?"

"Yeah."

They continued on, Rory's normal air of carelessness returning. Molly tried to copy him, but she couldn't stop scanning the crowds. So far she hadn't seen Blaise, but she couldn't afford to have him see her first.

"They're still keeping you away from the bar, I see, Nate," Rory said at her side. Molly turned and saw her brother shaking hands with a tall man in a dark security uniform.

The man smiled down at her brother. "It's not the drinks they have to keep me away from, Jim. It's the women."

Jim? Molly hadn't even thought about names.

"Speaking of women," Rory said, "I've got a tagalong tonight. You don't mind, right?"

The security guard looked down at her. Molly felt herself tense, but she attempted a smile and tried to think about what she had to do. *I have a reason to be here. I have a reason to be here.*

"Isn't she a little young for you?" the guard asked.

"Oh, please, mate, don't make me sick," Rory said. "This is my sister. She's been begging me to bring her. I finally caved."

"Oh, really? Here for the drinks or the men in uniform?"

"I want to sign up soon," she said. She looked at Rory and found an impressed smile on his face.

"Oh, well then," the guard said. "Who am I to crush a young girl's dreams?" He gestured for them to go in. "Just make sure you keep her away from the strong stuff," he told Rory.

"Of course." He took her arm and led her in through the crowd. "Nice one," he whispered in her ear.

The lobby of the hotel was large enough that the *Legerdemain* could have fit comfortably inside, and every inch of space exuded an opulence that Molly had never imagined. Golden filigree ran across the ceiling and along the banisters of the huge spiral staircase that led up to the balcony. Bars laden with a rainbow of bottles were dotted around the room, each one made of rich black walnut, a wood most often found in the dangerous Inner Continent—a place people would not go without being offered a fortune, for many never returned. High overhead, globes of fire that looked like miniature suns cast out all shadows. Both floor and balcony were filled with people in blue, gray and black uniforms.

Rory thrust a drink into her hand. While she had been taking in the scenery, he had dragged her through the crowd to the nearest source of alcohol. She looked at the tumbler in her hand, half filled with a reddish-gold liquid that clung to the sides of the glass. "I don't think this is the time for me to start drinking, Rory."

"Camouflage, Moll. Without a drink in your hand, you'll stand out a mile. Just put it to your mouth every once in a while and you should be fine."

"Okay, so..." She did as he suggested, then looked around at the ranks of red-trimmed uniforms. "Where's Bracebridge?"

"No idea. She'll be here somewhere. Why don't we split up? I'll go this way, you go that." He pointed her toward the east side of the hall while he moved west, drinking from his tumbler as he went. He exchanged greetings with several people in the crowd and even stopped to pat someone warmly on the shoulder.

He really looks like he belongs here, she thought. It made her feel all the more isolated.

She began walking through the crowd. The glass felt odd in her hand, so heavy and delicate at the same time. Aboard the *Legerdemain*, there had been nothing but tin cups, because anything else was either too expensive or too prone to break in rough skies. She held the glass delicately with two hands, not sure how tightly she could hold it before it would crack.

She scanned the crowd for familiar faces, either Bracebridge's or Blaise's, but she found neither. She noticed the way people tended to congregate into groups of the same color of uniform. She passed through clusters of black, blue or gray jackets, trying to remain unseen as she searched.

As she neared the east wall, a few words caught her attention. "...brand new, but she flies like an old crone. With a dozen level twos, we should be making eighty knots at least, even on a heavy ship like the *Gloria*. We're barely clearing sixty as it is."

The words came from a bearded man with scars on his face and hands. Despite the gaiety of their surroundings, his brow was furrowed. Many of the people he spoke to bore similar scars.

Engineers, Molly thought. She slowed.

"Sounds like faulty pneumatics, Saul," a dark-haired woman said. "When the pistons on the *Fairweather* jammed, we—"

"I've checked the damn pneumatics," the first man said. "I'm not new, you know. It's not electrics either. Got to be the spirit itself. We can't afford to have a feeble spirit in the aftmost engine."

Molly couldn't help herself—she stepped forward. "Do you engage all the engines at once?" she asked. A dozen sets of eyes turned to her, and she almost winced. *Great blending in, Molly.*

"What do you mean?" said the first man.

Too late now. "Do you fire up all the engines at the same time, or in sequence?"

"Same time, of course."

"Then by the time the air gets to the aft engine, eleven other spirits have already breathed it. She needs fresh air. Have you tried opening them up in sequence, aft to fore, to give the rear engines a few fresh lungfuls?"

The engineers shared looks between each other, saying nothing to her. The first man, Saul, looked intently down at Molly. "Who are you, exactly?"

"Molly Sanders," she said, hesitating only a moment.

"You seem awfully young to have advice for an old engineer."

Molly felt herself shrinking. "I grew up on airships," she said. "But I shouldn't have interrupted. I'm sorry, I'll..."

She walked away, feeling their eyes on her and chastising herself for being drawn into the discussion. *Remember why you're here*, she scolded herself.

Once she was out of the engineers' sight, she began looking for Bracebridge again, but only unfamiliar faces surrounded her. *This is hopeless.* She thought back to what Rory had told her. *Bracebridge isn't happy to be here. So where would I go if I was surrounded by people I didn't like?* The answer came to her instantly. *Up.* She started up the stairs.

The crowds were thinner on the balcony. Conversations were hushed and intimate. She discovered more than one couple wrapped in each other's arms, oblivious to the world around them. And at the far west end, leaning on the balcony's railing, was Bracebridge. Her angular face seemed softened by melancholy, and she had the sloppy look of someone who had been making good use of the open bars.

"Hello, First Mate Bracebridge," Molly said quietly.

Bracebridge turned reluctantly. "I'm not a first—" she began and then stopped when she saw Molly. Molly couldn't help but smile at the look of surprise on her face. "Molly? What on earth are you doing here?"

"I was looking for you, actually," Molly said. "Rory told me you started working for Haviland Industries."

"Rory knows?" Her head sank. "Your father probably

knows too then. I didn't take the job willingly, Molly. It's just that there's nowhere else to go."

"I doubt my father knows," Molly said. "He's not really talking to anyone much at the moment."

Bracebridge sighed. "No, I suppose he wouldn't be." She looked down at the drink in her hand. "How is he?"

"He's fine." She joined Bracebridge at the railing. "You're not a first mate anymore?"

"Third," she said, "and I was lucky to get that high. They don't usually put outsiders in officer positions." She didn't sound like she felt lucky.

"But you'll get to go aloft," Molly said.

"I will. Five more days. Once all this hullabaloo has settled, we'll be taking off."

"What's your ship?"

"The *Jupiter*. She's not a bad ship. A little sluggish for my liking." She looked sharply down at Molly and the drink in her hand, suddenly seeming much more like herself. "How did you get in here anyway? And where did you get that?"

"Rory helped. And don't worry—I'm not drinking it."

"Well, I doubt you crashed a party like this just to chat with your old officer. Spit it out. What do you want?"

Molly took a breath. She stepped closer and spoke barely above a whisper. "I need your help. I need to go aloft again, but I'm too young to get hired. I thought maybe you could help me get aboard a ship anyway."

"You want me to help you stow away?"

"No, I thought maybe you could add a name to a manifest. I can worry about the rest."

"Did you have a ship in mind?"

"The *Gloria Mundi*."

Her eyes sharpened yet again. "You want to go aboard the new flagship under a fake name and pretend to be one of the crew? Just to get aloft again? Are you mad, Molly?"

"I can't stand it down here," Molly said. "I feel so heavy. Everything's so close—there's nowhere to breathe. I need to see the skies again."

"You never spent much time down here, did you? Your da never wanted to come down." Bracebridge grimaced. "You know this will kill him, right? Having another daughter go over to Arkwright?"

"I know," Molly said, surprised that she felt a stab of guilt along with the anger that hid behind all thoughts of her father now.

Bracebridge stared down at the crowds below, brow furrowed.

"Please," Molly said. "I feel like I'm dying down here."

"Damnation," Bracebridge said softly, then swallowed the rest of her drink. "I wish you hadn't found me, Molly." She hung her head for a moment. Molly didn't speak, didn't move, afraid to disturb her further. Finally, Bracebridge turned toward Molly. "So what name am I putting on the manifest exactly?"

It took a little time to hash out the details with Bracebridge. The *Gloria Mundi* would be taking on its last crew complement at three o'clock the next afternoon and casting off at sunset. Molly Sanders, able sailor, would arrive at the muster point on the docks at two. Molly had wondered about signing on as an engineer, but Bracebridge said it was impossible.

"All their engineers are trained together at their own college, right down to the engine greasers. Deck crew sometimes get hired on from outside, like me, but you can't just have a new face show up among the engineers."

Molly agreed but silently cursed. She said goodbye to Bracebridge and then headed downstairs.

Despite having been at the party for less than an hour, Rory was already deep into his cups by the time she found him. His jacket had disappeared somewhere, and he and several other soused young men seemed to be haranguing every young woman who passed by.

"I thought you were helping me look for Bracebridge," she said.

"I was. I have determined that she is not in the bottom of any of the glasses."

"Well, I found her anyway. And now I need more help from you, so let's get you home."

"But I was just about to dance with the most beautiful woman in the room." He gestured to a nearby female officer, who cast him a scornful look before turning her back on him.

Molly had seen her brother like this many times. Unlike their father, Rory was a gregarious drunk, and the only time he had seemed to feel any brotherly devotion aboard the ship was when there were a few bottles in his belly. With a practiced hand, she grabbed him by the arm and steered him toward the exit. She spotted his jacket hanging off the end of one of the bars and grabbed it on the way. Rory protested briefly, but didn't seem inclined to fight her.

Just as they were about to leave, she saw a familiar scarred face coming through the doors. Blaise stood a head above almost everyone around him, and his cold eyes scanned the room. Her heart froze, and for a moment she stood staring at him, until her reason reasserted itself. She pulled Rory quickly toward a knot of sailors off to the side.

"Are we staying?" Rory asked, far too loudly. "Great—I could use another."

"Shut up, Ror," she whispered.

"Don't tell me to shut up," he said indignantly. "I brought you—"

"Rory, shut up! Please!" she hissed. Something in her tone caught his attention, and he fell silent. She stared at the floor, too afraid to look up, and hunched her shoulders as if trying to shrink straight down into the floor.

Several minutes passed, and nothing happened. She looked up and scanned the room. Blaise had moved on, away from the entrance and toward the back of the hall. She tugged on Rory's arm again.

"Okay, let's go." She hardly breathed until they were out of the hotel and walking away down the street. Her back prickled, and she waited for someone to shout after them. No one did.

"Was that the bald one you told Kier about?" Rory asked, his voice surprisingly normal given how drunk he had seemed a moment ago.

"Yes," she said. "His name's Blaise."

"Was he why we had to leave?"

"No. I've got a spot on the *Gloria* for tomorrow, but I need your help again. I need to know how to live on that ship and not get caught."

Rory looked confused. "So what do you want me to do?"

"I need lessons on how to be more like you."

As her family's house came into view, Molly began to feel sick. Her stomach clenched, and the muscles in her legs twitched as if trying to turn her around. But she needed her brother, and he needed his bed. She pushed on, despite the sweat breaking out on her forehead. Luckily, no one else seemed to be at home when they arrived. Once she had Rory safely tucked in, she fetched some water from their rain barrel and woke him just long enough to drink it. Then she sat down on Kiernan's empty bed.

Now that she was inside, she felt surprisingly peaceful. Her stomach had settled, and her legs were still. Handling her drunken brother had felt so familiar that for a moment it had overridden everything else, and for the first time in a long time she felt at home. She looked at her brother, twisted up in his blanket, and realized that though he was not exactly reliable, he was perhaps the most dependable person in her life. Through everything that had happened, he had not changed at all. She had a sudden urge to cross the room and kiss his forehead.

She went into the central room. On the table were a few scraps left from someone's sandwich, and she sat and ate these, carefully picking up any crumbs with the pad of her finger.

She looked toward her father's room, wondering if the journal was there. She could think of nowhere else it might be.

She crossed to her father's door and opened it.

The room was as bare as her own bedroom. The only piece of furniture was a double bed with a battered wooden frame. While one side of the bed was rumpled, the other side was immaculate, the sheets turned down crisply over the thin woolen blanket. In the wan light, she could see several bottles gleaming beneath the bed.

And there was the book, lying open on the floor. She picked it up. It had been open at the final page. Had it fallen that way? she wondered. Or had her father read the journal? She tucked it under her arm and left, closing the door behind her.

"Molly?"

She almost jumped a foot in the air. In the pale moonlight from outside, she could just make out the silhouette of a man in the middle of the main room.

No, not yet. I'm not ready to see him yet.

Then the figure stepped forward, and she saw its shoulders: lean and straight, not bowed.

"Kiernan." She stepped forward and hit him on the chest. "You scared me out of my skin."

"I scared you? I come home and hear someone rattling around in Da's room, when I just left him at the pub. Why are you here, Molly? Have you decided to come home after all?"

"No," Molly said. "I brought Rory back, and I'm waiting for him to sleep the party off."

"So you have further need of our brother's particular talents then?" As he spoke, he closed the front door and then returned to the kitchen and lit their oil lantern. He brought the lantern to the table. "Wish I had thought to grab one of the igneous lights from the ship before we left," he said. "Oil costs too much."

Molly shook her head. "No. This is good." She wondered what had happened to those small, flickering spirits that had lit the *Legerdemain*. At the thought of all the spirits that had been bound to the ship—and the fact that she hadn't even bothered with them after freeing Legerdemain—she suddenly felt weak.

"Molly, sit. What's happening to you?"

She hesitated a moment, then pushed the journal across the table to him. "Just read this."

"I don't want to read about it. I want you to tell me."

Molly shook her head. "The journal will do it better than—"

"Why can't you just answer a damned question?" Kiernan said, surprising her with the anger in his voice. "God, Molly, you'd think you don't know how to speak. Why are you always so closed up?"

She sat silent, uncertain how to answer, until she realized the irony of not responding to such a question. "I... don't know," she said. "I'm..." *How am I supposed to answer that?* "I didn't know you thought I was closed up."

"Of course you didn't. Just talk to me, Molly. Please."

She watched her brother, uncertain whether she could trust him with this—or if she wanted to. His entire life had been spent at their father's side, doing the family's work. What Molly had learned changed the meaning of all of that. Part of her wanted to protect him from knowing. But she couldn't help the spirits and leave her family untouched at the same time.

So she opened her mouth and spoke. She told her brother everything, talking until the lantern burned out and then continuing in the darkness, unable to see his face.

"And now I'm here," she finished, "and I'm waiting for Rory to teach me how I can live aboard that ship without being arrested. Or worse."

She stopped, and silence flooded back into the room like the ocean into a sinking ship. "Kier?" she said, when he said nothing.

"I'm here. I think...I should go to bed." His voice was oddly slow. "I need some time." She heard his chair scrape back, and then she heard his footsteps cross the room to her brothers' bedroom. The door closed, and she was alone.

She felt bewildered, uncertain what her brother's reaction meant. *Is he angry? Overwhelmed? Maybe I should leave before he can report me to Disposal.* She reached across the table, and her questing fingers found the journal.

Strangely, she did not feel scared. She felt empty—wonderfully, peacefully empty. The house did not feel so overwhelming; she could even think of her father, and though she felt anger, she found that her old, nervous love of him remained. Her brother could accept what she said or call Disposal on her, but for tonight she could sleep with no secrets weighing her down. Leaving the journal where it was, she went to her room, lay in bed and closed her eyes.

Molly's sleep was deep and long. When she woke, she had a vague memory of a bearded face looking down at her with unbearably sorrowful eyes, but she couldn't tell if it had happened or had only been a dream.

She got up without rousing the rest of the house and slipped out the front door. She made her way quickly to Toves's area. Ariel was waiting for her there, and Molly told her everything she had arranged with Bracebridge.

"Excellent, Molly. I will meet you at the docks."

"You're coming?"

"Of course I am. This is my fight. I will not let you fight it for me."

"But all the iron in the ship..."

"I believe that if I remain close enough to you, I will be able to bear it."

Molly did not try to talk Ariel out of her plan any further—she feared the spirit might listen if she did. "I should go back to..." She trailed off as she realized they weren't alone. A large pile of stones had sprouted beside them without her noticing. "Toves?"

The pile grew legs and strode over. "You're really going onto that ship? To shut it down?"

"Yeah. Well, to shut down the harvester."

"That's good, kid. When you're done, there are a few terric operations that could use your attention."

Molly laughed. "One at a time, I think."

"Good luck," Toves said, no humor in his voice. Then he was gone again.

When she got home, she was surprised to find both of her brothers awake and waiting for her. Kiernan grabbed her as soon as she came in the door.

"I need your measurements," he said, slinging a thin piece of rope around her chest.

"What? Why?"

"Because you're going to need a uniform that fits if you hope to even get on the *Gloria*." He took a few more measurements and then sat at the table, where Rory's uniform was waiting beside a needle and thread. "And we should cut your hair. Rory said someone almost recognized you last night."

"So…you're helping me?"

"Yes. You need it."

"So you believe me?"

He didn't look up from the uniform. "I trust you."

She felt an odd warmth suffuse her chest. "Thank you, Kiernan." The words came out as a whisper, and she wasn't certain Kiernan had even heard them until he looked up and gave her a tight-lipped smile.

"Okay," Rory said, "on to the lessons. Now, you're going to stand out no matter what, because you look fourteen. Most people who look younger than they are get a little brash to compensate."

She spent the morning working with her brother, with mixed success. She tried to be brash and confident but ended up sounding like a shouting child. Finally, her brother gave her a piece of advice that seemed to stick.

"Fitting in where you don't belong isn't really about being confident or acting a part. It's about *not* acting a part. You have to be natural, or people will sniff you out as a fake."

"But if I act natural, I'll just look terrified all the time."

"Well, how do you think a new crew member who doesn't know anyone is supposed to feel?"

They continued with more success. Just after lunch, Rory called her ready. Kiernan took her aside and cut her hair short. The scissors were dull, and her hair ended up a rat's nest, but running her fingers over her head, she decided she rather liked it. She felt lighter.

Rory whistled. "It's probably lucky we can't afford a mirror."

"She looks different, at least," Kiernan said.

"Different is right."

"I like it, actually," Molly retorted. "It feels good."

"It's not a perfect disguise. But it should help," Kiernan said.

Molly smiled at him. She donned her uniform, packed a change of clothes and the few tools she had salvaged from the *Legerdemain* and headed out the door.

She was stopped by something tugging at her leg. She turned around and saw Cog, standing behind her with his arms up like a small child asking to be lifted.

"You want to come with me?" He nodded. She looked over to Rory. "Rory, can I take Cog with me?"

"I don't care," he said. "If you think you can use it. It's useless, mind."

Molly bent to pick up Cog, but as soon as she lowered her arms, the little cogitant clambered up them and over her shoulder, and she felt him working his way into her pack. Once he was safely inside, she started for the docks.

ACT THREE
SIC TRANSIT

SEVENTEEN

Molly walked in a crowd of new crew members, following a tall young man across the docks. The others kept asking him questions, but all their guide would say was "Just wait. The bosun will talk to you." Molly kept her head down and walked.

From her vantage point at the back of the crowd, she didn't even realize they were crossing the gangplank until the sound of her footsteps changed. The plank was wide enough to accommodate twenty people walking shoulder to shoulder. As they crossed, the *Gloria Mundi* itself came into view around the sides of the crowd. Cranes and gantries stretched above them, as numerous as trees in a forest, and on either side the dark iron hull stretched away into the distance. Molly swallowed as her foot hit the deck.

"Welcome to the *Gloria Mundi*," said a familiar voice. Molly's head snapped around, and she saw Brighid standing in front of the new crew members, arms clasped behind her back.

As Brighid's eyes scanned the group, Molly ducked behind the others. Sweat sprang up on her forehead, and she itched to run in the other direction.

But Brighid kept talking, making no indication she had seen or recognized Molly. It took a minute for Molly's heart to slow enough that she could hear what her sister was saying.

"...under way only three hours from now, so we will need all hands on deck shortly. I will show you to your berths, you will have ten minutes to stow your gear, and then you will report back to me."

Report back to me? Molly thought. *Oh, great—my sister is the bloody bosun!* Brighid turned on her heels and started moving quickly across the deck. Molly and the others hurried to keep up with her.

"You okay?" Molly whispered into the collar of her shirt.

"Yes," Ariel said. The spirit had wrapped herself around Molly's chest, under her Haviland Industries jacket. It felt odd, and as they had entered the iron ship, Ariel had tightened uncomfortably, feeling surprisingly solid. "It does not hurt so much."

Molly opened her mouth to respond, then shut it tight. Up ahead, the sunlight glistened off the smooth skin of someone walking the opposite way across the deck—someone bald and very, very big. Molly immediately looked the other way. As they passed each other, she could feel him looming over her. Her already-taut nerves nearly snapped, and her breathing grew shallow, but again there was no cry of alarm. They reached a companionway and descended into the ship, and Molly breathed again.

Great. I've got to avoid both Blaise and my sister. Her plan to get aboard the *Gloria Mundi* seemed worse and worse by the second.

The other new recruits seemed disturbed by Blaise's presence as well. "Did you see him?" she heard one sailor whisper to another. "Gave me the shivers. Did you see his eyes?"

No going back now, Molly told herself. *I just need to wreck a few machines, and then I can hop off again.*

The interior of the *Gloria Mundi* was a network of dark, iron-walled passageways. Molly was used to the *Legerdemain*, which had only one, and she quickly lost her sense of direction. After a few minutes of quick walking, Brighid stopped and opened an unmarked door. "You will sleep here," she said, gesturing them inside.

The room itself was the exact width of the door, with berths sunk into the walls on either side. Molly swallowed. She hadn't been expecting quarters quite this close, but she followed swiftly after the others, making sure to keep people between her and Brighid as they filed past. As the others argued over beds, Molly hurried to the back of the room and hopped up to the topmost berth. She pulled herself inside. If she ducked her head, she had just enough room to sit. She looked out to make sure no one was watching and then opened her bag. Two small eyes glimmered inside.

"You can't come out yet," she whispered into the bag, "but I'll leave this open. Once everyone is gone, you can come out. After that, you can—"

"What was that?"

A girl with slightly greasy blond hair was looking up at her.

"Sorry," Molly said. "Just talking to myself."

"You don't do that while you sleep, do you? I'm going to be right underneath you."

"Not as far as I know."

"Okay." The girl pulled open a large drawer under her berth and threw her bag inside. "You didn't go to Arkwright Academy, did you?"

Molly shook her head. "Grew up on an airship. It's grounded now." She had already decided that her best bet was to keep her story as close to reality as possible. After all, it was not a unique enough tale to make her stand out.

The girl stuck her hand out to Molly. "Meredith," she said. "But people call me Mer."

Molly shook her hand. "Molly."

"You know you look like you're about twelve?"

"People have said that before."

Meredith shrugged. "Well, as long as you can keep up with us big people, I don't suppose it matters."

Molly actually found herself smiling. "Don't worry about me keeping up."

The rest of their bunkmates were starting to file out the door, so Meredith and Molly followed. Molly patted her bag lightly as she left.

Belowdecks, the *Gloria Mundi* seemed surprisingly small. The passageways went on forever, but they were just as narrow as those on the *Legerdemain*, and the living quarters were even more cramped. But when Molly climbed the companionway to the deck, she froze in her tracks, shocked by the ship's scope. The deck was so long that Molly could not see the docks at the far end. Speaking tubes sprouted from the deck like mushrooms, and huge gantries, taller than the *Legerdemain*'s mast, straddled loading-bay doors, lowering large spirit traps into the ship. Other spiritual machines that Molly did not recognize were congregated at the bow of the ship. People in blue uniforms ran everywhere, on the deck and in the rigging. Towering over everything were a dozen tall masts, each bearing an engine twice the size of the *Legerdemain*'s. The engines were shaped like blocky pears, narrow at the fore and then widening out to a large bulb at the aft end. Molly could see that the engines were closed full; no winds flowed in or out of their large vents.

She and her shipmates had come up close to the bow of the ship, next to the second mast. Molly heard a thump behind her and turned, then immediately knelt to retie her boot—Brighid had just dropped from the mast's rigging.

"All right, ladies and gentlemen, make yourselves useful. Six of you aft to help with the hawser, the rest with me."

Molly hustled to join the group moving aft. As they went, she stole a glance at her sister striding to the starboard side, the new crew trailing after her. Her sister walked with her head thrust forward, like someone entering a fight. Molly knew that walk well.

Molly and the five others hurried to the back of the ship, where the hawser—the thick rope used to moor the ship to the dock—awaited them. Molly had never seen a rope so large. It was broader across than her shoulders, and the winch that held the rope was more than two stories tall.

As they approached, Molly felt Ariel stir under her jacket.

"Molly, I am going to slip away," she said. "Even close to you, all this iron is overwhelming. I will be nearby."

The spirit flowed out through her sleeve and darted skyward. Molly looked around nervously, but though Ariel was obvious to Molly, no one else seemed to notice her. Molly returned her attention to the hawser.

There were already several sailors at the wheel that turned the winch, ready to push. One of them, with an extra patch on the shoulder of his uniform, shouted, "Sailors, hands on the wheel!" and Molly and the other five hopped to the task. The wheel was huge and had handles protruding every couple of feet. The sailors gathered at the handles and started to push. When the turn of the wheel put a handle too high, the sailor would run back and take up a new handle behind the others. Slowly, they brought the rope in around the winch.

As the hawser slid away from the moorings on the dock, Molly heard a voice like a god's echoing across the deck. It sounded like it came from the clouds above, and Molly instinctively ducked her head. But what it said was, "Ahead, half speed." Molly craned her neck upward as the words faded.

She heard a laugh and looked forward to see Meredith looking back at her with amusement. Some of the other sailors were smirking as well.

"I love watching ship brats hear that for the first time," Meredith said. "That was just an amplifier. It relays the captain's voice."

"Oh," Molly said. "Right." While the sailors around her chuckled, she struggled to regain her composure and focused on pushing the wheel.

The deck below them began to vibrate, and Molly looked up again. The wind above the ship had bent toward one of the engines. Molly smiled. The aft engine had started first. The others started in sequence, aft to fore, until half of the engines were running. The ship slid forward through the skies. It was almost alarming how quickly it moved for such a large ship. She had to look down at the deck—the swirling lights that passed through the engines were so quick and so intricate they made her dizzy.

They finished reeling in the hawser and then tied off the huge winch. Molly wiped her sweaty hands on her pants and stood uncertainly beside the wheel, wondering if she should be doing something else.

Suddenly one of the speaking tubes nearby started squawking, and a sailor—the one who had barked a command at them earlier—ran over to listen. "Some of the rigging has come loose," he said after a moment. "Who's handy with knots and has a good head for heights?" Molly put her hand up. The sailor pointed to her and three others. "You four, follow me." They all ran after him. Molly, to her surprise, found herself still smiling.

Exhausted and refreshed by a day of work aloft, Molly returned to her berth for a night of peaceful sleep. But when she closed her eyes, dreams were waiting for her.

She was swimming—or perhaps flying—through a sea that seemed to be made of light. She felt it flow over her face, its touch something like water and something like silk.

Other shapes moved around her, shadows in the brilliant light, but never came close enough to resolve themselves. She was moving steadily downward, and it occurred to her that she was not moving of her own accord. Something was pulling her.

"Legerdemain?" she said softly. The pull felt like the one she had felt from her ship's spirit, but stronger. Below her she could see a vast shadow, growing as she moved closer. "Legerdemain, is that you?" she called out.

The shadow shifted, and she heard a whisper from it, so low she could barely hear it. She was still moving downward, faster now, and the shadow continued to grow. It was large—much larger, even, than Legerdemain. It seemed strange to hear such a soft sound from such a huge thing. And then the sea of light parted, and she saw what was below her.

It was not Legerdemain. It was something much, much larger. Its body was thundercloud and wind-whipped waves and innumerable winds woven together into mandala patterns. Its wings, spreading out from its body by the dozens, were lightning blue and sunset red and blizzard white. A dozen eyes, gleaming like suns, swung up to look at her, twirling unsettlingly in the midst of the spirit's stormy face.

She could feel its attention, as if it were a physical force that plucked her from the air and held her tightly. She could hardly breathe, but she squeezed out the words "What are you?"

It answered, though not in words she knew. As before, its voice was shockingly soft for a being so vast, and she struggled to hear it. She could not tell what it said, but as she listened a storm of emotion washed over her: sadness, terror and a need so strong she thought she might disappear inside it. Her vision began to swim.

She woke on her bunk with her eyes wet, and she put her hands over her face. She ran her fingers across her eyes, her nose, her mouth, as if trying to convince herself that they were real, more real than the emotions that had followed her out of the dream. Slowly, so slowly, they faded and gave Molly room for her own feelings, her own thoughts.

As she lay there collecting herself, reminding herself that she was human, she realized that though the feelings had faded, she could still feel their pull. Something was drawing her downward.

Molly threw herself into her work the next day, using the physical labor to mask the pull she felt. She spent the morning working alongside her bunkmates, but shortly before lunch she was given an assignment with the rigging crew: carrying iron patches up to the engines. Her speed up and down the masts was enough to keep her there while the rest of the new recruits left to scrub the foredeck.

The rigging crew of the *Gloria Mundi*, Molly discovered, were little more than errand runners. The ship had no sails; it relied entirely on the power of the engines. However, with twelve second-level engines working at the same time, constant repairs were necessary, as the powerful spirits worked to break free of their prisons. The engineers assigned to each engine had small pocket-welders attached to their belts at all times. The third engine from the bow was especially cantankerous, and the flames of the welders lit its sides almost constantly.

Soon, Molly told herself again and again. *For now you have to fit in. Soon you can find a way to set them free.* Her reassurances only partially worked to assuage her guilt.

Returning from delivering a new set of spanners to the aft engine, Molly dropped from the yardarm and realized too late that there was someone below her. Someone with a bald, scarred head. She brushed his arm as she fell and then scrambled a few feet away.

"Sorry, sir, I didn't see you," she said in a rush, her head turned down.

She watched Blaise's feet turn and walk toward her.

"What's your name?" he said above her.

"S...Sanders, sir. Molly." She clenched her muscles, trying not to tremble.

A huge hand came down on her shoulder and began to close.

"Mr. Blaise," a voice boomed high in the air above them. "Mr. Blaise, please come to the captain's quarters."

The hand on Molly's shoulder relaxed.

"Watch where you land, Sanders," Blaise said and walked away. A few moments later Molly fell to her knees. She felt like she could cry, if she let herself. She wanted to climb back up the mast and just keep going into the clear, blue sky.

EIGHTEEN

"All hands on deck. All hands on deck."

The voice sounded like it was coming from directly beside Molly's bunk. She jumped up, banging her head on the ceiling above her bed, and then fell to the floor. She stood and rubbed her head.

Oh, right. Just the amplifier.

Around her, her bunkmates started rising. Molly pulled on her jacket and followed the rest of them down the corridors and up onto deck. Dark clouds stretched from horizon to horizon, crackling with lightning.

And we're aboard a metal ship, Molly thought.

She watched the lightning warily, but the tumult of bright winds was blinding, and she had to look away.

She saw several engineers working furiously at the bow, turning dials and adjusting valves on the spiritual machines clustered there. As she watched, lightning flashed down from the sky. She flinched, ready to be cooked along with the rest of the crew, but the bolt paused midair, changed its course and lanced directly into the machines, where it was absorbed without any apparent effect.

Someone grabbed her and pulled.

"Come on, midget," Meredith said, gripping her arm tightly. "The bosun assigned us to the aft gantry while you were gawking."

"Oh, right." She hurried to keep up with the others.

By the time they reached the gantry, several sailors were already climbing it, great sheets of rubber strapped to their backs. Molly and Meredith were given rubber sheets and sent up the starboard side.

The metal gantry was slick with rain, and even Molly had to concentrate to keep herself from falling back to the deck. When she finally made it to the top of the gantry, she scuttled across to the middle, where two men were wrapping their rubber sheets around it. Molly watched what they did and began working on her own sheet.

When she was done, she looked up—and then almost fell backward off the gantry.

Ahead, in the storm, was a vortex of light. Molly had to shade her eyes to look at it again, and even then it was hard to watch. One moment it seemed to swirl inward, bright multicolored lights flowing from the world into the dark orb at its center; the next, it seemed to reverse, with a rainbow bursting out into the world. It was as big as the *Gloria Mundi*, and for a moment Molly had the impression of a vast eye watching them. Then she looked closer at the center and recognized it.

It was a font. The energies around the black core looked entirely different to her now, but that telltale black center, the gateway between worlds, looked just as it had before Legerdemain had changed her.

Suddenly the thing that had been pulling her downward since her dream grabbed hold and pulled harder. Molly collapsed across the gantry with a groan. There was a hideous feeling inside her, like desperate fingers scrabbling at her soul, and it was so strong she could hardly think.

She gripped the gantry through the rubber sheet and forced her eyes open. She watched the rain splashing on the deck far below her. *I have to get down. If I fall from here...* She started back the way she had come, crawling on her hands and knees.

"You okay?" someone asked. Molly looked up and thought she saw Meredith.

"Don't feel good," she managed to say—or thought she managed to say; it was hard to tell with the pull scattering her thoughts. She crawled past two other people working on the gantry and then half slid and half fell down to the deck. From there she stumbled to the gunwale and hung there, trying to breathe deeply through the sheeting rain.

A hand came down on her shoulder. "Hey, are you all right?" Molly looked up into a face she didn't know, and tried to answer but couldn't. She felt as if she might be pulled directly down through the deck at any moment. They were moving toward the font now, and the closer it got, the more desperate the thing inside her became.

"Should I get the bosun?" the face asked.

Panic brought her voice back. "No! No, you don't need...to do that. I'll be okay, just..." She clenched her eyes shut, trying to concentrate on what she was saying. "Just a few minutes."

The light from the font was blinding now and mesmerizing. Molly stared at it as the *Gloria Mundi* drew up alongside the font, unable to take her eyes away. The ship matched the font's own speed and then began to slide sideways through the air toward the font. Molly held on to the gunwale so tightly that her fingers trembled.

Just before the font disappeared into the interior of the ship, there was a flash, and something burst forth. It was large, with tattered leather wings several yards across. The spirit's body looked tattered too, as if the creature were constructed from torn cloth. It sped out of the font and then wheeled and coursed back toward the *Gloria*'s deck. Lightning struck it and ran through it. The spirit didn't slow, but now it crackled with electricity, and its wings flexed back as it began to dive toward the ship's deck.

I need to move, Molly thought, but she couldn't. Her body would no longer obey her.

The spirit sped toward her, reaching forward with tattered limbs. From behind Molly came a bright red flash, and a plume of flame rose from the deck to meet it. The spirit flapped its wings, struggling to slow itself before it flew into the fire. Molly looked around to see where the fire had come from and found Blaise standing a few feet behind her. He had his arms raised, palms out, and the fire was coming from his hands. There was something on his hands, she saw in the flashing light of the storm. Gauntlets of some kind.

The spirit had flown up above the ship now, and each time it tried to descend, it was met with more fire. Finally, it seemed to reconsider and turned away, but as it shifted, the fire bent in midair and flowed to block the spirit's retreat.

Strands of flame flowed around the creature, caging it. Blaise made a pulling gesture with his hands, and the cage moved down. The creature flapped and dashed at the flame, but when it touched the fire there was a loud hissing, and it retreated.

The flaming cage descended to the deck, sailors scrambling out of the way. Blaise calmly walked forward and flicked his hands, and the fire vanished. The cowed spirit stood bewildered before him. And then Blaise was on it.

He moved like a spirit himself, something fast and brutal. He pummeled the creature with his ironclad fists. He tore off one of its wings with a quick wrench that seemed to take almost no effort. He scorched it with quick bursts of flame from his gauntlets. And when the spirit tried to strike back, he moved too fast to be struck or met its blow with a blow of his own.

She watched, unable to turn away, as Blaise broke the spirit piece by piece, until its limbs—Molly counted six of them—lay useless beneath it, and its remaining wing beat feebly against the deck. Then Blaise strode forward, took what must have been its head in his hands and squeezed. There was a surprisingly concrete crunch as his hands came together, and the spirit went limp.

Still utterly calm, as if nothing unusual had happened, Blaise began methodically blasting the spirit with fire from his gauntlets, reducing it to ash.

The pull inside Molly increased again, and she fell flat to the deck. She had never felt anything so strong, so desperate. Only half aware of what she was doing, she started back to the companionway, stumbling on legs as heavy as lead. With the fury of the storm and the aftermath of the fight as distractions, no one seemed to notice her leaving the deck.

The pull drew her on irresistibly, and by the time she had descended to the third level belowdecks, she was sprinting, her feet pounding the floor like a drum. She sped through the ship, down passageway after passageway, finding dead ends and turning back, moving faster and faster. Finally, with the pull so strong she thought it might yank her soul right out of her body, she turned one last corner and found a door. One with two guards in front of it.

The guards stood up straight as she ran toward them, bringing their guns to the ready. Molly called on every ounce of willpower she had to try to stop. She brought herself back to a walk but could not stop moving forward until one of the guards stepped in front of her and put his hand on her chest.

"Where are you hurrying to, miss?" he asked in a surprisingly gentle voice.

It was hard to hear her own thoughts over the unformed scream of the thing that pulled her forward, but she forced words out of her mouth. "Can I go through that door?"

"Why?" said the other guard suspiciously. "Only engineers and officers through here."

"Oh. I didn't…I'm sorry. I'm lost."

They both stared at her. Molly knew she must look half mad. It took an enormous effort just to hold still. She felt like she was trying to fly into strong headwinds with her sails unfurled.

"Go back that way," the first guard said, "and turn left at the end. You'll see the ladder."

"Thanks."

She turned around and began walking, slow step by slow step, feeling their eyes on her. She did not reach the end of the passageway; instead, she took the nearest turn and collapsed onto the floor, where she waited for the pull to either abate or finally succeed and draw her directly through the bulkheads.

A tremor shook Molly out of the half sleep she had sunk into. The *Gloria Mundi* rattled for a few seconds before all went still. As the tremor ended, the pull inside her finally eased. It was still there, but it seemed to have exhausted its strength. At the same time, she felt the slight vibration of the engines starting back up; the ship was moving on.

Done harvesting, I guess.

She rose. She wasn't sure how long she had been lying in the passageway. It felt like hours, but everything was just as it had been. She found her way, with some difficulty, back to her room, tiptoed past her sleeping bunkmates and hopped up onto her bed. There was an ache inside her that had nothing to do with her muscles.

"You okay, midget?" Meredith's voice whispered from below.

Molly cursed silently. "Yeah. I don't know what happened to me. Sick, I guess."

"No problem. I covered for you with the bosun. I remember the first time I flew through a storm, it felt like I would never stop vomiting."

"This wasn't my first time flying through a storm."

"Yeah, but your first time aboard a real ship, right? Not one of those measly little dinghies? It's different."

Molly clenched her teeth. "I guess."

"Tried to find you in the head. Did you make it that far?"

Molly thought back to her brother's advice on lying. "I was pretty confused. I ended up in another part of the ship."

"Huh. Well, next shift starts in two hours. Sleep tight."

Molly closed her eyes and tried not to whimper.

NINETEEN

By the end of her next shift—a full ten hours spent traveling up and down the masts—Molly was so tired that she almost didn't notice Cog on the way back to her room. The cogitant was sweeping in one of the side passages, but as soon as he saw her he stopped and began waving.

"Need to go to the head," she said to the backs of her bunkmates. "Be right back." They watched her as she walked off, but didn't say anything. A day of hard work, Molly had noticed, tended to make people incurious. She walked down the hall to Cog, checked that the others were out of sight and then crouched down beside him.

"It's good to see you," Molly said. Cog beckoned her over to the wall. He lifted a small flap like a cat door and gestured for her to go inside.

Why didn't I think of using those? Molly wondered. Most airships were riddled with vents to circulate conditioned air but also to allow cogitants and other spiritual machines passage without getting in the way of human feet. They were too narrow for most people, but Molly thought she could fit. She checked for watchers, then got down on her stomach and squirmed inside.

Halfway into the vent, she felt something on her leg and yelped, but as the thing scurried up her body and over her shoulder, she realized it was just Cog. He scrambled on ahead of her, gesturing for her to follow.

They continued on, Molly half crawling, half slithering along behind the small copper man. He took her through a maze of vents, down steep slopes, through branching passages that she couldn't have hoped to navigate alone. As they went, Molly could hear snippets of life echoing through some of the vents: conversations, music, the clang of cookware, someone weeping, shouts and apologies, hissing pneumatics.

I could get anywhere through these. And no one would know I was here.

Finally, Cog stopped at a downward opening. He gestured to Molly and then jumped through. Molly peeked over the edge. All she could see were a few crates and Cog, who was once again beckoning her. She crawled past the opening, slid her legs down through it and jumped.

They were in a large room stacked unevenly with crates, but for a moment Molly had the strange feeling that she had just entered a tavern. Everywhere she looked there were cogitants, of all shapes and makes. In the light of a gas lamp they glimmered in different colors: the reddish yellow of brass, the mirrored gleam of chrome, the matte gray-blue of zinc. Many sat on the crates, staring at her, but others seemed too busy to notice. Some were gesturing back and forth, seemingly in mute conversation. One cogitant, with arms as thin as nails, was tapping lightly on the side of an open crate, creating a beat to which several other cogitants were dancing, twirling around each other on their metal feet.

They dance? Molly was momentarily overwhelmed with sadness. *Why didn't I know that?*

As Cog brought her forward, the dancing stopped and then so did the beat. She paused as dozens of small lenses turned up toward her, but Cog kept beckoning her on. He walked up to a tall, spindly cogitant in the corner of the room, who had been sitting and watching the others. Its silvery frame was tarnished and dented, and when it moved Molly heard a rattle. Cog gestured wildly to this cogitant. It gestured back and then reached behind itself and pulled out a stack of paper. Cog looked up at Molly.

"What is this, Cog?"

Cog pointed to the old cogitant. It had stood up and was now leaning over the papers, which it had put on a low crate. When it straightened up, Moll saw a piece of charcoal in its hand and words on the paper.

You are Molly Stout?

"Yes," she said. "You can write? Cog, can you write too?"

But he shook his head. The older cogitant bent to the paper again and wrote, *Takes long to learn. You are here to stop the gate eater?*

"The...the harvesting machine? Yes."

We will help you.

"Can you get me to the machine?"

We can take you where you will see. The old cogitant rose and walked shakily to one of the others—a rather slight one made of brushed steel, with only one lens in its narrow head. The old cogitant took its arm and led it forward, then bent to write again. *Follow this one.*

Without waiting, the one-lensed cogitant ducked into a vent in the wall. Molly hesitated, remembering the pull she had felt the previous night. *Do I really want to go any farther?* She looked toward the single door into the room. She could walk through that and find her way back to her bunk.

Taking a deep breath to smother her fear and exhaustion, she followed the cogitant. Cog came behind her.

As they descended through the walls of the ship, the constant pull inside her stirred. She braced herself for the terrible desperation she had felt the night before, but it didn't come. The feeling fluttered lightly inside her but did not take hold.

They descended until Molly was certain they would fall out of the bottom of the *Gloria Mundi* at any moment. Finally, the cogitant leading them turned and held one finger up to his face. Since he did not have a mouth, it took Molly a moment to realize he was asking for quiet. She nodded and tried to move silently. Soon Molly heard the reason for stealth: footsteps reverberated through the vents above them.

They took one more turn, and then the cogitant opened a door at the end of the vent. Molly crawled forward. All she could see through the small door was open sky, clouds passing far below, ribbons of wind wending through them. She continued forward slowly, and a suspended walkway came into view just below the vent. She watched for a moment, but no one passed by. She poked her head out of the vent.

To her right, the walkway connected to dozens of others. They clung to the walls in every direction, a tangle of platforms and railings that hung all around the huge open space in the middle of the *Gloria Mundi*. At the edge of these railings were spiritual traps of all sizes, and men and women in blue uniforms were bringing in more traps as she watched. The thin metal of the walkways amplified their footsteps, turning them into a cacophony.

But Molly observed this for only a moment, for her eyes were drawn immediately to the object hanging down into the open space. It was a wide metal tube, with an array of metal arms at its end surrounding what looked like a large iris, now closed. It looked like some hideous mechanical eel—like a vast iron lamprey. It moved ceaselessly, shifting and rolling back and forth.

As it moved, creases in its metal plates opened up, and through them Molly saw bright lights, like winds moving underneath the metal. Sometimes these winds would burst forth, shooting out as if reaching for the walkways but always falling short. The entire thing seemed to flicker with energies Molly couldn't quite see.

As she watched, she felt the pull inside of her tighten, and the entire tube shifted in her direction, pointing straight at the vent. *It knows I'm here.* Molly heard the buzz of voices increase, people taking notice and leaning over the railings to watch. She pulled back inside the vent.

"They've got a level-one spirit trapped in that thing, don't they? I mean, something big. Powerful," Molly whispered to the two cogitants. The steel one nodded his head. Her mind flashed back to her dream. "How did they catch it?" she asked, not expecting a response. She leaned her head against the side of the vent, feeling the spirit tugging her insistently toward itself.

She peeked out again and followed the body of the harvesting machine to its base. The long metal tube was suspended from the ceiling, running toward the port side of the ship. In the upper corner of the chamber, the tube was connected to a knot of machinery unlike anything Molly had ever seen. This machinery was separated from the rest of the chamber by a cage with thick iron bars. There was a single door allowing access, and it was held shut by a huge padlock. There was no one inside at the moment.

"Can you get me inside that cage?" Molly asked the one-lensed cogitant. "Is there a vent that goes there?"

He shook his head.

Molly lay down on the floor. "What the hell do I do now?"

Whatever she did, she knew this was not the time. The area around the harvesting machine was too busy. She would have to come back.

"Can you lead me back to my room?" she asked Cog. He nodded. She considered the narrow vent around her. "Okay. Just give me some time to turn around. This isn't going to be pretty."

When Molly finally got back to her room, a dreamless sleep awaited her. But it didn't last; what felt like only moments later, something landed on her face, and she woke with a start.

"Come on, midget. Have to report to the bosun in ten minutes."

She pulled the thing—a pillow, she saw through her bleary eyes—off her face and sat up. Meredith was standing below her, arms crossed, while the rest of their bunkmates filed out the door.

"Thanks," Molly said, handing Meredith her pillow.

"Can't believe you slept through all that noise. Chris and Tom even got into a fight."

"I was tired."

"Well, if you don't get up now, the bosun's likely to throw you overboard. I hear she's done it to new recruits before." Meredith sailed out the door, leaving Molly alone. Still half asleep, she pulled on her uniform and followed, running to catch up.

She came up the companionway into a blazing sun. She breathed in the air and let the breeze wash away some of the fog still clinging to her, then ran after the rest of her team. She had just joined the others when Brighid strode up to them.

"No dawdling on duty today, sailors. You're all to report to the stern. Quartermaster Dobbs will have buckets and rags for you."

Everybody groaned except Molly. To her, a simple day spent scrubbing the deck sounded perfect. No moral qualms, no skulduggery. And it would be easy to avoid drawing attention to herself. She followed after her grumbling bunkmates.

She took a rag and bucket from Quartermaster Dobbs—the same man who had been barking orders on the hawser,

Molly discovered—and went starboard, just beneath the third aft engine. She sank quickly into the task, her arms growing sore and her mind peaceful.

A breeze skittered through her hair, and Molly looked up to see a flickering blue light. "Ariel?" she whispered.

"Let me in, please," the spirit said. "The iron stings."

Molly pulled the collar of her shirt down, then shivered as Ariel flew inside, bringing the cold air of the upper atmosphere with her.

"Molly, you will cross paths with another font within the next two days. I came to warn you. Have you learned how to stop this new harvesting machine?"

"Not yet," Molly whispered, returning to her scrubbing. "They keep it locked up tight. I haven't found out how to get to the machinery yet. Ariel, the machine is powered by a first-level spirit."

"I suspected. Oh, Molly. What it must be like inside a machine for such a thing."

"I know."

"We have to free it before it is forced to swallow another font. What have you learned?"

In fits and starts, speaking only when no one was around, Molly told Ariel what she had seen and learned since coming aboard the ship.

"Then we need to find who holds the key to that door," Ariel said.

"Do you…do you think you could stay?" Molly asked. "I might need help, and—"

"I think I can stay for a short time, as long as I remain close to you."

"Thanks." She took a deep breath and let it out, feeling Ariel's body swirling against her skin.

As soon as her shift was done, Molly made excuses and parted ways with Meredith and the others. She found a quiet corner with a vent and crawled inside.

"Ariel, can you find Cog? I'll get lost wandering around in here on my own." She was momentarily blinded as Ariel flowed out, her bright-blue glow filling the vent. She closed her eyes, and when she opened them again, Ariel was gone. Molly crawled farther in, putting distance between herself and the passage behind her, and then waited.

A few minutes later she heard a pinging sound drawing closer. The air in the vent began to flow past her, and Molly drew the collar of her shirt down just as Ariel flew around a corner. She looked slightly tattered and smaller than when she had left. She flew quickly into Molly's shirt. Following in Ariel's wake was Cog, each footstep pinging lightly on the bottom of the vent.

"Thanks, Ariel," Molly said. "Cog, I want to get back to the harvesting area. We need to set up a watch so we can see who has access to the machines."

Cog nodded and began walking back the way he had come. Molly followed him. "Ariel, are you all right?"

"Yes."

"Thank you for going. I know it must have been painful."

"Pain and I are not strangers, Molly. I can bear a little suffering."

They returned to the same vent that led to the harvesting area. It seemed quieter there this time, but when Molly looked out, she saw Abernathy, the chief engineer she'd met at the party, talking with Blaise on one of the higher walkways. Blaise's eyes roamed restlessly around the area, and Molly quickly ducked back inside the vent.

"Why is Blaise here?" she whispered.

"Perhaps it is the spirit. It is uneasy—can you not feel it?" Ariel asked.

Molly realized that she could indeed feel it. The pull the spirit had on her was growing stronger and weaker in waves. She peeked out again and saw that the large metal tube was thrashing, winds flaring out from it constantly.

"I am going to see if I can speak to it," Ariel said, flowing out of Molly's shirt and into the central chamber.

Molly waited for several uncomfortable minutes before Ariel returned. "What did it say?" she asked.

"It could not speak. It is half mad from its confinement already. Molly, we *must* find a way to set it loose soon."

"We're trying, Ariel."

"Those men, the one with the beard and the one with no hair, have gone now, though others have replaced them. You may be able to watch."

Molly stuck her head out of the vent, and true to Ariel's word, Abernathy and Blaise had vanished, replaced by two younger engineers who, thankfully, seemed much less attentive than Blaise. Molly made herself as comfortable as possible inside the vent and watched the cage that held the harvesting machinery. She stayed that way for an hour, until her eyes began to close of their own accord.

"I can't stay awake," Molly said. "Cog or Ariel, can you watch for a while?"

Cog nodded almost eagerly and stepped up to the edge of the vent. His lenses turned upward, and then he stopped moving, staying so still he might have been a statue. Molly retreated a little way into the vent and then stretched out on her back. It was uncomfortable, but her drooping eyes did not seem to care in the least.

"Wake me if someone comes to open the cage," Molly said and closed her eyes.

There was no transition this time, no fall through the clouds into a dream. When she closed her eyes, the spirit was there waiting, vast and crackling with energy.

It seemed more restless, its body in turmoil, its wings rippling and colliding with each other, stirring up storms. Its movements sent turbulence through the air around Molly.

Its swirling eyes turned to her, and again she felt a wave of need and anguish threatening to overwhelm her. In the midst of the wave an image came into her mind: a dark orb surrounded by loops of sky-blue energy.

"I know." Molly struggled to speak. "Ariel—my friend—saw it. She said it was close."

Another image replaced the first: a long metal tube cracking open, clouds full of lightning spilling out.

"I want to free you," she said, "but I don't know how yet."

She felt a tug on her hair and thought it was the wind from the spirit, but then the tug turned into small fingers tapping on her head, and the dream dissolved. She opened her eyes to find Cog practically dancing with agitation.

"Is someone opening the cage?" she asked. Cog nodded, and Molly hurried to the end of the vent. Ariel was already there, hanging in the air just outside.

"This does not bode well for us," Ariel said softly.

"What do you..." Molly began, but fell silent as the cage came into view. There was indeed a crowd gathered around the single door. Several engineers, arms full of tools and traps, were waiting to go in, while a familiar figure unlocked the gate for them. Brighid.

"Oh," Molly said. "Damn."

The return through the vents seemed to take much longer this time. Molly found herself stuck in a worried silence that none of Ariel's attempts could shake her out of.

"Molly, I know this is difficult, but we must—"

"I'm thinking. Let me think," Molly said, though she knew it wasn't true. She couldn't stop her head from spinning long enough to think. *Why did it have to be Brighid?*

"Perhaps it would be best if I handled this. I believe I could get the key without being noticed."

"No!" Molly said, surprised by her vehemence. The thought of sending a spirit to steal from her sister, of how her sister would feel if she knew, made her heart leap into her throat. "No, I need to do it. I'll do it. I just need...time, I guess."

"Time is short. Remember, we approach a font quickly."

"I know, but...please. She's my sister. I..." Molly found words abandoning her again, and she shut her mouth.

Cog led them on, looking over his shoulder frequently as if worried Molly might get lost. She had never noticed before, but the way his lenses gleamed made it appear that his eyes were constantly teary. Ariel finally fell silent too, and Molly hardly noticed the spirit nestled next to her skin the rest of the way back.

When they finally emerged from the vents, Molly checked the hallway and then turned to Cog. "Thanks. I guess I might need to find you again. Where should we meet?"

Cog stepped a short way back into the vent, then sat down.

"You'll wait right there? But I don't know when I'll be back."

Cog simply nodded his head and closed the flap at the vent's opening.

Molly turned and headed for her room, but the spirit wrapped around her chest stirred to life. "Molly, I must say again—"

"Not now, Ariel." Her eyes darted up and down the hall. An old Irish lullaby was playing incessantly in her head.

"I cannot be silent. I realize this is difficult because that woman is your family, but—"

"I just need time to—"

"You will listen to me, Molly!" Ariel's voice vibrated in Molly's ear as if she was speaking directly beside her eardrum. Molly clapped her hand over her ear, but Ariel pushed it aside with a gust of wind. "While you wrestle with the thought of stealing from your family, *my* family remains trapped all around the world, and this damned ship draws closer and closer to the door of my home. You must, *must* remember what is at stake!"

"I didn't…I'm sorry, Ariel. That spirit in the harvesting machine. Is it your family?"

"I do not know who it is, Molly, but all spirits of the air are connected. In our world, we are not as separate as we are here. The greater spirits, like the one trapped here and the one you call Legerdemain, have touched us all."

"I'm sorry, Ariel."

"Do you still wish to get the key yourself?"

Molly squeezed her eyes shut and tried to force the lullaby in her head to stop. *She hasn't been that Brighid for a long time.* "Yes, but…I'll do it now. I won't wait."

"Thank you, Molly."

"Will you be okay on your own? Can you make it to the air? I'd like to do this alone."

"I can reach the sky, yes. I will return tomorrow morning."

Molly felt Ariel flow out of her shirt and then watched the glimmering cloud disappear around the corner, heading for the companionway and the deck.

Molly turned and went back to the vent. She opened it and crawled inside, startling Cog. "Take me to her room now, Cog."

Brighid didn't return immediately, though Molly could see from the clock on her desk that it was only a few hours before dawn, when the bosun would report above deck.

Molly lay inside the vent, trying to keep herself awake. The vent let out under Brighid's bunk. Molly could see her sister's desk on the opposite wall, empty save for the bolted-down clock. There was a trunk tucked beneath it, presumably for Brighid's personal effects. If Molly stretched right to the edge of the vent, she could see the door on the left. The room was small, only slightly larger than Molly's room on the *Legerdemain* had been.

Molly watched the clock, the only source of movement in the room. *How long does it take to maintain one machine? She has to sleep sometime, right?* The second hand circled and circled, and suddenly Molly realized she could no longer see the clock. She snapped her eyes open. But watching the hand *tick, tick* its way around the clockface, she felt her eyelids droop once more.

There was a creak, and Molly's eyes snapped open. She rubbed at her bleary eyes as footsteps crossed the floor. When she looked again, her sister was at the desk, emptying her pockets and shedding her uniform. The clock's hands had advanced almost half an hour.

Brighid turned and went to her bed. Molly could only see her legs, but she thought her sister looked tired by the way she moved. Molly had moved the same way after a long day on the *Legerdemain*, her feet scuffing the floor as she walked. Brighid sat on her bed, one foot dangling in front of the vent. Molly could have reached out and touched her.

She heard a strange sound from her sister, as if Brighid was trying to talk through her pillow. Her leg disappeared, and the wood above Molly's head creaked as it took Brighid's full weight. The strange sound continued. Molly slowly crept forward, trying to hear more. She was at the very edge of the vent when the sound became clear enough for Molly to understand it: her sister was crying, the sound muted by her pillow or blanket.

A muddle of emotions washed through her. Part of her wanted to go and comfort her sister. Another part wanted to tell her that she deserved every tear for leaving her family behind the way she had. Molly lay frozen in the vent and listened to her sister cry, watching the clock count the minutes.

The sound finally faded, and there was silence in the room again. Molly stayed still and watched another half hour tick by before she moved. She slid out onto the floor, face up. Inches away, her sister's hand dangled over the side of the berth. Molly carefully stood up and looked at her sister.

She was struck hard by a feeling of recognition. She had seen Brighid, first on the docks and then as the bosun here, but the woman she had seen wasn't quite the one she remembered. She was crisper, sharper. But here she was her sister. Her own Brighid, who had shouted at her for dropping a favorite book overboard, who had once insisted on eating meals above deck so she could see the sky, who had locked herself away in her small cabin for hours, who had held Molly in her arms so long ago. She was still here, an arm's length away, the same sister she had always had.

Molly watched her, and what she intended to do came crashing in on her. She was going to loose a level-one spirit on her sister's ship. She saw again the *Legerdemain*'s engine torn apart as the spirit came free. What would happen to the *Gloria Mundi* when she released its prisoner—a prisoner that would be understandably angry and wielding the power of a god? How many would die?

She went to the desk. On its surface lay a brass pocket watch, a handkerchief stained with sweat, and a ring of keys.

Molly took the ring, wrapping her fingers around the keys so they wouldn't make noise.

She turned back to her sister. "I'm sorry..." she began to whisper before her sister's eyelids snapped open.

Molly was momentarily frozen, but Brighid was on her feet before she had even blinked.

"Molly?" she said.

"Hi, Bridge," Molly said. She looked at the door. It was closed, and she doubted she could get through it before her sister caught her. But the vent was still open.

"What are you doing here?" Brighid took a swift step forward. "Molly, what are you doing on my ship?" She grabbed for Molly's arm.

Molly pushed her off and then dove for the vent, wriggling inside as fast as she could.

"Molly, stop!" Brighid shouted after her. Molly glanced back over her shoulder and saw her sister's face framed perfectly by the end of the vent. "Come back here!" she shouted. "What are you doing?" The familiarity of her face had vanished again, leaving only the new and strange Brighid behind. Molly wondered if she had imagined the other Brighid, seeing her only because she wished to see her, because she missed her sister. She turned and continued down the vent, Brighid's shouts echoing after her.

TWENTY

Molly had been in the vents for hours. Her legs were cramped, her head hurt from banging against the ceiling, and her arms had bruises the color of ripe plums spreading up from her elbows. She had tried to leave several times, but the ship seemed to be swarming with the dark-coated security officers.

She stopped for a moment, laying her cheek on the cold metal floor. She considered closing her eyes, and then they seemed to close on their own, indifferent to her own wishes. They snapped open again when a voice rang through the vents.

"Attention. We have a stowaway aboard the ship, one Molly Stout. You may know her as Molly Sanders. She must be caught. All hands, report to the deck for search detail."

The voice was Arkwright's. And he had called her by her real name. Molly had held a slim hope that all the security she had seen was not related to her encounter with her sister, but if Arkwright knew who she was, it could only mean one thing.

Her eyes prickled, and she fought to keep from crying again. The tears came anyway. *Come on, Brighid's not worth this. Of course she told them about me. She's part of Arkwright's crew now, not mine.*

There was a tapping in the vent behind her. With difficulty, Molly wedged herself sideways in the vent. She had run across several cogitants, but they had all run away at the sight of her before she could speak to them. Maybe this time it would be Cog, if she was lucky.

Yeah, just look how lucky I am.

The tapping grew louder, until something emerged from a side vent a dozen yards away. But it wasn't a cogitant. It rolled through the vents, propelled by sinuous arms that sprouted from all sides, each arm capped by a hook. It rolled to a stop and then spun until a small lens came clear from the tangle of arms and pointed directly at her. *Ferratic.*

"Lucky me," she said out loud, and then she turned and began crawling away as fast as she could on her bruised elbows.

She heard a clatter as the thing began following. She looked back. It seemed as if it, too, wasn't intended for such narrow spaces, its arms getting wedged constantly. But despite its size and awkwardness, it was moving faster than she was. Through her tears, she searched desperately for some kind of hope.

Ahead—too far ahead—she saw an opening. As she struggled toward it, something glimmered across the vent's mouth, and then again. It looked like a weak breeze. She thought back to the day she had healed Ariel.

Please, she thought. *Please, I need help*. The breeze at the end of the vent flickered and bent. A glimmering tendril of wind began questing down into the vent.

Molly looked back. There were only a couple of yards separating her from the thing now. Its arms clanged against the vent's walls as they thrashed out toward her.

Faster! she told the wind. *Please, I need—*

She didn't have time to finish her plea. The narrow tendril turned into a torrent as wind began flowing through the vent. It hit her in the face and stopped her dead. She turned her face away and saw the wind flowing past her in sun-bright streams. The ribbons of wind converged on the ferratic, and it was blasted backward. It flew down the length of the vent, arms scrabbling at the sides, and hit the corner it had emerged from. Two of its arms sheared off on the wall. The wind faded and then stopped, leaving the thing lying twitching on the floor. It moved, rolling awkwardly on its remaining arms. Molly braced herself to flee, but the ferratic dragged itself away from her, not toward her. She watched until the thing had rolled out of sight, and then she clambered out of the vent.

She half expected to see security bearing down on her. But the long, narrow room she found herself in seemed to be empty—at least, of other people. It was crowded with small boats, each with a mast no taller than Molly and topped by a well-tied bundle of fabric. The boats were anchored to moorings in the floor, and in front of each one was a large hatch, hinged at the bottom. One of these hatches hung open, revealing the sky beyond. This was the source of the glimmering wind that had saved her, and which now skittered lightly between the boats.

The lifeboats, Molly thought, and hurried forward.

In the bottom of each boat was a stove, bolted down aft of the mast. *They're dirigibles*, Molly realized, looking up at the fabric atop the mast. She had heard of dirigibles, of course—the experiments in France and Germany that had let humans fly without the aid of spiritual machines were used as object lessons in lift and aerodynamics among engineers—though she had not known they were still in use.

People might need these soon, she thought.

She checked the moorings of one of the boats to make sure it was secure before going to the hatch and carefully unlatching it. With the aid of a rope attached near the top of the door, she let it down as gently as she could, wincing as it clanged against the hull.

The room stretched away out of sight, following the curve of the hull. Molly moved on to the next hatch. As it dropped, it revealed a blue glimmer in the sky beyond. The glimmer moved inside, taking on Ariel's familiar shape.

"Molly?" the spirit said. "The entire ship is in an uproar. Are they searching for you? What happened? What are you doing?"

"What does it look like I'm doing?" Molly retorted. "I'm getting the lifeboats ready." She opened another hatch.

"Molly, if you've been discovered, now is hardly the time to—"

"You said you didn't want to hurt anyone!" Molly shouted at the spirit. "You said, but now—"

"Molly, please keep your voice down."

"How many people do you think will die if I let that spirit out? Do you think it's just going to wander peacefully away?"

"I certainly hope not. I hope it will remember itself enough to free every imprisoned spirit on this ship before it departs."

"Why didn't you tell me what would happen? There are hundreds of people on this ship, Ariel! I don't want to murder hundreds of people!" Molly felt the tears returning to her eyes, though the wind pouring in the hatch dried them almost as fast as they came.

Ariel drifted closer. "What I said, Molly, was that I did not want to make you hurt anyone, and that is still true. Whether I myself want to hurt anyone is another matter entirely, and if you want to know how I feel, then please recall that your people have been enslaving and murdering my kind for hundreds of years. The number of us who have been killed is too high to count. How could I feel mercy in the face of that?"

"Not these people!" Molly shouted. "At least, not all of them. These are ordinary people. Some are even nice. I don't..." She took a deep breath, feeling the crisp air of the open skies filling her lungs. "You should have warned me, Ariel. I don't want to hurt anyone."

"Are you saying you no longer want to help?"

Molly wiped at her nose. "I'm getting the lifeboats ready, Ariel. Why do you think I'm doing that? But if you want me to help you, then you have to help me too. We have to give people a chance to escape."

"What help do you need? I cannot touch those iron hatches."

"Just check all the moorings—make sure they're tight. And when you're done, I need Cog. You can find him."

Molly continued on, opening hatch after hatch. After Molly had opened a few, Ariel began examining the boats. Molly tried to pay her no mind.

"You intend to carry through with our plan?"

"Of course," Molly said. "I'm bloody touched now, aren't I?"

"I have done nothing to your mind, Molly."

"I know that. I mean…all of this is a damned nightmare. I can't see a good way out, but it's got to end somehow. I have to make it stop."

"Thank you, Molly."

"Just check the boats. Please."

Ariel drifted across the rest of the boats and then left through the vent without a word. Molly scanned the closed hatches—a dozen or so left now—and kept working.

Seconds later Molly heard the *ping, ping, ping* of light footsteps and turned to see Ariel and Cog hurrying toward her.

"Apparently, he was looking for you as well," Ariel said.

Cog ran up to her and gestured for her to bend down closer.

"Why were you looking for me?" she asked him. Cog waited while she bent down and then stepped forward and wrapped his arms around her neck. It took her a moment to overcome her surprise, but then she hugged the cogitant back.

"Thanks, Cog. I'm okay. Now, I need you to do something for me. Will you help?" Cog nodded. "Thanks. Do you know the amplifier the captain uses to talk to the whole ship at once?" Another nod. "I need to find a way to get to it."

"It seems unwise to reveal our plans before they are complete," Ariel said.

"I know. But we can't just pull the ship out from under their feet. They need a chance to get—"

The ship jolted. A second later Arkwright's voice boomed from the air around them.

"Engineers to the harvesting chamber. Security, maintain positions. All others, on deck immediately."

Molly stepped to one of the hatches and leaned out, looking toward the bow. She saw dark clouds ahead, looming over the ship. Winds so bright they hurt her eyes whipped back and forth among the clouds, dancing around a central point where something sparked in a rhythm like a heartbeat.

"The font!" Molly said. "It's just ahead!"

Ariel came up beside her. "Molly, we must go."

"I know. Cog, please hurry. Come and find us at the harvesting chamber when you know where the amplifier is."

Cog turned and ran back into the vents. Molly had never seen him move so fast.

"Okay," Molly said. She took one last look at the storm ahead, and one back at the hatches still closed. With jaw clenched, she crawled back into the vents.

The chamber had been transformed. Dozens of cables and hoses ran out from the cage that held the harvester's machinery, connecting to the traps that lined the walkways. The cables were in constant motion, stirred by the storm winds that spilled in through the open sides. The harvester looked like some nightmarish beast, its tentacles spread to every corner of the chamber. And everywhere Molly looked, blue-jacketed engineers and dark-clad guards milled on the walkways.

The harvester's spirit seemed to sense the approaching font. It thrashed, straining at the chains that held it to the ceiling. As before, Molly felt its desperation as it pulled at her, and she had to press hard against the walls of the vent to keep herself from sliding out into the chamber, into the arms of the waiting guards.

"I forgot about…this part," she said with difficulty. *What good am I going to be if I can't even move?*

"I believe I can help," Ariel said at her side.

Molly felt the spirit flowing down into her coat again, across her skin. Winds like fingers played across her back, her ribs, her chest, and suddenly she could breathe again, the frantic pull easing away. She could still feel it, but it was like a distant call rather than a steel-tight grip.

"I have loosened its hold on you for now," Ariel said. "But if you plan to deal with such great forces and not be subsumed into them, you will have to learn to do this as well."

"Thank you," Molly said, "but I don't plan to do this ever again. Even if I survive."

"Regardless, we must work fast before the—"

"Not yet. We have to wait for Cog."

"Are you sure that will be safe?"

"Of course I'm not."

They sat silently watching the room for several minutes before the *tink, tink, tink* of metal footsteps echoed down the vent to them. Molly turned, heart in her throat, but relaxed when she saw Cog running toward them.

"Did you—" Molly began, but a loud *crack* from the chamber silenced her. She turned, and through the opening of the vent she saw a huge font sliding into sight.

"No," Ariel whispered beside her.

The font was large—bigger than the one Ariel had emerged from—and it shimmered like water, deep blues and oranges shining from its depths. *Crack!* The harvester came into view, straining toward the font like a dog on its leash. Molly could feel its desperation and unease.

"There is no more time, Molly!" Ariel shouted, straining to be heard over the crackling of the font and the shouting from the chamber. "We must act!"

"I know, but the amplifier! The people! We..." She looked around desperately, as if an answer might reveal itself, some hidden pocket of time that she could use. The ship slid sideways through the air, bringing the font into the center of the chamber. Molly watched in horror as the harvester spread the metal arms at its mouth and plunged into the font. The energy around the font parted, shying away from the metal of the harvester. The mouth of the harvester reached the black hole at the center of the font, looking like a whale about to swallow a fish, but when it reached it, something bent—the harvester, the world, twisted in a way Molly's eyes could not follow, and the harvester's mouth disappeared, its vastness vanishing into the small darkness. Its body, now strangely curved, drew a line from the font to the ceiling and shuddered violently.

"I will go," Ariel said.

It took Molly a moment to comprehend. "What? Go to the amplifier? But the harvester—"

"Molly, I cannot break through the iron in that machine. Only you can do that. We do not have time for you to give warning, so I will do that while you try to free the spirit."

"What about the ferratics?"

"Those poor beasts, so tortured by metal and electricity that they can hardly think? Do you really believe they can catch me?" Ariel turned to Cog. "Please, little one, show me the way."

Cog hesitated a moment, then reached out and squeezed Molly's arm with his tiny hand.

"I'll be okay, Cog. Thanks. And remember to keep yourself safe too."

He nodded and then set off. Ariel followed, turning into a narrow band of mist to avoid the metal walls.

"Thank you, Ariel!" Molly shouted after her. She looked out at the chamber, at the font hanging in the middle of the air, at the rippling cables spread around it, and the legions of people between her and the cage, where the machinery of the harvester whirred and hummed. She reached down and felt her sister's keys, heavy in her pocket.

I don't even know which key is the right one.

With all eyes on the font, no one noticed her emerging from the vent. Engineers were dashing everywhere, replacing traps, tightening connections. Molly gauged the distance to the walkway above her. She put her head down and walked fast, waiting for a moment when no one was looking her way, then stepped up onto the railing closest to the wall.

"Hey, what are you doing?" she heard behind her. She turned and saw a young man in black looking up at her from a few yards away. His eyes widened. "It's her!" he shouted. He pointed something at her. It looked like an elephant gun from the cover of one of her dime novels. She jumped.

Her hands clamped onto the walkway above. There was a *bang*, and something slammed into the wall just below her feet. She pulled herself up, and when she looked down she could see what looked like a burning stone embedded in the metal bulkhead.

The guard was shouting again. "It's her! She's here! She's here!" All around the chamber, eyes shifted toward her, and black and blue jackets began moving in her direction. The entire chamber rang with the sound of footsteps.

She looked toward the cage. Two more levels up, and a dozen yards to cross. And then a dozen keys to try. She didn't think she had time. *Too late to go back*. But the walkways were already crowded, and growing more so by the moment. She looked around the chamber and saw the wind of the storm pouring in from the starboard side. It swirled and eddied around the font.

It worked before, Molly thought. She reached out toward the wind, straining with her mind as well as her arm, and then pulled.

The bright winds shifted course, turning toward Molly. The wind hit the walkway like a tidal wave. People tumbled back against the railings, cables snapped, and traps teetered and fell, slamming into the walkways below. Molly watched a man snatch at the railing and miss. He fell, and she jumped to the railing in time to see him land, hard, on a cluster of people two walkways down.

Spirits began to leak from the ends of the broken cables, disoriented and weakened by their passage through the metal. Molly watched in horror as several people aimed weapons at them. Triggers were pulled, and clouds of shimmering metal rose into the air, slicing the spirits to shreds. All the while, the wind continued to buffet them, and more of the men and women were sliding toward the edges of the walkways.

I have to stop this! she thought, jumping to the next walkway above her.

She landed right beside two bewildered engineers. "H… hey!" one of them stuttered, but Molly pushed past her and ran in the direction of the cage. Up ahead, two security guards were sprinting toward her. Molly dashed to the railing and jumped up again, but one of the guards was too fast. She felt a strong hand grip her ankle—and a moment later let go.

She pulled herself up before he could grab her again, but when she heard a yelp from below, she risked a look back down. The two guards were dancing and kicking, slapping at their legs. They were moving so much that it took Molly a moment to recognize the strange shapes on their legs as cogitants—the small figures were clinging to the guards, refusing to be dislodged.

There were at least a dozen people between her and the cage—and at least a dozen guns pointed straight at her chest. Her heart thumped faster and then seemed to stop dead, as if it too was waiting for the impact.

One of the guards—a bright-haired girl who reminded Molly of Meredith—opened her mouth to shout, but Molly could not hear her words. The noise behind them—a clattering like hail against metal—wiped out her voice. And suddenly there were hundreds of tiny hands and feet gripping the railings, clambering onto the walkways, and the guards and their guns were disappearing under a swarm of cogitants. She saw the guards shouting but heard nothing beyond the sound of metal against metal.

The cogitants were writhing even as they pulled the people down, and several of them had wisps of smoke curling out from their joints. This attack, Molly knew, must be triggering every safeguard in their metal bodies. The walls of their iron traps would close in, and the electrics would send jolts straight through the spirits. In the face of this ultimate rebellion, the cogitants' own metal bodies were trying to kill them.

She stood still for a moment, trying to calculate if she had enough time to free the spirits. *If I turn back now, I'll be caught. That's not what they want. They're doing this to help you, to give you a way through. Take it!* Her legs tensed under her, and she jumped up onto the railing, running along its length, past the confusion of human and cogitant bodies. Then she was at the cage and pulling out her keys. Though she stared down at the lock, she was hardly aware of her hands running through the keys, testing each one in turn. Her focus was on the shouts behind her, the squeals of the dying cogitants, the roar of wind battering the chamber.

There was a click, and the lock sprang open in her hands. She looked back for a moment at the chaos behind her—the mass of men, women and cogitants, the wind bending the walkways below, cables and hoses rattling in the storm, the harvester driven deep into the font—and then she opened the cage door and closed it behind her, putting the padlock back on from the inside.

The metal tube of the harvester—still pulsing disconcertingly—entered the cage on her left and immediately disappeared into a dizzying array of machinery. Strange, intricate apparatuses clung to its sides, pistons firing irregularly, colored liquids flowing through spiraled tubes. The cables that filled the harvesting chamber converged here in a tangle, and they clacked and rattled against each other so loudly that it made Molly's ears hurt. She looked for intake vents or any other means of letting the spirit inside breathe, but she saw none. She tried to make sense of what she was seeing.

Low to the floor there was a squat, square machine that caught Molly's eye. It looked familiar somehow. Molly moved over to it. The front seemed like an access panel of some kind, with a metal door on sliders. A metal trap, open and empty, sat nearby. Molly stared at the machine for a moment and realized she'd seen it on a set of blueprints in the back of Croyden's shop. *This is how they feed the spirit. That must be why there are no vents—they feed it other spirits, not air.*

There was a lever on the side of the feeding apparatus. She pulled it, and the metal door slid up, revealing a compartment large enough to hold a medium-sized trap. There was another sliding metal door on the other side of the compartment. *It's like the airlocks they have on aqueous harvesters. Two doors, opening sequentially.* She reached toward the interior door—and snatched her hand back as the first door slammed down. A moment later she heard the second door opening. *The sequence must be automatic.* She looked around for a way to tamper with the second door, but its mechanisms were enclosed within the harvester itself.

She heard a thump on the interior side of the first door, like something slamming against the metal. *It's the spirit, trying to get free.* She looked around, found a toolbox and pulled out a wrench. *If I can take off this door, pulling the lever should create an open path for the spirit.* She tried to turn one of the nuts with her wrench, but it held tight. Leaving the wrench in place, she climbed halfway up the harvester's side. A kick to the wrench's handle moved it a quarter inch. With her second kick, the nut spun loose, and she jumped down to finish the job. She had to repeat the process for each of the remaining three nuts, but once they were all free, the door slid off easily.

She took a moment to look through the bars of the cage. The harvesting chamber was still in chaos. The wind Molly had called up had shifted now and seemed to be thrashing around the room, knocking people unexpectedly off their feet. Molly saw more than one person dangling from the railings. While some cogitants still struggled, dozens more lay lifeless on the walkways. In the center of the chamber, the bright winds of the font were dimming fast.

"Come on, Ariel," Molly whispered.

As the cogitants succumbed, people began to rise from the struggle. Some bent to help their comrades, but others immediately looked around, then located Molly inside the cage. Three security guards came toward her, two of them still holding their weapons.

Molly moved to the door.

"Hey!" she shouted, hoping her voice would carry to the lower walkways too. "I'm going to open the harvester! When I do, I doubt this ship will survive long! Get out now!"

The guards slowed, and then two of them turned and ran for the door. "Stop!" the other guard shouted at them. "We can stop her! She's just trying to scare you!" The two guards banged through the door and out of the chamber. The remaining guard raised her gun.

Molly jumped back until she was standing flat against the harvester, the angles of its machinery jabbing into her back. "If you fire into the harvester, you'll just do my job for me."

The guard came forward to the door but didn't fire. "You'll die though," she said.

"You think I'm expecting to survive releasing this spirit?" Molly said. *Please don't shoot me, please don't shoot me.*

"Can't reason with you, can I?" the guard said. "You're spirit-touched."

"I'm sorry. I wish I had time to explain."

"You'll have all the time you want once I lock you up," the guard said and pointed her gun at the padlock. Molly covered her ears.

"Hello?" said a familiar voice. It sounded tentative, and yet it was so loud that Molly heard it through her hands. She took her hands off her ears. "Can you hear me?" said Ariel. The guard lowered her gun.

Ariel went on in a firmer tone. "This is a warning. The spirit you have imprisoned in your harvester will soon be released. When it is, it will utterly destroy this ship. You are being given this warning so that you might have a chance to escape. If you do not make use of that chance, the consequences are yours to bear. Your escape craft have b—"

Ariel's voice stopped. Molly waited a moment, but nothing more came. The guard's eyes met Molly's.

"Please go," Molly said. "I don't know you, but I don't want you to get hurt."

Behind the guard, Molly saw people moving for the exit, blue and black coats. The guard at the door watched Molly for a moment more, then turned to run. Molly watched until the room was empty, then walked back to the feeding apparatus and pulled the lever.

A gust of wind blew her across the cage, slamming her into the bars, and then stopped abruptly. Molly opened her eyes, expecting to see the room around her being pulled apart piece by piece, but the room was still, save for the weakening font and the winds swirling outside. Molly crept forward and saw that the metal door of the feeding apparatus had closed again.

She stood safely to the side and pulled the lever once more. Another blast of wind came out, but after a split second the door slammed back down again. *There must be a failsafe of some kind*. She looked at the machinery. *If I can mess with the electrics, it might stop the failsafe*. But there were no exposed wires she could see. *Maybe I can wedge the second door open*.

She grabbed the toolkit and closed its lid, positioning it in the feeding compartment. With one foot on the toolkit, she pulled the lever and started to push, but both the toolkit and her foot were blown back by the force of the wind. She closed her eyes and rested her head on the machinery.

She sought inside herself for the faint pull from the spirit. It was weak now—so weak she hardly felt it—but it was still there.

"Please," she said, trying to cast her words along that line connecting her to the spirit. "I need to get to that door to set you free. But I can't if you push me back. I need you to try not to escape for a minute."

She felt a tremor in the pull. Not knowing what it meant, she pulled the lever and waited for the second door to open.

There was no blast of air, though she heard wind whipping against the side of the machine. She knelt at the mouth of the feeding apparatus, staring down its black throat. She shoved the toolkit inside, placing it under the second door. A moment later the door slammed down, shearing the toolkit in two. The spirit groaned as metal from the toolkit fell inside its home.

"Sorry, sorry!" Molly said, gathering up the remainder of the toolkit. She peered at it. The door had cut the kit and all the tools inside neatly in half. *They must have planned for something like this*, Molly thought. *I'm going to need to take the door right off. So how do I...*

She fell silent as she realized the answer to her question.

All the sensitive stuff is inside the harvester. I have to go inside.

She felt her heart fluttering. Climbing inside the harvester frightened her more than stepping into a room full of hostile people had.

What will that do to me? What will the spirit do? Can I even get in? She looked out on the empty chamber and saw the cogitants lying still on the walkways. *They sacrificed themselves just to get me here.* She closed her eyes and sought the spirit's pull again.

"My first plan didn't work. I think...I think I need to get into the machine with you to set you free. So please hold still again so I can come in."

Molly waited a moment and then pulled the lever. She crawled into the small compartment. The second door opened beside her a moment later. She flinched, but no wind streamed out. Quickly she pushed forward into the dark interior.

As soon as she was through, a strong wind took her legs out from under her and rushed toward the exit. The door slammed shut, and as darkness fell Molly heard a moan like thunder echo through the metal chamber. The moan passed through her ears, into the hollow caverns of her own body, between her bones and organs, between her molecules, and shook her to pieces. Whatever Ariel had done to weaken the spirit's hold on her vanished, and she felt the spirit's winds blowing through her, washing her away in its frustration and sadness and rage. She felt it fighting against its own hunger, trying to pull away from the font, but it had eaten so little, and it needed the taste of home so much, it could not stop drawing in the lives and energies on the other side of the door. It thrashed against its captivity, and Molly felt her own arms thrashing. There was a *clang* as her wrench connected with the metal sides of the machine, and she struggled to hold on to the tool, knowing somewhere in her dissipating mind that if she lost the wrench, neither she nor the spirit would ever leave this horrible trap.

She curled down over her knees in a protective ball, but this offered no defense against the spirit. It was everywhere in the machine, leaving no room for her. It was a landscape; she, a blade of grass. It was a storm; she, a single wind howling down toward the one brief taste of freedom on the other side of the font.

"No!" she howled in the wind. "No!" Her voice came from her own throat, still there, still somehow intact even as she came apart. She struggled back, trying to find her own skin, trying to remember what it felt like to *have* skin, to be a thing of flesh and bone. She felt fingers, wrapped tight around a thing that burned her—*the wrench!*—and she held tighter, letting the pain of the iron draw her back.

"I am...Molly Stout..." she said through lips that only half remembered how to speak. "I am...Molly..."

With one hand she reached up and behind her and felt the wall of the machine. Her fingers ran over it, seeking the door. There it was, the thick metal slab set into the side of the curved chamber. Her fingers continued up, finding the bolts that mirrored the ones she had removed on the outside, so long ago now, before she had known what it was like to be the wind, to spin in circles with countless brothers and sisters, to be trapped in a place that kept her still when movement was all that she was, all that she knew...

"I am Molly Stout," she said, each word bringing more of her body alive around her. "I am human."

She took her wrench—which still burned, though she could hardly feel her hands now—and placed it around the first nut. She pulled down, and the nut did not move. Feeling the resistance of the battered nut made her feel giddy somehow, like she was meeting a friend she had long thought dead. It was so purely physical, so basic and familiar, that it brought her back to herself. She planted one of her feet against the wall and pulled again, with every muscle she had. With a screech, the nut moved.

Molly kept working at the nut, her muscles burning. The physical exertion seemed to keep her grounded, but she could still feel the spirit everywhere around her, passing through her as if she wasn't even there. "I grew up on the *Legerdemain*," she recited to herself. "I tore the engine apart to let the spirit out." The first nut came off.

She moved on to the second nut, and then the third. Her arms were so tired they were trembling. "I have two brothers. I have a sister. I have a father." The third nut fell to the floor with a *ping*.

She put the wrench around the final nut and pulled. Like the others, it resisted. She pulled harder.

She felt the spirit shifting all around her. It knew she was close, and she could feel its attention turning from the font to her, like a weight descending on her shoulders. "I was a…I…" Her shaking muscles felt like they were coming apart, her body only so much detritus borne on the wind, her thoughts only the crackling static charge of storm clouds. She pulled at the wrench, but she could no longer tell where her fingers were. She dissolved into eddies and gusts. She rushed around the narrow space of her prison, throwing herself against the walls, even though the iron walls burned her every time she touched them.

No, she thought. *No! I am Molly Stout! I am fourteen years old, and I have upended my life just to get this far, and I am just one bloody turn of the wrench away from the end, and I am not going to get trapped in here!*

She heard an echo and realized it was her own voice—her human voice—shouting the words. She felt her throat, ragged now, and then her heart in her chest, and her arms and legs. She reached up and found the wrench—still miraculously holding on to the final nut. She pulled on it, pulled and pulled, until she felt her arms were going to rip from their sockets, and finally the nut moved. Molly twisted it once, then reached up and grabbed the door itself, twisting it on the single remaining bolt. And then there was light and air and a wind rushing past her that was so strong it took her with it, forcing her through an opening that was not quite large enough yet and back out into the world.

Her head hit something, and she was swamped by a wave of dizziness. She felt a cool metal floor beneath her, and then there was wind everywhere, spinning her around, and she was being lifted up on the crest of the storm clouds, lightning crackling across her skin in a giddy dance of exultation. She felt the lightning pass through her and part of her flinched, but there was no pain, only joy. *I'm free!* she thought. *I'm free! I'm free!* And then words were blown out of her mind, and she was soaring out, away from the scalding iron and into a sky that was already dancing in a wild storm of welcome. She was pouring out, out, out, until she filled the whole sky.

No, she thought weakly, though even to think in words was difficult. *Please. I don't want...this isn't...*She was still flying upward, but even as she rejoiced in the freedom of the skies, she knew this wasn't her freedom. She, Molly Stout, was disappearing.

Please. Let me go. Her body was still there—she felt it around her, less and less alive each moment. She felt the connection between her and the spirit, and she pulled back like she was pulling the cord of some great church bell, simply trying to draw the spirit's attention to her, away from the sky and back to what was happening in this tiny corner of its body where Molly was losing herself and becoming just another part of the spirit's own greater force.

I don't want this, she thought, and then she let words go and merely sent her anguish and despair along the connection.

The spirit seemed to hesitate for a moment, its winds curling back on themselves. Molly pulled on the connection again, and this time it came loose, and she—Molly herself, with arms and a heartbeat and a head that hurt so much it made her want to vomit—was falling. She landed with a *thud*, and everything went black.

TWENTY-ONE

There was a crash, and then an inhuman screech louder than anything Molly had ever heard. Her eyes snapped open.

Above her, the sky was black and starless. Clouds massed and swirled directly above the *Gloria Mundi*. Swirling throughout the clouds were bright points, like stars hidden in the storm. Several of them were concentrated at one central point, but others wandered through the clouds. The clouds shifted in unnatural ways that had nothing to do with wind, creating shapes almost like maws filled with rank upon rank of jagged teeth. There was another bone-shuddering crash that could have been thunder and could have been the voice of a god. Molly went to cover her ears and hit herself in the head with something. She looked down at her hands and saw that somehow she was still clutching the wrench.

She did not know how long she had been unconscious, but she knew it had been long enough for the spirit's initial joy to pass. Now the spirit, the sky itself, was one seething mass of anger.

The screeching came again, and the entire ship heaved. Molly sat up and saw that the aft end of the ship was tearing away, the metal screaming as it broke. It was being hammered by what looked like hailstones the size of elephants. The section finally tore away completely, and the rest of the ship tipped forward. Molly began sliding across the deck. She reached out and grabbed at a mast beside her, her short arms barely finding purchase. She looked down, toward the bow of the ship, and saw others who had not been so lucky, human shapes hurtling toward the ground.

"Ariel!" Molly shouted. "Ariel, can you hear me?"

Through the pounding storm, Molly heard a whine and felt the deck beneath her lift. She looked up to see one of the engines working at full capacity to hold the *Gloria Mundi* aloft, drawing in the wild storm winds and weaving them into a lattice around the ship. Despite its missing port section, the ship began to even out.

"Ariel!" Molly shouted again. "Where are you?" *Did she abandon me?*

The vast spirit above her had apparently forgotten her, not caring if she lived or died. *I must look so small from up there. Maybe Ariel sees me the same way.*

A memory rushed to the surface of her mind: Ariel's warning had stopped short. *What happened? Is she in trouble?* Molly looked around. The captain's quarters, and the amplifier, were near the bow, in the part of the ship that was still aloft. If Ariel was in trouble, that was the best place to look.

"Cog!" she shouted, but again there was no response.

The ship had come nearly level again. Molly got to her feet, tucked the wrench into her belt and began running, only to be stopped a moment later as a wall of wind slammed the deck in front of her. The wind was so bright it nearly blinded her. Dimly she saw one of the ship's masts blow away like it was nothing more than a piece of chaff. The metal engine atop the mast came apart like a dandelion in the wind, and there was a momentary flash as the spirit inside broke free. The spirit quickly disappeared into the vast, raging storm.

With that engine gone, the deck canted again, and Molly slid forward. She pushed herself sideways with her hands and feet, and just managed to land on the next mast. The ship had tilted so far that Molly could nearly stand on the side of the mast now. Around her the ship was being battered into pieces. Lightning lanced out again and again from the storm—or, at least, it looked like lightning, though Molly saw it shearing through the metal hull like a knife. Outbursts of wind descended from the storm, battering the ship like fists, while the sky above them shouted its anger.

There was another whine, and Molly looked up. The engine above her was the one that had been struggling so hard to keep the ship afloat. From this angle, she could see the silhouette of a person hanging from the engine's side—a silhouette she recognized immediately. Cursing into the wind and rain, Molly set her feet on the mast and began to run along its length. She made it halfway before the engine began to right the ship again, and she had to grab hold of the mast and climb.

"Brighid!" she called out. "Brighid, what the hell are you doing?"

The silhouette above her paused in its frantic motion.

"Molly? Molly, is that you?"

"Yes! What are you doing? Get out of here!"

"What does it look like I'm doing?" Brighid slid down the mast until she was across from Molly, and her fingers wrapped around Molly's neck. *I forgot how fast she is,* Molly thought.

"I'm trying to save the crew of the ship you just destroyed!" Brighid shouted. "How could you do this, Molly? You—"

"Get off me!"

"No! I'm not letting you go again! I'm not letting you slip off to do more damage!"

Molly struggled against her sister, but she couldn't break free without losing her own grip on the mast. "If you keep me here, we'll both die!"

As if to underline her point, a spear of lightning descended from the spirit above them and tore a hole in the ship. Molly and Brighid held tight to the mast as the *Gloria Mundi* shook with the force of the blow. The entire sky felt electrified in the lightning's wake, and the hairs on Molly's arm stood straight up. The metal deck glowed red beneath them.

The hole went straight through the ship, from top to bottom. Molly saw that the sky below the ship was cluttered with lifeboats, floating slowly downward. *I haven't killed* everyone *then.* The mast they were on teetered, snapping Molly's attention back to it. She looked up as the engine above them whined and started to struggle with its too-heavy load. The ship began to slowly tip again.

Brighid let out an inarticulate scream. "Why would you do this? Why are you trying to ruin everything?"

"Because I had to! Someone has to stop all this!"

"You've gone and gotten spirit-touched, haven't you? Was it the engine on the *Legerdemain*? I knew that old thing wasn't safe!"

"No, I'm not bloody touched! Just listen to me! I found—"

"Not touched? Molly, look at what you've done!" Brighid pushed Molly's head around to stare at the torn end of the ship and the spirit roiling above them, blocking out the sky. Its bright eyes had clustered together, all staring down at the remains of the ship, at Molly and Brighid. "You let that monster out of its cage! How many people did you kill today?" Molly watched the spirit for a moment more. The winds around the spirit were doing an impossibly intricate dance, weaving beautiful patterns before being thrown down to batter the ship.

"If it's a monster, we made it that way," Molly said. "And how many people? I…I don't know yet. I'll count later."

Just above them there was a loud *clang*, and something flew past their heads. Molly looked down and saw a metal flap hit the deck. The engine's spirit squealed.

"Rrrah!" Brighid shouted. She looked from Molly to the engine, then let Molly go and scrambled up the mast. Molly watched her open the engine's controls and heard a crackle as her sister sent a jolt of electrics through the spirit. With another squeal, the engine began to work harder again.

What should I do? Molly thought. *Should I free the spirit?* She imagined what would happen next, what the released spirit would do to her sister. She closed her eyes.

"I hate this!" she shouted. "I hate all of it! Why does everything have to be so bloody complicated?" If anyone heard her, Brighid or the vast spirit, they chose not to answer. Molly climbed a little higher. "Brighid! Please, just leave it! Save yourself!"

"Leave me alone!" Brighid shouted, and the words struck Molly like a fist. For a moment, were it not for the ship coming apart around her and the raging sky above, Molly could have believed she was back aboard the *Legerdemain*, tapping lightly on the always-closed door of her elder sister's room. She swiped at the tears that were suddenly in her eyes.

"You always were stupid!" Molly shouted up at her sister. "And if you really want to get yourself killed, I'm not going to stop you!" She slid back down the mast to the canted deck below. She let gravity pull her forward, aiming for the gap in the deck where the companionway came up. *Don't look back. Don't look back*, she told herself, but she couldn't seem to stop her head from turning. Her last sight before she went belowdecks was of her sister hammering at the engine with a wrench, the storm raging all around her.

Things were as bad belowdecks as they were above. Molly belted down the passages, dodging holes that led to lower decks or straight to open air. The passages were empty of people, but she saw a few ferratics rolling wildly from room to room.

As she moved forward, the passages narrowed and finally converged at a sturdy metal door. She pulled it open—then stumbled back with a scream.

Clinging to the other side of the door was one of the tentacled ferratics. The door swung open and banged against the bulkhead, and the ferratic dropped to the floor.

It began whirling toward Molly. Molly scrambled backward, but her hands met with open air. She turned and found herself looking out a hole in the hull. The starboard side of the ship looked like it had been torn off, and the winds were still buffeting it.

The ferratic was almost on her. Molly looked into the swirling winds and reached out to them. They responded so quickly, so eagerly, that Molly herself was blown off her feet as the wind rushed in through the hole and sent the ferratic spinning away. Molly grabbed at the door as she went past and caught hold of its handle. She held on as the mad rush of wind buffeted her, howling down the ship's passages. She dropped back to the floor and crawled through the door, closing it behind her.

After the rushing winds and screaming sky outside, the world inside the captain's quarters felt strangely silent. She could still hear the storm, booming like the hand of God knocking on the door. Were it not for the fact that the entire room was tipped forward, its contents collected against the far wall, she might have thought the crisis hadn't reached it yet.

The room must once have been an ornate foyer, based on the beautiful furniture that was piled against the wall. In one corner, Molly saw a desk that held a miraculously unbroken glass, a finger of dark-red wine still sloshing in its bottom. All around it, chairs were cracked to pieces, and a huge armoire stood with its doors lying at its base. Molly braced her legs and let herself slide across the floor. She shifted the pieces of a broken coffee table off the door and went through.

The room on the other side of the door had survived better, since its walls were lined with machinery bolted to the floors and bulkheads. A narrow path ran between all the machines. There were signs of damage here too though—several of the machines were cracked open, while others were dented, sputtering with a feeble life. The silence was oppressive, the storm barely audible. Molly opened her mouth to call Ariel but closed it again without making a sound. She moved forward, hanging on to the machines as she went past.

A skittering at her side sent her jumping back, but when she looked down she saw two familiar copper arms waving from beneath a machine.

"Cog!" she said. "Are you okay?"

She pulled him out from the machinery. His legs were mangled beyond repair, and his body badly damaged. "Oh, Cog," she said. "What happened?"

As always, the small copper man was silent. He simply patted at her arms and pointed insistently back the way she had come.

"Is Ariel here?" she asked, and he nodded. "Then I have to help." He shook his head and pointed again. Molly looked down at the broken cogitant who was still trying to save her. She picked him up and walked back through the foyer, her feet slipping on the sharply angled floor, to the hall outside and the great open hole in the wall.

Molly sat down, legs dangling over the torn edge of the passageway, and turned Cog over. He wriggled but could not move enough to stop her as she dug her finger into a fractured corner of his body and pulled. The plating on his back came away, and she saw the trap that was his heart, hidden in a nest of wires and tubes. Molly pulled the trap out, and Cog fell still. The trap was so small. Molly held it delicately for a second, then pressed in on the thin metal with her thumbs and pulled. The trap came apart as easily as an eggshell.

"Sorry, Cog," she said. "I should have done that years ago." A whisper of wind went over her hands, but she could barely make out the spirit. He was a tiny patch of turbulence in the air, nothing more. "Please go," Molly said. "You deserve to go home now."

The turbulence flowed out the gap—at least, Molly was fairly certain it did. She stared out at the storm for a moment, holding the empty shell of the cogitant in her hands. Her fingers were wrapped tightly around its body, and then she held it out and let it go. She watched it fall until it was swallowed by the clouds.

The ship groaned around her, and she heard more metal tearing. A cascade of lightning descended so close to the gap that she scrabbled back. She rose and hurried through the foyer and back to the room beyond, moving more resolutely. There was an open space up ahead, beyond the ranks of machines, and Molly could see a strange light coming from somewhere off to the left.

"Ariel?" she called out, breaking the silence. "Where are you?"

"Molly! Leave now, before—"

The reply was cut off suddenly, but it had definitely been Ariel's voice. Molly stopped in her tracks. *What am I walking into?*

"Come forward, Ms. Stout," said a voice like sandpaper. "No use in hesitating now. Unless you want us to dispatch your spirit immediately."

Molly moved slowly out of the alley between the machines. She entered the wider chamber and saw the source of the light.

It was the machine she had seen in Arkwright Manor, the tank filled with water that did not flow like water. Up close it was even more jarring, with its currents that seemed to arise from nowhere and then disappear just as fast, and waves that rose in slow motion across the surface and then fell down as quickly as regular water. But it was the figure inside the tank that held her attention.

Her first thought was that he could not be alive. Wrinkles covered his entire body, like the sun-dried husk of an apple. He was entirely submerged in the strange liquid, and as far as Molly could see, he was not breathing. Tubes ran from the machinery at the side of the tank directly into his body, glowing with a strange greenish light that made them visible even beneath his skin. His face was pitted and shadowed, a horrible wreckage of a human face. But that face was also smiling, and its blue eyes were very much alive as they looked at her. He was naked, she noticed, but she was too disgusted by his decay to care about that detail.

His hand rose and gestured her forward. "Come. As you well know, our time is limited, and I think your presence may help matters along." His voice was whispery and rough but still clearly audible, despite the tank.

"That's her," said another, deeper voice, and Molly's eyes snapped away from the old man in the tank. In the corner of the room stood Blaise, looking at her with undisguised hatred. "She's the one from the house." He had his metal gauntlets on, Molly noticed, and in one hand he was carrying a small trap with its vents shut tight. In his huge hands, it looked like a paperweight.

"Of course, Mr. Blaise," said the old man. "If you would be so kind..."

Blaise was on her so fast she didn't even have time to stumble back. His gauntleted hand wrapped around her neck, lifting her up onto her tiptoes.

"What...?" she spluttered, clawing ineffectually at his hand.

"Shut your mouth while the adults talk," he said.

"Indeed," the shriveled man said from his tank. "We do not need anything but silence from you, Ms. Stout. Now, Mr. Blaise, please open the vents again. I suspect we have the spirit's attention."

Blaise lifted the trap and used his teeth to turn the dial that opened the vents. A glowing blue whisper of wind emerged.

"Thank you, Mr. Blaise. Are you with us, spirit?" The man addressed himself to the trap.

"Yes," a voice whispered from the trap. Molly gasped. It was Ariel's voice, but the trap was far too small for a spirit of Ariel's power. It would be excruciating for her.

"Arie—" Molly began, but a squeeze from Blaise's hand cut off her voice.

"You cannot see, so I will describe the situation to you," the old man went on. "My associate, Mr. Blaise, has his hand around the girl's throat. I assure you, it would be no struggle for him to crush her neck. Do you understand?"

"Yes," Ariel said.

Molly could feel the gauntlets cutting into her neck and something wet running down over her chest. She couldn't look down to see if it was sweat or blood. She pulled at the gauntleted hand, but it didn't move.

"Good, good. Then if not for your own sake, perhaps you will save us for hers."

Molly looked frantically around the room. To her left, there were only more machines. To her right, there was something wedged between two of the spiritual machines, but it was so broken that it took her a moment to recognize it as a human body. A body with gold stitching on its blue uniform.

She stared at it. *Is that Tyler Arkwright?*

"How do I know you will keep your word?" Ariel said. "I have seen what you do to those you no longer find useful—even members of your family."

"You mean our captain?" The man in the tank gestured to the body. Then he laughed—or, at least, it looked like he did, but it sounded like two stones being scraped together. "You did not believe he was genuinely an Arkwright, did you? I have had no children."

Molly looked back at the body. *Not an Arkwright?* She could see for certain now that it was Tyler Arkwright; she could see his fine features twisted against the machinery. She struggled to understand what was happening.

The room shook, and Molly heard metal tearing somewhere above them. Blaise's grip temporarily faltered, and Molly twisted, but his fingers tightened again before she could escape. Now his thumb pressed painfully into the artery on the side of her neck.

"I never took you for the nurturing sort," Ariel said.

"He was a useful fiction, as were his predecessors."

What are they talking about? It was clear to Molly that Ariel knew this man, but how? She watched the man closely, trying to find some clue.

"As for your question, it is simple. The girl does not matter enough for me to kill her. I can keep my word because it costs me nothing."

The closer she looked at him, the more unsettling the man became. When he was not speaking or smiling, his face went slack, not moving at all. Not blinking, not even shifting subconsciously. She felt a sudden revulsion—he looked like something inhuman using a human body as a disguise. And yet there was also something familiar about that sharp chin and those inquisitive eyes.

"Even after she destroyed your ship?" Ariel asked.

"I am not interested in revenge. I am a pragmatist, as you well know. The ship is already destroyed, but I am not, and I will take whatever path is needed to see that I survive. As I always have."

"Is that how you justify all of this? Your own meager survival?"

The ship shook again, and the door of the room rattled on its hinges.

"We haven't time for this," the man said. "Now, you will bring us safely to the ground, or I will have Blaise kill the girl. I know you have an attachment to her—you have an apparent weakness for Stouts."

It was something in the way he said her name that gave Molly a spark of recognition. Hidden in that wreckage of a face were features she had seen over and over again. A face that should have been long dead.

"Arkwright!" she burst out hoarsely. "You're Charles Arkwright..." She wanted to say more. *How are you still alive?*

Why did you kill Haviland? He was your friend! But she'd spent all the air she had and could say no more.

The man in the tank—Arkwright—spared her only a brief glance. "Yes. Now, Mr. Blaise, please show the spirit we are serious. Break her hand."

Without hesitation, Blaise brought the metal trap down on Molly's left hand where it gripped his own. Molly felt a sharp pain, which was quickly joined by the overwhelming feeling that something was wrong, fundamentally wrong. She struggled to look at her hand and saw her fingers splayed at strange angles.

"Stop!" Ariel said. "Please! I will…I will help you."

Molly did not want to see the wreckage of her hand again, but she thought she'd seen something beyond her broken fingers. She looked down—and confirmed it: Blaise's legs were as thick as steel girders, but he was standing with his knees locked. He wasn't braced properly for flight.

"Good. Then we should begin. For myself, we will need the machines immediately to my left, and…"

Molly aimed carefully. She knew she would have only one chance at this.

Her heel caught Blaise directly in the knee, knocking his leg sideways. He tried to catch his balance, but the ship was shifting too much under him. His fingers clenched her throat, and then he fell. Molly rolled away from his hand.

"Molly!" Ariel shouted from inside the trap, which was now lying wedged under one of the machines. "You must—"

"I know!" Molly said. She ran to the machines Arkwright had just spoken of and reached for a cluster of metal-lined hoses with her unbroken hand. She pulled and they came loose, spilling smoke that glittered sunset-red in the air.

Something pounded on the outside of the room like a giant fist, but Molly ignored it. She went for the next machine.

"Mr. Blaise! Stop her!" she heard Arkwright yell. Molly pulled the wrench from her belt and swung it at another machine. It buckled under the first blow and then broke under the second. A geyser of water shot out, hitting her in the chest. The water flowed toward the door, defying gravity.

She turned and saw Blaise rushing at her, Ariel's trap tucked under one arm. He raised a gauntleted hand, and flames blossomed from his palm. Without thinking, Molly reached out and frantically pulled at the air in front of her. The air shimmered under her hand, and suddenly there was a wind where none had been before, bright and clear as a full moon. It rushed across the room, snuffing the flame and knocking Blaise into the wall.

Molly pulled again, and she shot forward on a wave of wind toward Blaise, reaching for the trap. But with a shake of his head, he recovered and focused on her. She flew straight into his arms.

"You think I won't kill you 'cause you're a little girl?" he asked. He wrapped one arm around her body and dropped the trap to grip her neck. His fingers dug between her muscles. She kicked at his legs, but he seemed not to feel it, so she kicked at the trap. It bent, and she heard Ariel shout, but it did not break. She tried to draw breath to scream, but she couldn't. She kicked out at the room in blind panic, and the wind kicked with her. Waves of wind slammed into the machines, sending metal fragments flying, flames and water and clouds of dust flying with them as spirits fought their way free. She heard glass shattering and wondered if she'd broken Arkwright's tank, but the fingers around her neck were still tightening, her vision was clouding, and she could see no farther than Blaise's furious face staring down at her with teeth bared.

"Wish I had time to break your bones one by one, the trouble you caused," he said, "but I've only got time to—"

The room around them cracked open like an eggshell. *Did I do that?* Molly thought, but she knew the answer when the two halves of the room stopped in midair and then moved upward. *The spirit.* She could see it above them, its sun-bright eyes all focused on the three tiny humans it held. It bellowed with the fury of hurricanes, a sound so loud Molly felt it pressing against her skin. Blaise's grip loosened. As her throat opened and air poured in, Molly found the strength to reach down and wrap one arm around Ariel's trap, and then the vast spirit tore Blaise from her, and the remains of the ship came apart around her, and they were all sent hurtling across the sky.

She was falling, with nothing but empty air between her and the ground far, far below, but for a few moments all Molly could do was cough. It felt like the muscles of her neck had been tied in knots, and breathing felt like swallowing blades. She wrapped herself around Ariel's trap as she arced toward the ground.

"Molly! Molly!" a voice was shouting at her from the trap clutched in her arms. Molly tried to reply but could not speak.

"You have to do something!"

"I...I..." The two syllables sent her into a fit of coughing.

"DO SOMETHING!" Ariel shouted.

Molly fumbled at the trap with her one good hand, trying to open it. She found one of the catches and twisted. It came loose, and she moved to the second, but her trembling fingers could not make it budge. Molly let go of the trap and reached out to the sky, which was retreating above her. She closed her hand tight and pulled, and saw bright rivers of wind flowing down toward her and the trap, faster and faster. They rushed in around her, holding her tightly, trying to pull her back up to the sky. The wind slowed her fall, but she was moving so fast, and the ground was so close, that even the wind was not enough. She watched the grassy ground rushing toward her and felt the winds wrap themselves around her, trying to protect her.

I wonder what it will feel like, she thought. And then she landed—hard—and felt nothing at all.

TWENTY-TWO

Something was trying to work its way into the dark, still place Molly had found. She could feel it pressing at the shell of her peace, but she pressed back.

No, no, no. Don't make me leave.

She felt something slap at her cheeks, and her eyes opened to brightness. She slammed them shut again. She wrapped the darkness back around her.

But the quiet was gone. There was a sound in her ears, a ringing, a drumming, like the rumble of a storm moving quickly toward her. She heard the shouts of an angry sky, and memories began to invade her peace. Every part of her body cried out in pain. Her eyes opened again, and the world flowed in.

The sky above her was clear and blue. She could still hear the storm ringing in her ears, but there was no storm above her.

"I'm alive," she said. The ringing was so loud that she couldn't hear her own voice. All the same, she whispered, "Thank you" to the winds far above.

A patch of wind, brighter than the sky's bright blue, floated into her vision and took the shape of a person.

"Ariel? You're okay."

Ariel floated down closer and plucked at Molly with gentle hands. She made odd gestures toward the sky.

"Ariel, I can't hear you. My ears...the storm..."

Molly pressed her hands into the ground to sit up but immediately fell with a cry. *Right. I forgot.* She forced herself to look at her broken fingers. Three of them were bent backward in a way that made her stomach lurch. Her thumb and index finger seemed whole, though, and these she moved tenderly. There were new pains, too, from her landing. Her back was a map of bruises, and when she breathed there was an awful scraping sensation in her chest.

Moving slowly and painfully, she managed to sit up and look around. She was on a grassy field in the midst of rolling hills. To her left, a handful of wind-stunted trees clung together. Scattered here and there were the remains of the *Gloria Mundi*—bent iron plates, fractured walkways, tangles of machinery.

Ariel floated down until her head sat directly beside Molly's ear. "...is coming," Molly heard through the rumble of thunder. The sound of the storm seemed to be fading.

"What?"

"Help is coming!" she heard Ariel shout.

Molly struggled to her feet, ignoring her body's protests. "What help? Who?"

She saw the shape descending from the sky and closed her eyes. *Am I dreaming? Am I dead?* But when she opened her eyes again, it was still there.

It was the *Legerdemain*—or, rather, what was left of it. The hull was still cracked open, and it was canted to one side, flying wounded. But above the ship, where the engine would have been, was Legerdemain himself, just as she had seen him when she set him free. His long, sleek body swam through the sky, wings spread wide, towing the ship in his wake. The winds he wove around the ship cradled it like a basket.

"What is…how long have I been out?" Molly asked.

"Almost an hour," Ariel said. "I could not rouse you, so I went to fetch help."

"You brought Legerdemain? And the ship?"

The sound of the storm finally faded from her ears, and she became aware of another sound. Aboard the ship, someone was calling her name. There was a figure at the bow. Against the bright sky he was nothing more than a silhouette, but Molly knew him immediately.

"Da!" she shouted, and she was surprised by the feelings that washed through her: relief and love and anger and a bone-deep need. The fear was gone. As the ship touched down, gently as a feather, she started limping toward it. Her father jumped down from the bow and ran to her. They stopped several paces apart.

"Moll, are you safe? Are you hurt?" he asked.

"I think I'm okay," she said. "I mean, I'm hurt, but I'm not dead, which I probably should be." Behind her father, two figures jumped down from the ship. "Kier! Rory! What are you all doing here?"

"What do you bloody well think we're doing?" Rory asked as he and Kiernan raced to Molly's side and hugged her.

"Ow! Ow, please stop!"

They drew back. “We heard the *Gloria* went down,” Kiernan said. “And then that came.” He gestured up at Legerdemain.

“Terrified half the city,” Rory said. “Including me, I’m not ashamed to admit.”

“He flew into the city?” Molly stared up at Legerdemain, and for a moment she could not speak. He dipped his head and regarded her with stormy eyes. The oxygen of his breath washed over her, and she breathed it in deeply, and it felt like she hadn’t taken a breath since they parted. It tasted like the sky, like home.

“Thank you for coming,” she said. “Ariel, thank you for bringing him.”

“He was not far. I found him searching the wreckage.”

Molly reached up, and Legerdemain bent one of his wings low to brush her fingers. He felt surprisingly solid, and when she touched him it felt like there was a wind stirring up beneath her skin, between her bones. He let out a high, fluting trill.

“He says thank you for stopping the harvests,” Ariel said. “A sentiment I share. Thank you, Molly. You cannot know how many lives you have saved.”

Or how many I ended. She pulled her fingers away from Legerdemain’s wing.

“Ariel, how did you escape the trap?”

“The fall cracked it open. I tried to wake you, but I could not, and I did not want to move you until I knew how badly you were hurt.”

“And you all agreed to come with her?” She looked around at her family.

"Come on, Moll, don't be dense," Rory said. "'Course we came."

Molly looked at her father. "Yes, Moll. I knew enough to trust her. I know why you did what you did," he said, answering her unspoken question. "I know you're not touched. Or at least that it's not what I thought it was. Molly, I'm sorry. I—"

"We don't have time to sort this out now," Kiernan said. "There are Disposal ships out searching for you already, Molly. We have to leave."

"We can't," Molly said. "We have to search the wreckage. People might have survived."

Ariel brushed Molly's arm. "Molly, they are hunting you. We must get you away from here."

"But Brighid...Brighid was aboard the ship when it went down."

She watched her father's face as he took in the news. The skin around his eyes sagged and then trembled. His mouth opened and shut several times. She wanted to look away, but she couldn't.

"Brighid?" he whispered. He looked around at the wreckage. "Did she...do you think she..."

"I don't know," Molly said. "But she wasn't leaving. I tried to get her to leave."

"She never did listen."

She waited for him to say more, but he stared silently at the horizon. "We can look for her," Molly said. "She might—"

"You must go," Ariel said. "You cannot help her. I will search while you escape."

"She's right, Molly," Kiernan said. He gripped her shoulder, and she flinched, but she didn't draw away.

"Where will we go? Where can we go?"

"The open ocean," Kiernan said. "They can't search the entire Atlantic."

Molly nodded. She watched her father, who still hadn't moved.

Ariel flew between them, forcing Molly's eyes onto her. "I will begin my search."

"Thank you," Molly said.

Ariel flowed forward, wrapping herself around Molly and speaking softly in her ear. "Thank you, Molly Stout. I will see you soon."

"Please stay safe."

Ariel released Molly and flew away fast. Molly watched until her glimmer disappeared into the blue of the sky.

Kiernan took command, getting them all aboard the ship and working to stow cargo. They had come in a hurry, it seemed, bringing supplies but not taking the proper time to ready the ship. Rory and Kiernan bound Molly's broken fingers, and her ribs, two of which were broken, and then tried to lay her down to rest.

"No. I want to help."

"Molly," Kiernan began, "you've just been through a wreck. I think you—"

"Kier, I'm going to help. Now, is there something you want me to do, or should I go loose the sails with my one good hand?"

Kiernan looked into her eyes and sighed. "There's a lot of wreckage still in the hold. You could go clear it out."

"Good. Thank you." She turned to leave, but Rory put his hand on her shoulder, and she stopped and looked back at him. He was grinning. "What? What is it?"

"Molly Stout versus the *Gloria Mundi*," he said and smiled so brightly that she could not help but smile herself, despite the pain, the worry and the guilt roiling in her stomach. He punched her shoulder lightly, then let her pass.

The ship lifted off the ground just as she kicked the last broken timber through the hole in the hull, and she stopped to watch the earth receding. She took as deep a breath as her ribs would allow, and let it out slowly.

She heard footsteps behind her, and her father came down the ladder into the hold. He surveyed the room for a moment and then walked over to stare out at the sky with her.

"This is all going to take some getting used to," he said. "Having an engine that can have its own way and could drop us all out of the sky if it chose to." He stepped forward and leaned out of the hold to look up, showing no fear of the open sky. "How did it ever fit inside that little engine casing of ours?"

"That's what I thought when I saw it too." She clenched her good hand. "Da, I'm so sorry about Brighid. I really, really—"

"Don't. She might still be alive," he said.

Molly thought of her sister clinging to the side of the engine and could kindle little hope. "She might." She pulled at the bandages around her ribs. "You read the journal?"

"Yes. That night, after I threw you out." He still wasn't looking at her. "Took me some time to come around, to believe it."

"Some time? Or some whiskey?"

There was a long pause before he answered. "Both, I guess. That's true enough." He finally turned around, and Molly was surprised to see tears in his eyes. "Molly, I'm so bloody sorry. I can't even..."

He started sobbing. Molly took one of his arms and pulled him away from the hole in the hull. He put his arms around her and hugged her tightly, and Molly winced but let him. After a few moments she hugged him back, closing her eyes and letting herself feel like a child again. Longing for the safety of her father's arms. The safety was still there, she felt, but it was different. Broken.

"I'm sorry," her father finally managed to say.

"I know you are, Da."

"I won't ever do anything like it again."

"I know you won't."

"Can you forgive me?"

"I don't know." She felt his arms slacken around her, and she held him closer. "But I'm glad you're here."

They had been flying at speed for over an hour, but they were still passing over the wreckage of the *Gloria Mundi*. Molly sat on the engineer's loft, Legerdemain looming above her. It had taken quite the effort to climb this high with only one hand, and her broken ribs burned like fire in her chest, but she had wanted to be closer to Legerdemain. She looked up at the splintered top of the mast, a few feet below the spirit's belly. *We could put a crow's nest up there, maybe a yardarm and some rigging to make the climbing easier.*

"Do you know what happened to the harvester's spirit?" she asked Legerdemain.

Legerdemain let out a long, low tone. Molly had no idea what it meant, but its familiarity was comforting.

To starboard they passed a particularly tangled mass of metal that looked like it might have come from the bow of the *Gloria Mundi*. Molly leaned out to examine it. She saw broken glass glittering on the green earth below, and what might have been a leg protruding from the wreckage. *Might that be Brighid? Meredith? Blaise or Arkwright?* She was surprised by the anger that rose at the thought of Arkwright, frail inside his tank. She felt no guilt at the thought of his death.

"Ship to port!" Kiernan called out. He stood at the *Legerdemain*'s bow, spyglass fixed to his eye. Molly looked out and saw a black speck against the blue sky. "Silver sword on the hull. It's a Disposal ship."

"Ten degrees to starboard!" Molly's father shouted. "If you please," he added after a moment. Above them, Legerdemain dipped his right wing, and the ship went into a graceful turn, pointing them away from the other ship and picking up speed.

Molly leaned back against the mast. She remembered the way it had once trembled subtly from the working of the engine. Now there was no need of an engine: Legerdemain carried them all, as he always had. She closed her eyes. "I missed you so much."

Legerdemain responded with a small huff, and Molly felt the winds inside her warm. This close, her connection to the spirit was strong. When she concentrated, she could feel his wings beating, the winds rustling through his feathers, the sun hot on his flank.

"What do you think we'll do now?"

He gave a long keening, rising from a low rumble to a high squeak.

"I don't know either."

The coast was coming up to the fore. To starboard, Molly could see the fug of Terra Nova, and the docks atop the long umbilical, like a great dandelion rising out of the wasted ground of the city. She turned her eyes forward. Out over the water, the winds were dancing capriciously. Several flew toward them and then darted away, as if inviting Legerdemain to chase them.

They sailed on until the land disappeared behind them, the stars glimmered between the glowing winds, and the *Legerdemain* itself disappeared beneath her as the day's light was extinguished in the waves.

ACKNOWLEDGMENTS

This book was begun years ago, pecking out the first draft in the wee hours before my sons woke for the day. So I owe them thanks for those small pockets of time.

Thanks to my earliest readers—Amber Bassett and Luke Hill and my family—for kind words and kinder commentaries. Kathleen Wall, an early reader and a longtime writing mentor of mine, deserves special thanks. She devoted herself to this book, to making it better and to seeing it get into the right hands. Without her gracious help, it might never have seen its way to publication. A million thank-yous are not enough, Kathleen.

Thanks to the entire team at Orca Books, who put their faith in Molly and worked so hard to bring this book into being. Special thanks to my editor, Robin Stevenson, who labored with me to plaster over the cracks in my literary walls. It was invariably a pleasure to work with you, Robin.

I owe a huge measure of gratitude to my parents, who encouraged me to keep writing, keep dreaming, throughout my childhood and beyond. I wouldn't have been able to write this book without that support.

Last, and most, I must again thank my wife, Alexis. Writing when you have small children is always, always a team effort. She devoted herself to this book no less than I did and sacrificed to see it through to completion. Thank you for every minute, my love.

SHANE ARBUTHNOTT grew up in Saskatoon, Saskatchewan, and now lives in Guelph, Ontario, with his family. When he is not writing, he can be seen chasing after his three adventurous children, trying to convince them to eat green things occasionally. His short fiction has previously appeared in *On Spec* and *Open Spaces*. This is his first novel. For more information, visit www.shanearbuthnott.com or follow him on Twitter @SMArbuthnott.